CHILD
OF
ETHERCLAW

CHILD
—OF—
ETHERCLAW

MATTY ROBERTS

Twilight Fox

Child of Etherclaw is a work of fiction. Unless otherwise indicated, all the names, characters, businesses, places, events and incidents in this book are either the product of the author's imagination or used in a fictitious manner. Any resemblance to actual persons, living or dead, or actual events is purely coincidental.

Copyright © 2022 by Matty Roberts

All rights reserved. No part of this book may be reproduced in any form or by any electronic or mechanical means, including information storage and retrieval systems, without permission in writing from the publisher, except by reviewers, who may quote brief passages in a review.

Publisher's Cataloging-In-Publication Data
(Prepared by The Donohue Group, Inc.)

Names: Roberts, Matty, author.
Title: Child of Etherclaw / Matty Roberts.
Description: Denver, Colorado : Twilight Fox, [2022] | Series: [Etherclaw] ; [1] | Interest age level: 012-018. | Summary: "When an engineering student discovers the connection between her adopted brother and her mother's necklace, she must save him before he is used to reshape humankind"-- Provided by publisher.
Identifiers: ISBN 9798986065809 (hardcover) | ISBN 9780578394169 (paperback) | ISBN 9780578395562 (ebook)
Subjects: LCSH: Engineering students--Family relationships--Juvenile fiction. | Adopted children--Family relationships--Juvenile fiction. | Necklaces--Juvenile fiction. | Magic--Juvenile fiction. | Family secrets--Juvenile fiction. | CYAC: Engineering students--Family relationships--Fiction. | Adopted children--Family relationships--Fiction. | Necklaces--Fiction. | Magic--Fiction. | Family secrets--Fiction. | LCGFT: Fantasy fiction.
Classification: LCC PS3618.O315867 C45 2022 (print) | LCC PS3618.O315867 (ebook) | DDC 813/.6--dc23

Library of Congress Control Number: 2022905179

Printed in the United States of America

Published by Twilight Fox LLC
Denver, Colorado
www.twilightfoxpress.com

To Amanda, Holland, & Laina.

The panda, the wolf, and the cat that make everything worth it.

"Our brothers and sisters are there with us from the dawn of our personal stories to the inevitable dusk."

— **Susan Scarf Merrell**

CHAPTER 1
UNDERCITY

Fenlee strained against the pile of collapsed scaffolding pinning her to the wall, but couldn't dislodge herself. She smacked her palm against a bulky cross brace one last time, then slumped against the rubble in defeat. It was clear that she was going to lose her leg. Again.

Pipes and brackets, undisturbed for centuries, clattered as a small boy fought his way through the wreckage toward her. She hadn't wanted to bring him, given all the dangers in the undercity, but Elliot was her brother—*younger and far less experienced brother*, she kept reminding herself—and he refused to let her explore down there alone.

"Lee! You okay? I told you if you squeezed back there that thing was going to tip over and smash—" He stopped short

when he saw her, his soft voice reverberating through the still, dark chamber. "Oh. You don't look so good."

"Right, thanks for the reminder, Elliot. But yeah, definitely feeling a bit smashed up at the moment." Fenlee was extremely not in the mood, but this wasn't his fault, either. She tried to refocus and calm herself with one of those deep breathing exercises he was always trying to get her to do. Big mistake.

The abandoned undercity below New Cascadia always smelled foul, but the recent rains and summer heat had simmered the odors into a nauseating stew. A thin layer of sludge covered everything, and the crash had released a fresh stench of mold and fermenting rat carcass. It was so pungent she could taste it. She gagged on a bit of floating particulate and spit-drooled as she forced every last bit of the nasty vapor from her lungs.

It was supposed to have been just another late afternoon scavenging run with her brother. Simple and quick, like usual. Unfortunately, the areas were so picked over, she had very little to show for the day's efforts. They were heading to the exit before the autodrone patrol showed up when Fenlee's curiosity had gotten the better of her. Against her brother's objections, she'd slipped behind some old scaffolding to get at a hidden panel that had caught her eye. It hadn't seemed all that rickety at the time, but how was she to know the decades of decay had reduced its structural integrity to that of toothpicks? One misplaced elbow and the entire mess had tumbled down around her.

Now she was trapped, and the next autodrone patrol was due to come through any minute.

Elliot eased in beside her, dripping with sweat. He was paler than usual in the dim light of their lamps. With his scrawny frame, Fenlee wondered if it would have been more effective for him to have gone in instead.

Nah. If this garbage was going to fall, better it fall on me.

She growled through her teeth and again tried to pull loose, but the mountain of cross braces, rails, and couplers wouldn't budge. "I'm all right. Left leg's a little stuck."

Elliot looked down and gasped. "Dad's going to murder you when he gets back."

"Yeah, well, when is he *not* going to murder me?" She tried one more time to twist free, but the prosthetic refused to cooperate and splintered with each movement.

"Fair. But we have to get you out of here. The drones—"

"I know! Just give me a sec."

The old service tunnels and transport bays were a great place to hunt for mechanical parts or other junk the waves of looters had missed over the centuries. Sometimes Fenlee lucked out and found scrap useful for her academy projects, or at least exchangeable for a few crednotes. She was the only academy student daring—or stupid—enough to brave the undercity for parts, and the quality of her work was better for it. The day had been fairly disappointing so far, so this little setback only bolstered her stubbornness and she wasn't about to return empty handed.

The panel's hinges were stiff with fresh rust, but after a few tugs, it finally gave. Other scavengers had stripped out any wiring long before she was born, but it wasn't wiring she was after. She shined her lamp inside and found that her intuition was correct—someone had been using it for storage.

"Real nice, Lee." Elliot peeked over her shoulder. "Two moldy ration packs, a totally corroded comm unit, and..." He poked at the last item and recoiled, twisting his face in revulsion. "And a nasty bag of who-knows-what? Told you it'd be a bunch of junk."

She punched the panel in frustration. So that was it. The sum total of their lame afternoon adventure. Elliot was right, as usual, he just didn't have to sound so smug about it. She skipped over everything else in the storage compartment and stuffed the little bag in one of her side pouches. Better be something decent inside, unlike last time. The only other bag she'd found secreted away in the undercity had ended up containing a severed finger and a wad of hair. That had been a fun surprise when they got back to their apartment.

Now for the crushed, useless leg. Her heart sank. The prosthetic had been a gift from her father, and the cost had to have been extraordinary. It was a sleek, lightweight model with an advanced bio interface. Fashionable and high-tier, it was the first leg she'd ever been proud to wear. And now she'd wrecked it. She bit her lip, snapped the pin release connecting the leg, and pulled free, leaving the broken prosthetic behind.

Together, the pair stumbled out from behind the scaffolding into the main tunnel where she wrapped her arm over her brother's shoulders. At sixteen, Fenlee was two years older and two inches taller, forcing her to lean into the lopsided arrangement and causing both to keep tripping on the cracked floor plates that littered the underground chamber.

A hot tickle crawled up the back of her neck. The drone? No, something else, something *alive*. They needed to hurry. "Don't worry, I'm going to get you out of here."

"Oh, *you're* going to get *me* out of here? Have you seen yourself?"

"We still have a little time, we'll make it." But with some quick calculations, she determined limping speed wasn't going to cut it; they'd have to find an alternate route. If one of the Sentry-class autodrones found them, they'd be dragged away by the Cascadian Authority Security Forces, locked up, and forgotten. Her stomach went cold. SecForce probably wouldn't even bother to notify her father. Like so many before them, they would just disappear.

"Oh, no." Elliot stopped so suddenly that Fenlee almost fell forward.

"What? What's 'oh, no?'"

He whimpered like a puppy in a thunderstorm. She followed his gaze toward the main entry tunnel behind them. "Um, drone's a little early today," he said in a broken whisper.

She yanked a pair of goggles out of one of her pouches. The infrared function was flaky and the lenses were scratched, but the basic optic enhancement was good enough; there was no mistaking the horizontal red beam combing the walls in a slow, deliberate search pattern.

Voiding hell! Why, today of all days, did the patrol have to be running ahead of schedule?

"Kill the lamps," Fenlee whispered. Two soft clicks and the room plunged into a charcoal murk. "Okay. All right. We can do this. We can definitely do this." She looked around, but without the lamplight, it was nearly impossible to make anything out. "There should be another small tunnel around here and then it's maybe a quarter mile to surface access. I think."

"You think."

"Well, yes. If Casper's maps are correct."

"Seriously?" Elliot sighed. "You didn't tell me you got it

from Cas. His mapping data always sucks. I don't get how you two are even friends—"

"There. Go!" Fenlee cut him off and pointed toward the far side of the room, opposite the way they'd arrived. Another tunnel opened into the darkness beyond. She jerked her head to the side as something small padded through a nearby puddle, just out of sight. It wasn't just the drone, there was something alive in there with them after all.

They hurried toward the smaller tunnel, stepping lightly to avoid kicking debris piles, splashing in muck, or anything that might alert the Sentry autodrone. There was no telling if it was equipped with an auditory sensor package, and Fenlee didn't care to find out.

The autodrone had entered the main chamber with them, conducting its slow, methodical scan. The menacing red light illuminated the single train track bisecting the room, elongating the rail's shadows toward them like pincers.

After a painfully slow pace, they arrived at the far wall. Elliot dug his fingers into Fenlee's arm as he trembled beside her. It turned out that Casper's maps had been junk after all—what had appeared to be a tunnel opening was nothing more than the vague shadow of a large domed fuel tank. They were staring at a dead end.

There were only a few smaller fuel tanks and a long row of overturned shelving units nearby. Not much to work with, but it was what was under the shelving units that now captured her attention: a pair of glowing green eyes sat a few feet away, staring back at her.

Elliot squinted to see what she was looking at, then smacked his hand over his mouth, stifling a yelp. He backed up and tripped, knocking them both to the ground.

The creature slowly emerged from under the shelves. Fenlee scrambled backward on all threes until her head hit the wall. They were caught between an autodrone and…a giant undercity death rat?

"Wait." Elliot bent down and extended his hand toward the creature. "There. It's okay. You got a name?"

"Death rats don't have names, and—what are you *doing*?"

"It's all right, he might be lost." The creature nuzzled his hand and looked up at Fenlee. "And he's not a death rat."

An orange cat with deep brown stripes stretched its claws and twirled its long, ringed tail around Elliot's legs. The patterns on its body reminded her of images she'd seen of tigers or other large exotic cats now long extinct. But this was just a scrawny old house cat, what was it doing here? The cat trotted off, disappearing underneath the row of overturned shelving units. A moment later, it paused to look back at them from within the crawlspace. Elliot was quick to follow.

"Lee, check it out, there's a passageway back here. It's kind of cramped though. Can you crawl for a bit?"

Fenlee eyed the Sentry as it hovered closer, almost within scanning distance, then considered the little creature beckoning them with its enigmatic eyes. "Fine," she grumbled. "But your little furwad friend better not be leading us to another dead end."

Once they'd crawled a few feet in, there was enough room to stand up. The passage was covered in black mold and blocked about twenty feet down by a jungle of green growth dangling from the ceiling. On their left was a door, slightly ajar, and on their right was a heavy retractable gate, slouching in its tracks. The cat ran to the door and looked back expectantly.

It was dark beyond the door and Fenlee didn't want to take the chance that it was a storage room where they'd end up cornered. She eyed the gate—a faint light was coming from the other side. "That looks promising. Come on and help me get this gate up."

Elliot felt along the jagged edges of an upturned corner. "Sure, but *what* is it promising, Lee?"

"Got any better ideas?"

"Pretty sure we should follow the cat," Elliot mumbled. "He seems to have some thoughts about the best route."

"We don't have time to debate with a cat. There. Is. A. *Drone* behind us. Anyway, it's probably trying to lead us back to its cat lair with its cat family, and they'll all cat-attack us and have us for their cat dinner. And I refuse to be mauled to death by a fluffy flurry of displaced house cats. Not today."

Fenlee tried to pry the gate up. It opened a few inches, but with a deep metallic groan. The autodrone rotated, accelerating toward them. *Of course we'd get a drone with audio sensors.*

"Help me lift it!" cried Fenlee.

"I'm trying! It's jammed or something!" Elliot strained against the weight of the gate, but it didn't budge.

"Move." With her butt on the ground in the tight corridor, Fenlee braced her leg against a piece of broken flooring and shoved upward with all her strength, but it was hard to get leverage. The gate abruptly shifted and she fell hard on her back, the impact knocking the wind from her.

Elliot made it to the other side and tried to help drag her through. "You're…too *heavy*," he gasped.

"Not helping, *little* brother." She ground the words out through clenched teeth and clambered past him.

It was doubtful the autodrone could get through the cluster of shelves, but Fenlee wasn't going to risk it. The cat let out a low growl behind them as she slammed the gate down with a grating screech.

They emerged from the gap in the gate to find a vast underground loading bay. Several dozen lengths of track ran parallel with platforms between each at regular intervals. Stacks of heavy intermodal shipping containers sat empty, the contents salvaged or ransacked long ago. A few cranes were left, all but one toppled on their sides. The light they had seen was coming from a bank of thin windows at the top of the opposing wall, giving the impression they were inside a massive bunker.

Fenlee stretched and the tension left her muscles, but the anxiety remained. In all the years she'd been scavenging, she'd never had such a close call. From falling, crawling, and trudging through the dampness, she was a sopping wet mess. Nearby, Elliot wiped the filth from his hands while chewing on a few strands of his hair—a nervous habit he'd had as long as Fenlee had known him.

She leaned against the grimy metal wall and activated her holoquip, one of the cheap, compact wrist computers common among low-tier citizens. It had a small holographic projection display and a few other features, but it was nothing fancy. She had no maps for their current area, and she couldn't find any positioning data to calibrate against. If mapping data even they kicked everyone out of these places, they meant for them to stay out. Rumor is, they killed any stragglers."

As she spoke, a rumbling hum approached from behind to underscore her point. Fenlee froze. "Not after all this." Her voice shook as she breathed the words. "No way."

Too late, Fenlee saw this autodrone wasn't like the Sentry from earlier whose duty was to survey and report. This was a shoot-to-kill Guardian-class autodrone. And the offensive models never hesitated.

"Shit! Elliot, *run!*"

But there was no time. The moment the Guardian hovered into view, the housing around its mini-turrets retracted and the guns rotated toward them. Without thinking, she wrapped her arms around her brother and dove on top of him.

Fenlee's world went supernova, and she collapsed into a black hole.

"Not helping, *little* brother." She ground the words out through clenched teeth and clambered past him.

It was doubtful the autodrone could get through the cluster of shelves, but Fenlee wasn't going to risk it. The cat let out a low growl behind them as she slammed the gate down with a grating screech.

They emerged from the gap in the gate to find a vast underground loading bay. Several dozen lengths of track ran parallel with platforms between each at regular intervals. Stacks of heavy intermodal shipping containers sat empty, the contents salvaged or ransacked long ago. A few cranes were left, all but one toppled on their sides. The light they had seen was coming from a bank of thin windows at the top of the opposing wall, giving the impression they were inside a massive bunker.

Fenlee stretched and the tension left her muscles, but the anxiety remained. In all the years she'd been scavenging, she'd never had such a close call. From falling, crawling, and trudging through the dampness, she was a sopping wet mess. Nearby, Elliot wiped the filth from his hands while chewing on a few strands of his hair—a nervous habit he'd had as long as Fenlee had known him.

She leaned against the grimy metal wall and activated her holoquip, one of the cheap, compact wrist computers common among low-tier citizens. It had a small holographic projection display and a few other features, but it was nothing fancy. She had no maps for their current area, and she couldn't find any positioning data to calibrate against. If mapping data even existed, it wasn't publicly available, and there hadn't been a functioning global positioning system in over two hundred years.

"Looks like this thing is useless," Fenlee said, shutting down her holoquip. "But I'm pretty sure I know where we are. This has to be one of the old freight transfer hubs. It's where bulk cargo would come in from the sea before they shipped it underground to distribution centers around the region." She cocked an eyebrow. "Probably worked much better than what we have now. People could actually get what they needed. Anyway, hubs like this in the Waterfront District were built right beside shipyards, so there has to be an exit close by. If we hurry, we might still have time to catch a maglev back home before the station shuts down for the night."

Fenlee peeled herself off the wall and wrapped her arm around Elliot. Together, they started forward. She swore this would be the last time they'd venture together into the undercity. The only problem was, the loot she'd scrounged together on these scavenging trips was expensive elsewhere or, in many cases, outright impossible to find. But she needed it. She loved her mechatronics projects, and it was imperative that she rise to the top of her class if she was ever going to get a job that paid enough to get her and her family out of the low-tier.

About the only route up and out of the bottom rungs of society in New Cascadia was through Norfayne Labs, the global science and engineering conglomerate. She would have to prove herself, and her academy studies alone wouldn't be enough. She excelled in working with mechanical and electronic components and the bits of code that glued them together. And if she could get a position at Norfayne, it would be the path forward that she needed. It wasn't that she really minded life in the low tier, but she wanted something better for Elliot and her father. Like it used to be.

"So, um, have you figured out how you're going to explain your leg this time?" Elliot asked.

Fenlee grimaced. "I have my old one as backup, so I can just wear that for a bit. Dad won't be back planetside until tomorrow, so I have a little time to get this all sorted out."

"Sure. But isn't your old leg still about an inch too short?"

"Half-inch," she said through clenched teeth. "I'm used to dealing with this. I'll be fine."

"Check it out—I bet we could get out that way." Elliot pointed to a set of stairs with a landing at the top. It was high enough to be partially obscured, but there was a hint of light coming from an opening with rainwater dripping down.

Relief washed over her. "Makes sense to me. Let's go."

They walked past several open shipping containers, but not all of them were empty—a few held bedding and other personal objects. Elliot stopped and stared inside one. "Lee, do people actually *live* down here?"

"Nope. Well, I mean, supposedly, people tried living in these hubs for a while. Climate refugees from the south who couldn't get citizenship, mostly. But the Cascadian Authority wasn't having it, so they kicked them all out."

"But this area isn't used for anything. Why would they force out refugees with nowhere to go?" Elliot asked.

"Because the Cascadian Authority SecForce is full of terrible people. You know that. As little as they care for us, they care even less for…" She trailed off, the blood draining from her face. Her voice dropped to a whisper. "Elliot, we have to get out of here. This place should be crawling with autodrones. When they kicked everyone out of these places, they meant for them to stay out. Rumor is, they killed any stragglers."

As she spoke, a rumbling hum approached from behind to underscore her point. Fenlee froze. "Not after all this." Her voice shook as she breathed the words. "No way."

Too late, Fenlee saw this autodrone wasn't like the Sentry from earlier whose duty was to survey and report. This was a shoot-to-kill Guardian-class autodrone. And the offensive models never hesitated.

"Shit! Elliot, *run!*"

But there was no time. The moment the Guardian hovered into view, the housing around its mini-turrets retracted and the guns rotated toward them. Without thinking, she wrapped her arms around her brother and dove on top of him.

Fenlee's world went supernova, and she collapsed into a black hole.

CHAPTER 2
BAREFOOT & COMBAT BOOTS

The world was dark and empty. From somewhere within the void, ravenous tendrils unfurled, creeping into the depths of her existence, probing, stealing. It was invasive and wrong, but she couldn't fight it. She wanted to scream, or maybe just sleep for a while.

"Lee..."

She began to regain her senses as reality slowly glued itself back together. Everything was cold, and the pit of her stomach was hollow. Her body felt as though it had aged decades.

She opened one eye.

"*Fenlee!*"

She opened her other eye. Why was her face touching Elliot's? That was weird.

"Hey. You okay?" Elliot asked. His arms were wrapped around her, but he wasn't quite in focus. "I thought you were about to get shot and then when that thing just exploded, I couldn't tell if maybe part of it hit you." His eyes were glistening. "I didn't know if you were going to wake up."

Fenlee pushed his arms loose and rolled off him. She lay on her back, staring vacantly at the ceiling. "Wheat bar." She exhaled the words.

"Sorry, what?"

"I need food. You have a wheat bar."

"O-okay, but you hate wheat bars—"

"Now, please."

Elliot handed the remaining wheat bar to Fenlee and she quickly devoured it. They rested next to each other in silence.

After a few moments, Fenlee had a bit of her strength back and her head was starting to clear. "So, what the hell even happened? What did you do?"

"I didn't do anything. You fell on top of me, and the autodrone blew up. Then you passed out."

"Uh, I didn't 'fall' on top of you, Elliot. I covered you. I was trying to save your life."

She sat up and looked at the pieces of the deadly autodrone scattered on the ground. It appeared to have been torn apart. There were chunks of shredded metal, but no evidence of a blast or burn marks.

"Hold on, what do you mean, 'it blew up?'" Fenlee asked.

"I don't know, it just suddenly exploded or something."

She rubbed her pounding head. None of this was making any sense. "How long was I out?"

"Not long, maybe fifteen or twenty seconds," Elliot said.

Her stomach twisted at the thought of the danger she'd put him in. "I'm real sorry about all this. I have to get you home."

He stood up and offered his hand. "It isn't your fault."

She tried to pull herself up but didn't have the energy. "I'm, uh…" A whitish blur washed over her vision, and she dropped her hand. "I'm still really out of it. Even between you and a handrail, I don't think I can make it up all those steps."

They were interrupted by the small, but husky, voice of a young boy coming from the shadows beside a shipping crate. "It's them."

Fenlee and Elliot watched as two figures emerged. A tall woman walked toward them with the confident gait of a soldier. Well-maintained muscles flexed sharply under her deep black skin. A silver tattoo ran from her neck to her shoulder, shimmering as she moved.

Behind the woman peered a strange little barefoot boy. He had a warm brown complexion like many of the refugees and was probably no more than eight or nine, though it was hard to tell. He had a fluff of poorly dyed green and black hair and wore tight cloth wraps all over his body.

The pair could not have been more different in appearance or presentation.

"Are you sure?" the woman asked the boy. "These two look like they were just in the wrong place at the wrong time."

The boy gave a curt nod. "Sure. She has one."

The woman turned to Fenlee, her expression carved in granite and braced with steel. "So, tell me, girl, what have you done here?"

Like I know what happened here, and like I'd tell a couple of freaks like you if I did. If they thought she or Elliot had anything to do with the destruction of the autodrone, there was no telling what trouble they might find themselves in.

Fenlee relaxed her face and turned her eyes up in the innocent expression that often worked on her father. "What are you talking about?" she asked. "We were just hanging out and got lost. Then that thing came"—she pointed to the scattered metal bits—"and it must have malfunctioned or—"

"I'm afraid you don't understand the situation you're in here, girl," the woman said. "This place is strictly off limits to civilians. Most of the access to the undercity is tightly controlled, so you didn't wander in accidentally. Don't play dumb. I will ask again: *why* are you here?"

Fenlee considered the pair for a moment. Despite the woman's intimidating air, she lacked a uniform or any other characteristics that might indicate she was with the Cascadian Authority Security Forces. And the boy was just weird. She watched him pick something out of his hair, smell it, and flick it away. SecForce surely wasn't employing him.

She was certain that this strange woman and boy weren't supposed to be roaming around the undercity either, and Fenlee was not about to be bullied. "Yeah, well, it looks like we were here first, so why don't you tell us what *you're* up to?"

Elliot fidgeted with one of his hoodie straps. "Lee," he whispered. "I don't think making enemies is a great idea."

Ignoring Fenlee and Elliot, the woman turned to her young companion. "If she has one, where is it?"

The boy folded his hands behind his back and skipped over to Fenlee. He stopped a few feet away, leaned over, and stared. His eyes drifted to Elliot as he scrunched up his brow. "Neck," he said, sliding his gaze back to Fenlee. "Around her neck."

Before Fenlee could react, the woman strode over, grabbed the black opal Fenlee wore on a chain around her neck, and held it in a vice grip. "Where did you get this?"

Fenlee gritted her teeth. "Let *go!*" she said, yanking it from the woman's grasp. No one was going to touch her mother's opal without her permission. She managed to take it back, but the small exertion left her woozy and she slumped backward on her elbows.

Elliot reached behind to help steady her. "Leave her alone," he begged the woman. "Sure, maybe we shouldn't be down here, but we really did get lost. All we're trying to do right now is go home."

The woman's jaw relaxed and her eyes softened. "You really don't know what you have there, do you, girl?" She paused for a moment. "You need to get some calories in you." She pulled a small flask from her tactical belt, unscrewed the lid, and put it to Fenlee's lips. "Drink."

Fenlee turned up her nose. "And why the hell should I? How do I know what's in that?"

The woman sighed. "If I wanted to hurt you, I could have easily done so already. Drink, and I promise we'll help you get out of here."

True enough, the woman could snap Fenlee like a twig, and she hadn't so far. Fenlee sniffed the top of the flask and took a tentative sip. Discovering it was only syrupy sugar water, she grabbed the flask and drank deeply. Before she finished, she had already started to feel better.

"Thanks, I guess," Fenlee said. "No idea why, but I wasn't feeling all that great." She narrowed her eyes. "But you knew that. How?"

"What's your name, girl?" the woman asked.

"Fenlee. And why do you care about this?" she asked, brushing her hand over her opal.

The woman nodded. "Fenlee. I'm Kyara, and this is Nico," she said, looking at the boy. "And that thing around your neck is etherclaw."

The word hung in the stillness of the undercity. *Etherclaw* sounded cryptic and dangerous, like the faint, intangible remnants of a nightmare. But it was just a word, and this woman was clearly crazy, so why did it send her heart racing? Elliot shifted beside her, breaking the silence.

"I don't know what you're talking about, but this is a black opal," Fenlee said. "It was my mom's before she died, and now it's mine." The opal was one of the only physical reminders she had of her mother. It meant the world to her, but beyond sentiment, it was nothing more than a cheap stone.

Elliot still had a tight grasp on her arm and looked as though he'd prefer to crawl under the nearest shipping crate. "You said you'd help us get out of here," Fenlee said. "I really need to get my brother home, so, if you don't mind—"

"Yes, we do need to get you out of here," Kyara said. "There are other autodrones patrolling this area, so we cannot afford to linger. But you also need to understand what you've just done." She crouched close to Fenlee, forearms draped over her knees, and spoke in a severe tone. "That opal is no mere stone. Your mother, or perhaps someone else, fabricated it to hide something."

"Hide what? What the hell are you talking about?"

There was a distant look in Kyara's eyes, as though she was weighing her response. "You recall how the Void Pillars were constructed, yes?"

Of course she knew. Fenlee, and anyone else who'd been made to suffer through courses on history and modern religion, had it drilled into her head. Two centuries ago, just before the Great Collapse, the weird creatures known as Aeons had appeared on Earth and built the Void Pillars. The massive iron columns had helped cool the catastrophically hot planet, which had paved the way for the rebirth of humanity. She didn't know *how*, exactly, they were built, but then, supposedly no one really did.

"Well, yeah," Fenlee said. "The Cascadian Pillar is kinda hard to miss." It sat in the heart of the Cascade Range and was one of twelve found all over the world. At over fifteen miles in diameter and reaching over a hundred miles high, it shrouded parts of the megacity of New Cascadia in its shadow during much of the year. "But again, what does this have to do with anything right now?"

"Very few are aware of the full history," Kyara said. "When the asteroid miners accidentally uncovered the Aeons, those biomechanical creatures came to life headed for Earth. They left most of the human miners dead in their wake. When the Aeons arrived, they immediately set about constructing the Void Pillars. During that time, all life directly around the pillars diminished. You see, the life was being drained, Fenlee.

"Most of the Aeons buried themselves deep within the Earth when they finished building the final pillar. Perhaps they died after fulfilling their task, or maybe they're just in hibernation." Kyara shrugged and paused for a moment. When she resumed, bitterness tinged her words. "But one was left broken. Humans being humans, they cannibalized the remains and sought to steal that poor creature's power. You have part of that Aeon,

Fenlee." Kyara put her hand over Fenlee's. "You have an etherclaw fragment. And it is yours, whether you like it or not."

Whether she liked it or not? The hell was that supposed to mean?

Fenlee stuffed the opal back down her shirt. "Right, so aside from the part where none of that makes any sense, what exactly are you getting at?" she asked.

"I'm saying that you used this etherclaw to destroy that Guardian drone." Kyara indicated the pieces scattered behind her. "And it also appears you did so without knowing it, meaning it required a strong emotional burst from you as a trigger."

"My emotions fueled this thing?" Fenlee asked.

"No, *triggered* it," Kyara said. "Your life energy fueled it."

"Hey!" Elliot shouted. "Get out of her stuff!" Nico was rummaging through the contents of one of Fenlee's pouches like a starving street pup drooling over a discarded dinner. Elliot tried to intercept him, but he dashed away and, with a cat-like leap, perched on top of one of the shipping containers. In his hand was the small canvas-wrapped bundle Fenlee had retrieved earlier.

"What in the Void is wrong with you? Give it back!" Fenlee yelled. "I found that earlier, and it's the whole reason we're in this mess."

Nico cocked his head to one side. "Finders keepers." He sniffed the little bundle, then shrugged, hopped down, and gave it back to Fenlee. "You found, you keep."

"Um, thanks?" Fenlee stuffed it back in her pouch. The hell was up with this kid?

Nico pressed his grubby finger to Fenlee's lips and motioned for everyone to be quiet. Before she could protest, a low hum in the distance caught her attention as another autodrone entered from a tunnel several hundred feet away.

Kyara surveyed the parts from the destroyed Guardian, seemed to find what she was looking for, and pocketed a small metallic module. "Time to go," she whispered, turning to Fenlee. "Get on my back."

Fenlee let out a short laugh. "You have to be kidding." She shook her head. "I can do this." Elliot grabbed her arm to help her stand.

"Don't argue with me, girl. You were lucky the first time; you won't be the second time." Kyara moved to within a few inches of Fenlee's face and bit out her words. "Get on my back now, or Nico and I will leave you."

"Lee, I think maybe you should listen to her," Elliot said.

"Fine," Fenlee growled.

Kyara bent down and Fenlee climbed on, glad to at least be in the undercity with no one around watching. The woman picked her up effortlessly as though she were an empty rucksack. She broke into a light jog and headed toward a tunnel opposite from where the Guardian autodrone had emerged.

"The stairs are back the other way," Fenlee said. "Where are you taking us?"

"Those stairs do indeed lead outside, but they are secured up top. You wouldn't have made it very far," Kyara said.

Despite the woman's swift pace while carrying Fenlee on her back, Kyara still spoke evenly and without labored breath. She wasn't just athletic; her muscles had been trained with purpose. Fenlee glanced behind them at the distant hum and suspected, if it came to it, Kyara could rip apart an autodrone with her bare hands. *Mental note: don't piss off the crazy lady in the undercity.*

Elliot, on the other hand, was already winded running alongside them. A small orange blur trotting next to his boot caught Fenlee's eye. "Looks like your little beastie is back," she said.

Elliot was panting, but grinned at the cat. "Hi, little guy! Thought…we thought you ran off."

"That's Kavi," Nico said, skipping along on the other side of Kyara.

"Kavi? How…how do you know his name?" Elliot gasped as he ran. "He live down here or…?"

"Kavi lives where Kavi wants," Nico replied.

They finally entered the sanctuary of the side tunnel. A single track cut deep through the center with narrow walkways on either side. The ceiling arched high above, and any light from the loading room they came from quickly diminished, leaving them in near-total darkness.

They came to a halt, and Elliot leaned over a guardrail, breathing hard. "We…we have lamps," he said.

"No lights," Kyara said. She felt along the wall until her hand wrapped around a door handle. With a light push, it swung open easily, as though it had seen recent use. They followed her through, and she silently shut the door. "Now you may turn on your light, boy."

"Thanks. And my name's Elliot, since no one ever asked," he said, fumbling for his lamp.

He fumbled with the switch in the darkness and, sensing his embarrassment, Fenlee leaned over and discreetly flicked it on. The light revealed a small room of concrete and metal panels, similar to the passages she and Elliot had come through before. There was a background odor of ammonia that burned her nostrils.

Fenlee waved her hand in front of her nose. "So, is this Kavi's kitty bathroom or what?"

Kyara eased Fenlee down and walked over to the wall. "The mycotoxins are strong here, as is the case in many of these old tunnels. It's best not to linger." She pulled off one of the rusted metal panels and picked up a large pack. Digging around inside, she produced a small, tightly sealed bag with several black fabric masks. "Put these over your mouth and nose," she said, handing them to Fenlee and Elliot. Nico had already taken canvas wraps like those on his arms and wound them tightly around the lower half of his face.

"How much farther until we're out of here?" Fenlee asked.

"Not far," Kyara said. "But this is where we part ways. You and your brother will head down this passage in a northwest direction. Take the first ladder you see." She glanced over at Nico, who nodded back. "That will lead you to the surface where you can catch a maglev to anywhere you need to go."

"And what about you?" Fenlee asked. "Where are you two going?"

"We have business to take care of. Business that is none of yours," Kyara said, stashing the bag back in its hiding place. She gripped Fenlee's shoulders. "You have a bond with your etherclaw, Fenlee. That is hard to achieve. There are those who would seize it from you given the opportunity. Stay vigilant." Kyara hesitated, her expression inscrutable in the faint light. "I would tell you it's best not to use it, but that is unrealistic advice. If you take care, you can learn to control it. Focus and practice will allow for more efficient operation so you don't nearly kill yourself each time."

Fenlee started to ask, "How do I know if—"

Kyara squeezed her shoulders tighter. "Be very aware, if you use it for ill gain, I *will* find you, and it will not be pretty." She released her grip and flicked on a dim red lamp strapped to her belt. "Go now."

Fenlee watched them start down the southwest passage and called out, "Why do you know all this stuff about etherclaw?"

Nico giggled as Kavi leapt up on his shoulder.

Without breaking stride, Kyara replied, "There are many things you're better off not knowing."

Fenlee opened her mouth to respond, but the odd trio had already disappeared into the gloom of the passage.

"Who do you think those two were?" Elliot asked. He secured his arm around Fenlee's waist as they limped down the other corridor toward the ladder. The walls glistened with inky growth, the caustic odor growing more intense as they plodded along. Even with the face masks, Fenlee's lungs burned and her eyes watered.

"No idea," Fenlee said. "Probably a couple of misplaced refugees with brain damage from breathing in all the mold down here."

"Do you think what they were saying was true? About the etherclaw or whatever?"

"I think they're insane. I just hope they were right about this being a way out." They had better have been insane. If any part of what Kyara said was true…Fenlee shook the thought away. There would be time to figure things out later, after a hot shower.

CHAPTER 3
SINISTER ASSIGNMENT

Fog rolled across the city below, thousands of colors from millions of lights softly diffused under the drifting, suspended moisture. Spires punctured the cottony surface which otherwise obscured the filth of the lower tiers.

Dr. Seth Arkamis normally admired the view during the evenings, but tonight he was unsettled. He paced, alone in his office in the old chateau atop an abandoned tower on the eastern fringe of New Cascadia. As Chief Researcher of the Xenobiology Division at Norfayne Labs, he normally would have conducted his studies and experimentation in the state-of-the-art facilities at the company's primary campus, but his research deviated from the Norfayne mission—*Research, Rediscover, Rebuild*—and he preferred the isolation. While the global

corporation was busy fulfilling their mandate of redeveloping technologies lost to the Great Collapse, he was busy exploring and innovating outside the boundaries of traditional science. Instead of merely rebuilding the past, his work would move humankind into the future.

But he was running out of time.

The world, once again, was careening toward disaster, and he was the only one who understood how to stop it. Arkamis saw the fractures deepening: climate refugees continuing to pile up at the borders of city-states around the world, an eager populace stumbling blindly into a new era of resource deficits, and, most importantly, world governments that seemed determined to repeat all of humankind's mistakes. There would be another collapse, and there would be no rising from the ashes next time.

Dr. Arkamis may have been as human as anyone else, but he saw himself as something greater: an architect of a new age. It was time for the next iteration of human evolution, and he had the means to see it happen.

The Aeons. Awoken centuries ago by accident, the strange biomechanical beings constructed the mighty Void Pillars, giant heatsinks built from asteroid metals. Those enormous black structures pulled humankind from the brink of climate apocalypse, and many regarded the work of the Aeons as humanity's salvation. But few understood the true nature of the Aeons as he did, and he would see to it that their power would save—no, *replace*—humanity.

He had been fending off some anxious inner tension all day, and couldn't figure out why. The calm of his office was disturbed only by the steady tapping of his thumb against the hilt of his ceremonial saber. His vintage narcissus tea grew cold, neglected on his desk. He tried desperately to unwind, but he was restless, distracted. It had been years since he'd made any true progress in his research. Not since...

A soft tone at the office door interrupted his scattered thoughts.

He closed his eyes and took a few meditative breaths to ground himself. *Control. Always maintain control.*

"Enter," he said, hoping it wasn't his attendant. The insufferable little girl would likely reprimand him for wasting such fine tea but then wander off and forget to clear it. Instead, a heavily augmented man of appreciable age strode in with no regard for formality, no respect for etiquette. What was left of his stringy black hair blended with a few thin cables running directly out of his ghostly white cranium. He had replaced his left eye with an unnerving dull red sphere that saw well more than most people realized.

"Ah, Dr. Morrow," Arkamis said, addressing his colleague. "To what do I owe the pleasure at this late hour? I was under the impression you were deeply engaged in conducting the biofixation trials. I haven't seen you in days." He was quite happy to have not seen him around. Morrow may have been a brilliant engineer, but he was also an uncultured mess. Arkamis hoped he wouldn't stay long enough to take a seat as the man tended to leave a residue behind.

"There're more important things at the moment." Morrow's harsh rasp was more grating than usual. "An incident in the undercity today has been brought to my attention, and now I'm bringing it to yours." He turned around and shouted into the hallway. "Lieutenant Cano, get on in here!"

A young woman in uniform with skin the richness of his

now-cold tea and crisp-cut hair the color of the leaves from which it was brewed crossed the room to stand beside Morrow. She gave a curt nod and remained silent.

"Lieutenant Cano has valuable intel to share," Morrow said. "And she's here on her own, not on behalf of SecForce or the Cascadian Authority. Right, Lieutenant?" He waved her forward. "Go ahead then."

Cano looked Arkamis up and down, her mouth agape. "You…didn't mention he was on the Divine Council," she stammered. "I thought everyone here was a researcher with Norfayne."

Dressed in the traditional cream and crimson suit and cloak worn by members of the Divine Council and carrying a ceremonial saber, Arkamis knew he struck an imposing image. That was the point. There was no need to wander the halls of his own chateau or his research labs in such formal attire, but it served as a constant reminder to those around him who he was. The Divine Council was the theocratic seat of power in New Cascadia, affiliated with the global Telluric Ascendancy. Arkamis' membership afforded him some of that power, but his allegiance to them was merely for show.

"I hold an advisory seat on the Council, yes, but my research here always takes precedence over Council matters. You needn't be concerned that anything shared with me here will get back to those fools."

"Right then." Cano glanced at Morrow then squared herself with Arkamis. "In that case, I'm here to report an incident that was just flagged under the Waterfront District. The old underground tunnels and shipping bays are routinely patrolled to identify and report or, depending on the area, eliminate trespassers. We've had ongoing issues with vagrants in certain sectors, and with our resources being stretched as they are, we have elected to terminate on-sight in the highly restricted zones. Earlier this evening, one of our offensive Guardian-class units was destroyed. There is no meshnet connectivity in that area for it to make contact, so we only became aware when it never made it back to the proper checkpoint. When the security team found the drone, it appeared as though it had been blown up, but they couldn't find evidence of a blast. The audiovisual and infrared recorder was nowhere to be found. We searched—"

Arkamis rubbed his aching temple. "Can you please get to the point, Miss Cano—"

"*Lieutenant* Cano, Mr. Arkamis."

"*Dr.* Arkamis, Lieutenant." He suppressed an amused grin. "As I was saying, my time is valuable, it is well past the end of my day, and I am a fair bit exhausted. Dr. Morrow may be content to humor your ramblings, but I am not. Now, *what* do you have to tell me?"

Cano's eyes dropped, but her composure slipped for only a heartbeat. "Of course, Dr. Arkamis," she said. "While we were unable to recover the recording component, the destroyed Guardian unit happened to be one of a few also outfitted with biosensors." She handed him a small datacard. "This is what it picked up moments before the blast."

Arkamis held the datacard over his wrist, and a small holographic display appeared above the holoquip on his forearm. "It's a biosignature, but I'm afraid I don't have every single one in the world memorized. Care to elaborate?"

"Compare it to Rook," Morrow said. "See what you think."

Arkamis frowned and manipulated the display in front of

him, pulling up a second set of data. He stared, and he didn't dare breathe. This didn't seem possible, yet there was no mistaking the overlapping biosignatures. Shutting down the display and pocketing the datacard, he closed the remaining distance between himself and Cano, forcing her back a step. "Why did you know to bring this to me?" he whispered.

Morrow cleared his throat. "Don't be so damn dramatic, Arkamis. Lieutenant Cano's done several off-the-record favors for me in the past. Few years ago, I gave her that biosig and told her if they ever identified a match to bring it to my attention. She's good at what she does." He rubbed his scruffy face and chuckled. "She should be—we pay her enough."

"I see," Arkamis said. "A job well done, then." He backed up but remained so tense that it was all he could do to keep from shaking. "I need this child, Lieutenant Cano. Bring me this child, and your reward will be an order of magnitude greater than whatever Dr. Morrow pays you."

"Thank you, Dr. Arkamis," Cano said. "But we have extremely limited resources, and I don't have the authority to conduct biosignature scanning. There simply aren't that many autodrones that can do it. It was pure luck this one even had the necessary module installed."

Arkamis began pacing again, deep in thought, and resumed the light tapping on the hilt of his saber. He paused for a moment and pointed his thumb at Cano. "Suppose some reliable tips were to come in indicating increased terrorist activity in the Waterfront District. Would this be sufficient to justify allocating the resources necessary to perform bioscans among the civilian population in that area?"

Cano stared out Arkamis' office windows. She slowly

nodded her head as though weighing the possibility before committing. "Well, it's true that it would be easy to attribute the destruction of the drone today to terrorism," she said. Her eyes brightened. "And it's not unheard of, either. Ever since the attack on your labs years ago, we've periodically found members of the Snowdrop Collective skulking around in the undercity. It's completely plausible they would be seeking to reestablish themselves." Her confidence returned with a hint of pride. "This can be done, Dr. Arkamis, and I'm the one to do it."

"Then I have two requests, Lieutenant Cano," Arkamis said. "One: I need you to see to the destruction of all other copies of that particular biosignature. You are the only one in the entire Cascadian Authority who is to know it even exists. Two: the child is to be treated with the utmost care and shall be delivered unharmed *and* unafraid. Again, if properly executed, this endeavor could earn you far more than anyone in the SecForce is taking home. Clear?"

Lt. Cano smiled. "Yes, Doctor."

"Excellent," Arkamis said. "I look forward to seeing results. You are dismissed, Lieutenant Cano."

With another curt nod, Cano left the office.

When she was out of earshot, Arkamis turned to his colleague. "This is it, Morrow! Our etherclaw work has stagnated for so long, but this changes everything. We can finally dust off the Osiris Project." He picked up the cold tea from his desk and swirled bits of leaves around the bottom. "But tell me about this Cano woman. Can she truly be trusted?"

"She's ambitious," Morrow said. "And she might appear green, but she's better informed and more cunning than you can imagine." His malevolent grin put his rotted teeth on full display. "She's had no qualms about engaging in various unsavory acts for me. Cano can be trusted. She's proven to be a highly beneficial asset."

"Then we need to fulfill our duty quickly so she can fulfill hers," Arkamis said. "I hope you don't have plans. We need to move on this immediately."

He took a whiff of his tea. The porcelain was cool on his lips as he downed the entire cup in a single swig. He'd never tasted it cold before. It was unconventional, yet crisp and invigorating. He would have to summon that servant girl for a fresh pot. It was going to be a long night.

CHAPTER 4
THE DISCOMFORTS OF HOME

Fenlee and Elliot arrived home late.

The maglev from the Waterfront District took a circuitous route, forcing them to change trains multiple times. Inhaling the undercity air for so long had made them both sick. They grabbed some fortified water from a self-serve bodega, and after a brief rest, both their pallor and demeanor improved. Fenlee could still catch the occasional whiff of the foul gunk on her clothes, but at least they were both out of that nightmare.

Once home to almost a billion, the population of New Cascadia had been devastated two centuries ago. The Great Collapse was the culmination of multiple civilization-shattering events: catastrophic climate change, resource depletion, and a global economy wrecked by strong artificial intelligence. After

the Aeons constructed the Void Pillars, the structures stabilized the climate and allowed humanity the opportunity to catch its collective breath. With broken nations and a worldwide power vacuum, a single global religion emerged. The Telluric Ascendancy required the worship of the Aeons, but also served as a guiding light as humankind climbed out of the darkness. Corporations such as Norfayne Labs were created to fulfill the Acendancy's mandate of renewal.

Now, a mere fifty million lived together in various wards and districts that had been rebuilt in the years since. Lower Ashe Ward, home to the Harpers, was one of the safer inhabited zones in the lower tier.

As they stepped off the final maglev platform, Fenlee sighed in relief at the familiar sights and sounds. It was night, but there was still a good amount of energy. Pushcarts, bicycles, and the occasional delivery drone shared the uneven streets. The hazy glow of the high-tier platforms and the colorful lights from shops, cafes, and tearooms danced in an ever-changing kaleidoscope along the wet avenues. Comforting smells of fried street food, peppery and pungent, made her stomach growl. She breathed deep. They were finally home.

Their building was a standard serviced apartment complex. An array of single-task bots and drones performed simple maintenance, upkeep, and basic security. But it was not, by any means, glamorous. Neighbors' arguments easily penetrated the paper-thin walls, and the poorly sealed windows let in moisture while heat escaped in the winter and invaded in the summer.

The glow panel lighting flickered to life as they entered. The apartment was small, but sufficient—a kitchenette attached to a common room, two bedrooms, one bath, and a converted utility room that Elliot used. Fenlee slumped over the cold steel table in the kitchen while Elliot went straight to work on some noodles and tea. He typically prepared dinners in the evenings and prepped lunches in the morning. After too many of Fenlee's inedible messes, he had insisted.

A fistful of dry brown rice danced around a hot pan and a bit of the tension slipped from Fenlee's shoulders. Rice tea was usually so bland, but Elliot's genmaicha was special. The comforting aroma of the crackling grains filled the kitchen. He steeped the roasted rice and added a spoonful of matcha powder. They ate and sipped in exhausted silence.

The comm unit on the end of the counter lit up with a chirp.

They both stopped eating and stared. Messages were expensive to send and consequently rare. Elliot raised an eyebrow at Fenlee. "Expecting something?"

"Nope," Fenlee said. She clutched the edge of the table as she made her way to the comm unit. The green light atop the dusty old box pulsed with an impatient urgency. Like most low-tier residents, they didn't have a meshnet connection. Instead, they relied on couriers to deliver messages via short-range wireless transmission once or twice a day. Local messages from in and around their ward were delivered in a similar way, but those were free and would have gone to one of their holoquips. The Harpers hadn't received a message on their household comm unit in years. Receiving one after the night they'd endured made her uneasy, but Fenlee went ahead and hit the play button.

"*Hey there, crew!*" It was Maxwell Harper, Fenlee's biological father and Elliot's adoptive, and she immediately picked up on the nervous tone in his voice. His likeness filled the small screen—a broad-shouldered man with fiery red hair and dirty freckles smiled and offered a thumbs-up against the backdrop of a grimy maintenance bay. It was a static image, the same profile picture he'd been using for years.

He continued, "*Hope everything's going well, but if I know my Fenlee and Elliot, y'all are fine. Not worried. No way. Hey, I'm fine too! Company only gave me a little slice of time to record this though, so I gotta be quick. Good news and bad news. Well, depending on how you look at it, maybe good news and good news? Aw, hell. Anyway, bad news is, I won't be back around tomorrow like we planned. Gonna be off-planet a few more months. I know, I know, and I'm sorry. But, the good news is they want me on that new orbital platform and I might be able to make team lead if I stay on a little longer. Saw an opportunity and I took it.*"

It was at that point that Fenlee tuned out, ignoring the rest of the message. He did this to himself. He did this to them. After her mother died, he had promised he'd never leave her. The two week off-planet rotations these days were bad enough, but he'd already been gone a month this time and now he was extending it. She slammed her hand down on the comm unit shutting it—and him—off.

Elliot kept quiet, chewing on his hair and contemplating his boots. She looked through the tiny forest of plants her brother grew in their small common room and out the window to the murky sea of metropolis lights beyond. Everything was compressing on her shoulders, and her anxiety levels were about maxed out.

The dangers on the orbital platforms were real. Since her father's company had been acquired by Norfayne Labs, they'd been desperately trying to restart asteroid mining for the first time in two hundred years to make up for the critical resource shortages. But they were moving too fast and accidents were common.

"What are we going to do for that long?" Elliot asked.

"Same thing we always do. We don't need him around anyway." Bracing herself on the wall, she hopped down the hallway toward her room. "Sorry, I just need to be alone." She tried to close the door behind her, but the stupid thing was jammed again.

The automatic sliding mechanism on her pocket door had started malfunctioning a week before and she hadn't fixed it yet. She tried to force it closed manually, but the door kept slipping in her grip and she couldn't get the leverage she needed. Her eyes stung in frustration, which only made her angrier. She grabbed the multimini tool from her workbench, stabbed one of the sharp bits through the thin aluminum door, yanked it shut, and collapsed on the floor.

She ran a finger over the multimini. It was a gift from Elliot four years ago for her twelfth birthday, and it was perfect. It had spring-action pliers, an array of blades and screwdrivers, and even a micro torch. She never figured out how he'd saved up enough for it, but the fact that he had meant everything to her.

The same birthday, her dad had given her the most ill-fitting garment she'd ever owned. It was an amazing-looking dress, and he probably paid a helluva lot more than he should have for it. She'd been excited to wear it but hid her tears when she tried it on. It was cut for her mother's figure. All these years after her death, that's where his attention remained. If he'd shown more concern for his own daughter, maybe he'd have noticed she had more of his big-boned genetics and very little of her mother's slight build. Even now, years later, he still saw

Fenlee as an extension of her mother—when he bothered to see her at all. That was why the leg had meant so much. It was an uncharacteristically informed gift, as if, for at least a moment, he *had* paid attention.

She pulled off her filthy outer layer of clothes and threw them across the room. Her shoe had dried on the outside, but the ball of her foot was one big saturated blister. She eased on a dry sock, then dug around in a bin under her workbench for her old faded blue leg. Each nick, dent, and scratch covering the leg had its own story. It would be a little short, but at least it had the same interface.

The pin snapped into place. She felt a little better, but still incomplete.

Fenlee pressed her hand over her heart and took comfort in the small lump under her tank top. The opal was a tangible reminder of her mother's love, and to Fenlee, proof of her existence. Just as her mother had never been without it, Fenlee took it everywhere. She had switched her mother's fragile silver chain with a black tungsten replacement, one she trusted would never fail.

When Fenlee's mother died, her father had fallen into a deep and distant depression. After he recovered from a night of drinking that almost killed him, he had promised he'd always be there for her from then on. The eight-year-old girl accepted his solemn vow and the security it afforded her. He was true to sobriety, but in recent years, work had taken him further and further away from her. *At what point is that promise as good as broken, Dad?*

They had been living a good mid-tier life on her mother's salary, but after her death, her father sold almost all of their belongings to purchase their modest low-tier apartment. The only items of her mother's that remained were the opal and an odd ceramic statue that looked like a cross between a fox and a cat. They were Fenlee's most precious treasure.

She took off the opal to examine it.

Multicolor flecks caught the city lights from outside her window and shimmered deep within the blackness of the stone. Over the years, she'd spent countless hours gazing into it as though another universe lived within its depths. She held it close and felt its warmth on her lips. As a little girl, she had equated the heat that radiated from the opal as her mother's love. But as she'd gotten older, she'd come to realize that warmth was just her own body heat being transferred to the opal as it hung against her chest…wasn't it? Or was it something more? She'd never given it much thought, but the little rock had almost become a part of her. On the rare occasion she had to take it off, it left her feeling anxious and exposed. It was as though it had somehow become an extension of herself. But for the first time, it also gave her a sense of unease.

Mom…what the hell did you give me?

She was beyond exhausted, but her brain was electric, still wired from the day's events. Picking up her side bags, she cleared a space on her workbench, switched on a small lamp, and dumped out the contents.

Her workbench was directly under her bunk. For a brief period after they'd found Elliot, he slept beneath her. It had been therapeutic in an odd sort of way to have him around after her mother died. It helped for her to have someone to take care of. She had never had a sibling, and this pale, quiet, frightened little boy needed her. And she had needed to be needed. After a couple of years, they both wanted their own space, so Elliot took the utility room down the hall. It was cramped and windowless, but he seemed to be comfortable sleeping there. Her privacy was important, but his presence brought tranquility and she missed that sometimes.

The day's haul was not impressive. She stashed a set of springs and a handful of fasteners in a parts drawer and set the rest aside to try and sell later that week. All that was left was the small canvas bundle.

She held it with reverent uncertainty, like the apprehension before opening a brilliantly wrapped birthday gift knowing the contents may well turn out as disappointing as a half-eaten wheat bar. The fabric was soft in her hands, well-worn without the coarse feel typical of canvas. It had an organic smell, a musky sweetness that it wouldn't have picked up from the conduit run. She turned it over revealing a dark red stain on the bottom.

Blood. *I swear, if this is another severed finger…*

After a brief battle with the cloth tie at the top, the bundle came loose. She peeled back the strips of canvas, revealing a curious assortment of objects. Before her sat a piece of unpolished quartz, a standard datacard, a logic chip, and what appeared to be the mushy remains of four or five blueberries. She was relieved to see that the berries were the apparent cause of the "bloodstain" on the bottom.

She wasn't about to pop unknown datacards in her system, but she was more interested in the chip, anyway. She rotated it with her fingers. There was no imprint on it, and the serial number was gone. Or maybe there had never been one.

It looked like…

On the back of her workbench was a scavenger bot she'd been working on for the better part of the last year. The matte black, eight-legged little robot was about the same size as her open hand. Grinning, she picked up the little bot, and in short order had its outer casing removed. Inside, she had embedded a small coprocessor board for pluggable modules. So far, she had a few specialized chips to help with sensory input, navigation, and movement. These component chips were swappable and easily tied together through a central program she'd written.

She tried to pop the new chip in, but the pin alignment was slightly off. This was not an insurmountable problem. Her old friend Murdok would surely have something available to get this new chip seated correctly.

Right. Need to add "socket adapter" to the list.

She held the chip under her lamp, a thrilling tickle running up the back of her neck. The little chunk of nanotransistors could be dead and worthless. But it certainly *looked* like an Elixir chip, the basic AI unit fabricated—and highly regulated—for use in high-end robotics. They were expensive and required a license to use, so she'd never entertained the possibility of getting her hands on one. Of course, an unlicensed Elixir chip was contraband in the eyes of the Cascadian Authority. It may be worth a fortune, but it'd be impossible to sell without a license.

She didn't care—this could be the finishing touch on the scavenger bot project she needed to be able to prove herself at the academy. If she could get it working for her final practical exam by next year, then she'd almost be guaranteed a position at Norfayne. And, if this truly was a working Elixir chip, she would never have to go into dangerous areas looking for parts and scrap again.

The possibilities were thrilling. Her necklace, her father, her leg, and all the world's troubles could wait.

CHAPTER 5
CAN WE KEEP HIM?

THE MORNING SUN cut through the layers of the city and atmospheric particulate to arrive, uninvited, smack in the middle of Fenlee's face. She opened her eyes, decided that was a horrible idea, and rolled over. As she began to sink back into the sweetness of sleep, a few taps on her bedroom door jolted her into the reality of the day.

"Lee," Elliot said from the other side of her door, "you've got to get up or we're going to be late." He hesitated for a moment. "I made you some tea."

"M'kay." Mornings were always the worst and her fatigue from the day before wasn't helping. But she wasn't about to miss school. As she climbed down from her bunk, she was overcome by a horrific smell. She looked around for the source of the

otherworldly odor and, realizing it was her, headed straight for the bathroom.

The humidity and filth from their expedition through the undercity had angered her acne. She was choking the life out of a particularly deep zit a few inches from the bathroom mirror when Elliot slid the door open.

"You'll never guess—"

"Agh! Elliot, I didn't say come in! Get out! Out out *out!*" Fenlee yelled. *Elliot and his dumb perfectly moisturized soft clear stupid face.*

He shut the door with a meek meow-like sound, and Fenlee went back to work on the few remaining mini-volcanoes dotting her skin.

After a quick shower and some fresh clothes, she went to apologize to her brother. The last thing she wanted was to project her stresses onto him or make him feel worse than she figured he probably already did.

"Elliot, I'm so sorry. I didn't mean—"

"Check it out!" Elliot was seated in the kitchen grinning ear to ear as he picked up a medium-sized ball of orange and brown fur from his lap. "Kavi came and found us." The cat hopped out of his hands and sauntered across the table to Fenlee.

"Ah, great. The cat." A cat was not something she ever expected to see in her home, let alone the weird cat from the day before. "Why is he here? *How* is he here?"

"No idea how he followed us, I mean with all the train switching and rain and everything, but here he is. Isn't it great?" he said, putting away a small dish of water. "What do you think? I'm guessing he wants to live with us!" Elliot was happier than the first time his pet cactus bloomed.

Fenlee gave the cat an experimental pat on the head. Her hand vibrated with a soothing purr. There was a comfort to it, similar to the way the rumbling warmth of their old heating system kept the winter cold at bay. Kavi yawned and turned around, his tail went vertical, and he presented his backside.

"I think he likes you," Elliot said.

"He seems real proud of his butthole, at the very least." Fenlee was torn. She'd never really been into animals, not like Elliot was, and their father would never allow a cat around. But her father wasn't going to be back around for a while, so who the hell cared? "I tell you what, why don't we see if he even wants to stay with us? That green-haired kid from yesterday said Kavi pretty much does whatever he wants, right? This cat might be here today, gone tomorrow. But if he wants to stay, maybe we can figure out how to make a place for him. Sound good?"

"Yes! You're awesome. You won't even notice he's around. I mean, unless you want to notice him. He can stay in my room. I mean, unless you want him to hang out in your room, then that's fine too. Maybe we can share him?" Elliot's smile took over her face like a contagious yawn.

"This isn't exactly the largest apartment, so it won't be easy. Also, Kavi's a hundred percent your responsibility while he's around."

"He might be scared here alone while we're gone. I think he should come with me today."

Fenlee laughed. "To the academy? Yeah, right. And how exactly would that work?"

"Don't worry." He gave the cat an affectionate chin scratch. "Kavi and I got this figured out." He opened the main section of his backpack and the cat hopped in as though it was a totally natural exercise they had gone through a million times.

"Huh," Fenlee said. "Well, good luck with that. If anyone discovers him, that's on you." She grabbed her hoodie and backpack as they left the apartment. "By the way, I was going through some of the stuff we found last night, and I want to stop at Murdok's after school. Turns out yesterday wasn't a total loss." She checked her chrono. "But we have to run. I'll tell you about it later."

They rolled their bicycles out of the secured repository next door. The sun was still low enough in the cloudless morning sky to paint last night's puddles a fiery pink. Daytime street vendors were setting up their food and wares. The aroma of fresh spiced breads and the oily tang of not-so-fresh synthetic meats clawed at the hole in Fenlee's stomach where her forgotten breakfast should have been.

The ancient temaki cart man had just opened for business. He spent every day, rain or shine, across from their building. With all the money she'd given him over the years, she could probably have purchased her own temaki cart. Though he never said anything, his gaze seemed to bore straight through his eye patch as though judging her lack of fiscal responsibility. Before Fenlee could get out the two crednotes to pay, he was already preparing a plain red rice roll for her. After a wordless exchange, she hopped on her bicycle, breakfast in hand.

"Oh, come on," Elliot said. "Don't ride one-handed."

"Oh you come on. I can ride no-handed," Fenlee said. "And I'm not the one with a cat in the bag. Just don't get all clumsy and fall, or we'll be having crushed feline for dinner."

Elliot clamped his mouth and tightened his grip on the handlebars.

The school day inched by. Fenlee's exhaustion from their adventure the day prior had caught up with her. In Civic Religion, she napped through a lecture on pilgrimages to the Void Pillars, her mind weaving its way through a nightmare about etherclaw. In Mechatronics, she daydreamed about her Elixir chip instead of programming a servo. In Applied Mathematics, she sketched out a clever way to cram a socket adapter in her scavenger bot. And in Intro to Control Systems, she melted into the desk, overwhelmed with thoughts of her father.

"Hey, Fenlee." A light breeze tickled her ear. "*Fenlee*, you awake?" More like a hot gust.

Casper.

"What? Geez, what's up, man? What are you doing?" Fenlee said, cleaving through her mind's fog. She typically sat by Casper in Control Systems class. He was her lab partner and friend, but his whispering had put him unnervingly close to her face. Casper was a little taller than she was, though she figured he weighed half as much. Out of her small group of friends, he was the only one whose acne was worse than hers, or at least it was more prominent on his pasty skin. They traded skin care tips, but she often wondered if it wouldn't make more sense to get those tips from someone with a clear complexion instead.

Casper contorted his scrawny frame to lean in close. "You were totally zoning," he said. "I was trying to do you a favor and bring you back to life before you got called on or called out."

The instructor droned on in the background. "...*but here we are interested in feedback stabilization...*"

"I'm fine," Fenlee said.

"Didn't look so fine," Casper said. "I mean, not that you don't look *fine*. Because you totally do, you know?" He recoiled from his own words like trying to choke back surprise vomit. "Er. Not what I meant. Sorry."

They had been best friends growing up, doing everything from working on mechatronics projects or exploring the Lower Ashe Ward together. Casper had even stayed over more than once when things got a little rough at his place. Then, a few years ago, he started seeing her as more than friends and decided to act on his feelings. She had just gotten over a total joke of a relationship and was in no mood to have another one of her friends start drooling all over her whenever they were together. There were only a few people she'd been into over the years, and Casper was not one of them. She made it clear they weren't going to go down that route. Ever. He seemed to get it, and apart from an awkward slip here or there, he'd left it alone since.

"Don't worry about it," Fenlee said. "I'm just a little tired today."

"*...recall that we are concerned with overall system stability...*"

"Yeah, you looked like you were either gonna pass out or cry or maybe both."

"*...therefore the eigenvalue placement...*"

"I don't know, maybe I was," Fenlee said. She started to melt into her desk again. "Found out last night my dad's going to be up on that new orbital platform for several more months."

"Ouch, yeah, that sucks," he said. "I mean, I guess I should've figured. Sounds like my dad's stuck up there a while longer, too, but man, it's gonna be so great having him gone that long. But your dad's pretty all right, you know?" The instructor glanced their way, so Casper messed with his notes display to look busy. "That's kind of a long time. What are you gonna do?"

"...*and so we have a stable transfer function...*"

"Dunno. The same old crap I always do, I guess," Fenlee said. She stifled a yawn and recalled the main reason she was exhausted. "Oh, Cas! I didn't even tell you what happened yesterday. You know those schematics you gave me? The ones with access and mapping data over in Waterfront? Yeah, so the mapping info was mostly correct, but there were live Guardian drones. Elliot and I almost got killed!"

Casper went bug-eyed. "What the—"

The chime rang three times, indicating the end of the day. Fenlee checked her chronometer, gauging how much time she and Elliot would have to get to Murdok's. "It's okay, not your fault at all. But I've got to tell you about this later."

"Maybe come over tomorrow?" he said, hurrying to catch up as she walked out the door. "I don't have any classes, so I'll be around all day." He dropped into a conspiratorial tone, again leaning just a little too close. "And Alex is gonna be there."

Fenlee felt her cheeks flush. Lately, she was finding it hard to be around Alex without seeing her friend through a different lens. And Casper seemed to have picked up on it. "Yeah, sounds great. Let's catch up then. I have something I have to look into today." The warmth from her opal seemed to pulse in time with her heartbeat. *Well, two things.*

CHAPTER 6
MURDOK

It had started drizzling again. Most of the daylight not already obscured by the buildings and upper platforms was diminished by the low cloud cover. After the academy let out, Fenlee and Elliot wasted no time heading off together, trying to beat the worst of the rain. Hoods up, they biked along the bustling thoroughfare that cut through the middle of their ward until they arrived at the entrance to a winding alley. They hopped off and walked their bikes toward the Lunarinto Market, and Murdok's, where Fenlee hoped to find a socket adapter. And maybe some answers.

As they turned off the main road, the back of Fenlee's neck tingled as though they were being watched. She stopped and looked over her shoulder. A green-haired figure ducked behind

a large, slow-moving service bot. She thought about calling out, but the figure quickly darted through the crowd and disappeared.

There was no way. Those two wanted nothing to do with her, right?

She shrugged it off. They'd probably passed a dozen people with various shades of green hair just on the way here, and there was no reason to think that weird kid from the other day was tailing them. Still, the eerie feeling wouldn't leave her alone. But it didn't matter; she could easily lose almost anyone in the Market.

"You okay?" Elliot asked.

"Oh, yeah. Hundred percent," Fenlee replied. "Sorry, let's just get to Murdok's."

The Market was labyrinthine, a tangled knot of alleyways that acted as a hub where a thousand subcultures mingled. Lanterns and dimly lit signs hung at irregular angles above the faded awnings and recessed doorways. Fenlee nodded to a few people she knew and avoided those she didn't want to know. Spice and incense blended with petrichor, making her feel tired, hungry, and fiercely alive all at once.

They continued past small tea cafes, medicine dealers, run-down bordellos, questionable credit brokers, and even a toy shop that had not changed its window display for as long as she could remember. No one here was perfect, and no one aspired to be. But everyone had something to sell. It was a threadbare tapestry of commerce.

After a purposeful sequence of twists and turns that would disorient most newcomers, the pair arrived at a faded red door. The small hand-painted sign above would be easy for most to miss.

Murdok's
Salvage and Collateral

A door chime sounded as they entered and leaned their dripping bikes against a wooden bookcase. Outside light streaming through a single barred window cast shadowy ribbons across piles of artifacts, some centuries old.

The only other light came from a few orange-y filament bulbs hung at arbitrary intervals highlighting a stack of papers here, a box of gears there, or, in one case, a fluffy robotic bear that had seen better days. Dust tickled Fenlee's nose along with her favorite aromas of well-worn metal, machine oil, and musky vanilla.

An old woman standing behind the counter looked as ancient as anything else in the shop. The light gave greater warmth to her weathered skin and deepened the creases lining her face. She had on a pair of loupes and was studying a palm-sized circuit board.

"Fenlee Harper," the woman said without looking up. "It's been a few weeks. Things were starting to get dull around here." She pushed the loupes up on her forehead. "And you brought Elliot this time!" She looked him up and down. "You look like a wet dog. A skinny wet dog. Does your sister not throw you any scraps?" She picked up a wrapped candy from a bowl on the counter and tossed it to him.

"Thanks, Murdok," Elliot said, catching the buttery vanilla sweet. "Nice to see you too."

"Of course, Elliot." The old woman smiled. "And there's no need to hide your friend. Why don't you let the cat out of the bag? Let him run around and get some air. He won't hurt anything in here."

Elliot blinked. "Um, sure. How did you know...?" He shook his head and let Kavi out. "Never mind."

"So, Dok," Fenlee said. "Got a few things for you today." She dropped a bag on the counter. "How much for all this?"

The old woman dumped out the bag and picked through the items Fenlee had taken from the undercity. "Not much. I'll test these capacitors and see if they're any good, but that's about all that's of any value here." She put everything else back in the bag. "You should hang on to the rest."

Fenlee sighed, but she wasn't surprised. "Not what I was hoping to hear," she said. "Thanks anyway though."

Murdok leaned forward on her elbows. "What else have you brought me? You never start with your most impressive pieces."

"You're right about that. I need a socket adapter or some way to interface with this." Fenlee handed Murdok the chip from the canvas bundle. "I think it might be an Elixir chip. Pretty unbelievable, right?"

Murdok turned the precious chip over in her hands with a mixture of reverence and...something else Fenlee couldn't quite identify. "I know what it is. I don't think *you* know what it is."

"Do you have anything that will work with it?" Fenlee said.

Murdok passed the chip back, stepped down from her side of the counter, and walked around to stand in front of Fenlee. At about four feet tall, she may have had to look up at Fenlee, but her presence always filled the room. Murdok shook her head. "Wait here."

She rummaged around in her back rooms and returned moments later with a socket adapter in hand and a grave expression on her face. "I'm parting with this against my better judgment, Fenlee." She broke into a wide grin. "But far be it for me to deny a girl an adventure."

Kavi hopped up on the counter and sauntered over to the old woman for a scratch behind the ears. "I think I like your new friend, Elliot." She dumped out the candy bowl and filled it from a water bottle under the counter. Kavi lapped it as though it were a spring in an oasis. "Now, as I was saying, there's the matter of payment. That little piece of hardware is not cheap, and I'm afraid what you've brought for me today is terribly insufficient for a trade."

"I thought we were on a budget, Lee," Elliot muttered.

He was right, and she knew it. They were going to have to be careful with the crednotes while her father was away. Still, she really, truly needed this socket adapter. It was this small piece that could bridge the gap between a kid's toy robot, and a fully functioning autonomous scavenger.

"Well…" Fenlee arched an eyebrow. "How about I go ahead and take it now, and pay you what I owe over the next few weeks?"

"Oh, Fenlee, my little Fenlee. Do you have any idea what your current tab looks like?" Murdok pointed to the box Fenlee was carrying. "Do you have any idea how much that item alone is worth?" She activated a flickering holographic display in the counter and sorted through some customer account logs. "I can't bankroll your hobbies like I've been doing. You're more than old enough to start accounting for yourself." She reversed the display so Fenlee could take a look. "See this?"

Fenlee gawked. "Oh. I…that's more than I thought," she said. There were records going back years. Until seeing the comprehensive list in front of her, she'd never realized how much

Murdok had let her have without payment. There was a shortwave RF amplifier from years ago that she had never gotten to work, bevel gears, pinions, and even a barometric sensor that she had never found a use for, but had looked neat at the time. And Murdok had tracked it all.

A surreptitious smile played across Murdok's face. "Perhaps I have a solution," she said, shutting off the display. From her vest pocket she pulled an old wooden pipe, packed some sweet-smelling leaves, and lit up. A few puffs later, Kavi had left the counter area. "I have all this…*stuff* everywhere," Murdok continued, waving her hand around as though being the proprietor of the most interesting shop Fenlee had ever seen was little more than a nuisance. "It's unorganized. And filthy. Those bicycles of yours likely pick up more dirt inside here than they leave."

Murdok leaned across the counter close to Fenlee and blew a sharp jet of smoke out the side of her mouth away from the two of them. "You come in here a couple of days a week to help out and I'll pay you. Half of that goes toward your outstanding balance, and the other half goes in your pocket." She leaned back and laughed. "What do you think, Elliot? You think your sister's up to it?"

Fenlee didn't know what to think. On the one hand, this was Murdok's, a place of wonder, a place she felt safe, and a place where, maybe, she could learn a few things. On the other, this would mean an actual *job*. Work was fine, Fenlee loved burying herself in a good project. But a job? Jobs were where imaginations went to die, and that terrified her. She had watched jobs and careers chew up her father and the parents of all of her friends, stripping their passion and humanity.

But maybe this could be different—it was Murdok, after all. Fenlee couldn't justify passing up the opportunity, and it also appeared to be the only way she could get her hands on that damn socket adapter.

"I'll do it," Fenlee said.

Murdok smiled. "Of course you will."

"Since I guess I'm an employee now, can you do an *employee* a favor and take a quick look at something for me?"

Murdok squinted, twisting the corners of her mouth in odd, opposing ways, like a sideways integral. "You're quick to try and find an angle, my little worker," she said. "By, 'take a quick look,' I imagine you mean you want an appraisal or a forensic analysis? No go."

"I don't mean break out a mass spectrometer and destroy it or anything," Fenlee reached down her shirt and pulled out her opal. It was ridiculous to think it could be anything other than a smoothly polished stone, but she had to know the truth. "I don't even care how much it's worth. I just need to know if it's real or not. I need to know what it is."

Murdok's smirk deepened and she raised a single eyebrow. "I'll do it this one time without an appraisal fee. We can call it a signing bonus, I suppose." She took the necklace and stone from Fenlee and dropped the loupes over her eyes again. "But no more favors and no more freebies. You're working a real gig now, kiddo."

Taking the opal gently but firmly, Murdok rolled it around in her rough fingers, inspecting it. She frowned and flipped down an alternate lens, activating the miniature elemental scanner in her glasses.

Fenlee held her breath. If Murdok, with her years of experience and skill, couldn't identify it by sight alone, there must be something significant about the opal, something different, something special.

The old woman flipped the loupes back up on her forehead and gave the stone a final odd look. "Here you go, my little geologist," she said, passing the opal back.

"So what do you think? What is it?"

"It's fake, Fenlee." Murdok offered a sympathetic smile. "I'm sorry."

"But what's it made of? And is there anything inside of it?" The mere fact that it was not a genuine opal made no difference to her. It was from her mother, and had it been a chunk of cement, it would still be priceless. But if it were fake, that meant maybe there was something to the whole etherclaw thing after all.

"It's just a synthetic resin. A strong, higher quality one, sure, but nothing fancy. Certainly not worth much. Apart from some peculiar fabrication defects inside, there's nothing terribly out of the ordinary about it. I would date this as no more than two decades old, likely manufactured in one of the Chinese Industrial Provinces."

Fenlee didn't know why she should have expected anything different. She wondered if her mother had known it wasn't a real opal. There wasn't any backstory or history Fenlee was aware of that made it significant. She just knew her mother had worn it every day she could remember. Maybe it was only a phony rock that her mother happened to like.

"It's pretty enough, though. And if it's important to you, the authenticity and quality don't matter one little bit," Murdok said. "Now, it's about time for me to shut down for the night. I'll expect to see you here at the shop around the first of next week."

"You better believe it. I'm a woman of my word." The phrase felt funny leaving her mouth, but in Murdok's case, it was true. She would be there, and she would fulfill her obligations.

"You two take care getting home."

"Thanks, Dok. See you."

Fenlee and her brother rode home in a hazy drizzle. Nightfall made the glow of the high-tier platforms more pronounced in the gradiated dusk. She tried to shove the opal out of her thoughts and focus on getting to her workbench to install the Elixir chip, but too many things gnawed at the corners of her mind. Her mother would never have cared about a fake piece-of-junk rock, so why had she valued the opal so much? No, none of it added up, and only left her with a growing sense of unease.

CHAPTER 7
CIPHER DROP

THOUGHTS OF ETHERCLAW and worries about her father had kept Fenlee up, so she'd spent almost the entire night installing and integrating the Elixir chip to keep her mind elsewhere. She got it working, but sleep still wouldn't come, so she composed a message to her father. It'd be expensive to send, but she had to say something.

> *Hi, Dad. Hope you're well. Me? I'm great. Except that I've been shitting myself because, you know, after Mom died, we all promised we'd never leave each other. And that's kind of what you're best at these days. But, hey, it's all fine because I found a chip that's most likely stolen and worth probably half this apartment block, but in order to get it to work, I*

had to go into the Lunarinto Market for an adapter. But the adapter wasn't exactly free, so I'm going to start working a part-time job while you're gone to pay it off. In the Lunarinto Market. You know, the place you hate for me to even go near. One of my legs is just short enough to be constantly uncomfortable because I decided to wreck the one you gave me, my underwear is somehow still riding up my ass from the bike ride home yesterday, and I'm hyperaware of how bad my pits stink. Doesn't matter because I got no sleep and I don't have time to do much about it before academy. Also, Mom's opal, which isn't real, by the way, might actually be some kind of weird magic device from aliens. Woo! Oh, and your adopted son is smuggling a stray cat. Thought you should know. Don't get yourself blown up. Love you!

She stared at the comm unit for an eternity before deleting it. Her opal felt cold on her chest in the morning gloom.

After school let out, sister and brother hopped on their bikes and headed to Casper's place. Fenlee's leg was starting to throb. The difference in length was minor, but she could feel it in her hip. To offset this, her right leg did more of the work, and the ache in her muscles from overcompensating was a constant reminder of how dumb it was to have destroyed her other leg in the first place.

Casper lived close to the academy. The short ride there took them through a gauntlet of fried temptations hawked by vendors so eager to sell, Fenlee was certain at any moment she'd find a still-steaming mutt stick made from back-alley meat stuffed in her mouth and an outstretched hand demanding payment. Even Kavi stuck his head out of Elliot's backpack to locate the source of the aromas. Fenlee was glad to be surrounded by the noise and chaos of the city, as she was certain the sound of her stomach rumbling could have been heard for blocks in every direction otherwise.

Two adjoined towers rose hundreds of stories high in front of them. The twisted hulks of steel and cement formed a single structure that acted as a cornerstone for the Central Platform in New Cascadia. The patchwork of living spaces on each tower appeared as growths, tumors that had infested the structures over time. Leaking pipes, steam vents, conduits, and an assortment of machinery obfuscated the original building facade. The odd array of characters standing around paid Fenlee and Elliot no mind as they secured their bikes in a lock station and went inside.

A timeworn man, looking as though he'd been recently unearthed, glanced up from his reading material as they entered one of the branching sub-lobbies. Fenlee imagined rust flaking from his eyes as they rolled in the sockets. Normally, lift access and control would be a duty left to a bot, but there weren't enough to go around, and some human or other would often have to take over instead. Judging them innocuous enough, or simply not caring, he hit the lift authorization. Fenlee and Elliot shot up fifty-three levels before the old lift car shuddered to a halt.

Casper greeted them at the door in a stained, too-big tank top, a pair of old warmlite goggles dangling around his neck. "Heya, Fenlee! And you brought your bro! What's up, Ellie?"

Casper said, leading them inside. "Sorry about the mess. Mom left for work a little bit ago, and I don't think she was really awake between shifts. I'd pick up and stuff, but if she can't find her things, then it goes...not well. Plus, she's pretty pissed my dad's going to be away for so long. She doesn't get it yet, but she's gonna love not having his sorry ass around."

He laughed and kept walking, but Fenlee caught a sliver of pain flash in his eyes as he turned. "Anyway, Alex is already here."

They walked into the common room where a girl lounged at the table, study materials spread out in front of her. Fenlee immediately wished she'd taken the time to shower and just dealt with being late that morning. Every part of her felt self-conscious about something. "Oh, heya, Alex. Got capoeira today?"

Casper and Alex, different in nearly every way, were the most unlikely of study partners. Fenlee found it hard not to feel like she was in the presence of perfection whenever she was around Alex. Apart from being utterly brilliant, she was strong and impossibly hot. Her rich, dark skin contrasted sharply against the bright white of her crisp, form-fitting workout gear, the top of which exposed her trim, cut midriff and round, muscled shoulders. Long, thin braids were done up atop her head in a coiled bun, with a few strays draped around the contours of her neck. Each was jet black with sparks of pink and beads of silver. As she turned to greet Fenlee and Elliot, her abdomen flexed like corrugated steel conduit.

Alex had moved with her aunt Lily from one of the last habitable equatorial zones to the city-state of New Cascadia two years before and she had kept mostly to herself at the time. After seeing her lonely day after day, Fenlee and Casper approached her, and they'd all been friends ever since. Alex was quiet about her past, and Fenlee didn't want to pry. She'd gathered bits and pieces over time, but never enough to paint a full picture. She knew her move had to do with Norfayne pushing resource extraction in the equatorial zones too far. And as an employee of the company, her aunt was forced to flee with Alex or risk getting caught up in the unrest. Maybe there was more, but Norfayne was politically complicated, and Fenlee preferred to tune out a lot of the details.

"Hey, you two." Alex smiled. "I wanted to stop by and swap some quick study time with Casper before capoeira practice, but timing's tight, so I just wore my stuff. What brings you both here?"

Kavi poked his head out of Elliot's bag and looked around. "Whoa! Ellie, you got a cat?" Casper ran over and met Kavi at eye level. "Seems...nice? Just don't let him piss on stuff or my mom'll blame me again, you know?"

Alex allowed Kavi to sniff her hand. "What's its name?" she asked.

"His name's Kavi," Elliot said. "He's only been around a couple of days, but he's really great. We found him in the Waterfront undercity and he ended up following us—"

"Following *you*," Fenlee interrupted, throwing a sideways glance at the cat. "Which reminds me—Cas, that undercity map you gave us was insane."

"Well, he suits you," Alex whispered to Elliot and sat back down. "Why are you two still playing around down there? You know how dangerous it is. One wrong turn, and they'll never find your bodies." She bounced a wadded-up food wrapper at

Casper. "Those maps are hard to come by for a reason. You all don't seem to know the history of that area."

It was true. Despite having only been a New Cascadian resident a short time, Alex was well-studied in the history and politics of the city-state. Fenlee had no idea when she found the time.

Casper threw the wrapper back and managed to miss Alex's head by a foot. She didn't flinch. "Yeah, well, that's why you're here. You teach me history, I teach you mechatronics. Can't expect everyone to know everything, you know? And plus, Fenlee's tougher than she looks. She always fine down there."

Fenlee crossed her arms. "Oh, really? Tougher than I *look*?"

"Well, I mean, do you want to look tough? Because you totally do. Unless you don't want to, in which case—"

Alex laughed and hit Casper square in the mouth with the wrapper. "You need to watch what comes out of your face, Cas."

"You know I can't watch my own face," Casper said. "But whatever. I wanna hear about what you found, just lemme grab something first." He went into his room and emerged a moment later with a small metal box Fenlee recognized as casing for a ventilation controller.

"You building out an airflow system or something? What is that?" Fenlee asked.

"This," Casper replied, "is my most magnificent creation!"

Fenlee suppressed an eye roll. Like her, Casper always had a project going. However, despite tutoring Alex in the subject, mechatronics was not Casper's strong suit. He was exceptional at systems and programming and one of the only people Fenlee knew who could reliably patch into the meshnet without getting caught. But when it came to manipulating anything in the physical world, most attempts ended in disaster.

Casper smiled. "It's not what you think. Check this out." He popped open the casing to reveal a medium-sized glass jar with a tight canvas wrap on top. "Been brewing for weeks! I just sampled some a couple days ago and decided I really need to share. So, I present to you: Casper's Super Secret Small Batch Sake! I got ahold of some yeast balls a while back and threw in a fistful of short grain. A little time in a box under my desk and—"

"Wasn't that the fart jar?" Fenlee asked.

Casper flushed down to the neckline of his tank top. "Uh, yeah, but you know, I cleaned it real good first."

"Well? Was the fart still in there? You weren't supposed to open it without me."

Alex leaned forward with a slight sideways grin. "I think Elliot and I might be missing out here. What exactly is the 'fart jar?'"

"Oh, Casper ripped a brutal one and trapped it as an experiment years ago when we were little kids," Fenlee said. "I'd forgotten all about it. Nice to see the old fart jar alive and well, though."

"Okay, if Cas had a stinker fermenting in there for years before the rice, I think I'll pass," Alex said.

"That's fair." Fenlee shrugged. "Gimme that jar, Cas, I'll give it a go." Casper passed her the jar and she took a deep swig. Fire cleared a path down to her stomach, and the back of her jaw tightened just enough to help her hold in a cough.

Casper leaned forward and studied her face. "What do you think?" he asked.

"I think," Fenlee said, taking a controlled breath, "that maybe…Casper, how long was this sitting under your desk?"

"Oh, I dunno. I actually kinda forgot about it until a few days ago, you know? I'd say almost a year?"

"Damn, Cas," Alex said. "That's got to be close to pure ethanol at this point."

"Yup. Not much flavor, but it gets the job done nice and fast," Casper said. "How 'bout it, Fenlee? Pretty good, right?"

"Definitely impressive. Probably better for cleaning wounds."

"Well, that's good to hear because"—Casper reached back into the casing and pulled out a second, smaller jar—"I made some just for you."

"Oh. Neat. Thanks." Fenlee flashed half a smile and stuffed the jar into her bag. "Now I want to show you my little project." When she pulled her hand back out, she was holding her little scavenger bot. "Meet Cipher. I stayed up all night putting the finishing touches on him. He's a completely operational, semi-autonomous bot. Well, at least I'm pretty sure he is. He's not field-tested, but we're gonna take care of that right after we leave. He's using some of the learning data I trained my old clunked-up junkbot with, so that should get him started." She activated his power source and he came to life, his circular sensor emitting a dull red glow. "There's a lot I have to tell you about the past few days."

Fenlee explained how they had used the mapping info provided by Casper to explore new areas of the undercity. She described losing her leg and running from the Sentry patrol drone. Knowing how expensive Elixir chips were and that she wasn't licensed for one anyway, she glossed over that part. She flicked another few drops of sake at Casper. "And your data was outdated or just flat wrong. We were almost killed by a damn Guardian down there." Then she told them about the close call and meeting Kyara and Nico. "It was all really weird. I was wondering though...Alex, you know the hell out of some history. You ever learn anything about something called etherclaw?"

"Etherclaw?" Alex pursed her lips and considered for a moment. "Can't say I have. Sorry."

Fenlee shook her head. "Yeah, it's fine," she said, pulling at the red stripe in her hair. "No one has, I guess. I kinda doubt it's actually a thing. It's just that the whole experience was so bizarre, I feel like I've gotta ask."

Alex stood up and grabbed her bag. "I totally didn't realize what time it was. I'm going to be late for practice." She walked toward the door and stopped, leaning close to Fenlee's shoulder.

Fenlee's world narrowed as she became fixated on whether or not Alex was close enough to see the fingernail marks around the giant zit she'd tried to annihilate in the bathroom before leaving for the academy. She wondered if her lips were still dried out. All the odors of the day clinging to her suddenly popped into focus.

Please don't smell my hair. Please don't smell my hair.

"You know, Fenlee, you've never been over to my place and met my aunt. She does biomech research for Norfayne and has a bunch of body parts lying around that—well, okay, that sounds bad. She has a lot of *artificial* body parts lying around and might be able to help you with something so you're not wearing that undersized leg until your dad gets back. Maybe you can come for dinner?"

Fenlee looked down at her worn-out leg and massaged her hip. She hated the idea of accepting charity, but Alex was a friend. Besides, she'd never been to her place and had always wanted to meet her aunt. "Yeah, I mean, I'd love to!" Fenlee said.

Alex nodded. "Elliot should come too. With your dad gone, I'm sure it'd be good to have a decent dinner."

"I make decent dinner," Elliot mumbled.

"Perfect, then I'll let my aunt know you'll help with prep." Alex winked at him and headed toward the door. "See you both this weekend."

"What, I'm not invited?" Casper asked.

"Nope!" Alex raised an eyebrow and pointed to the screens and markup on the table. "Maybe if you could at least recite The Tenets of Rebirth, but from what I've seen this week, you need to be head-down with those materials every chance you get. Dogma-based history's hard, I know, but you've got to know it or they'll kick your ass right out of that academy."

"Yeah, yeah. Still lame," Casper grumbled.

It was getting late. Casper's family had one of the less expensive interior apartments, so there was no natural light. Instead, they relied on an old envoscreen integrated into the wall, which mimicked outside conditions. Another hazy evening was settling in.

Fenlee checked her chronometer. "Damn, we have to run if I'm gonna release Cipher before it's dark out."

By the time they arrived at the Waterfront District, the deepening fog had obscured the remaining daylight, forcing night's early arrival. The lamps above the sparsely used avenues created voluminous glowing patches in the dense air. Fenlee typically enjoyed a little break from the noise and chaos around her home in Lower Ashe Ward, but tonight the quiet was unsettling.

The maglev wasn't crowded and they had made good time

getting there, or so Fenlee thought. She checked her chronometer. "Weird. It's still pretty early, but I have no idea where everyone is."

A lone street vendor finished putting away his goods and began pushing his cart toward a storage facility. The district may not have typically had the activity she was used to, but this was unusually desolate.

"I don't feel very good about this," Elliot said, pulling his hood further down over his face.

"No need to worry. This is perfect. We can drop off Cipher with zero risk of anyone seeing what we're up to. Now all we need is the access route." She activated the holoquip on her wrist. The translucent screen hovered above her forearm with the undercity map data, but she wasn't able to make sense of the layout relative to their current position. "Problem is, I'm not really sure where we are." She slammed the off button. This would be so much easier if they were allowed to patch into the stupid meshnet.

"I don't think we should waste time wandering around. Let's just go ask," Elliot said. He walked toward a crusty-looking bodega that was still open and had a human proprietor.

Clean water, snacks, bio-packs, and other goods lined the shelves in the small store. The dim photoluminescent lights painted everything bluish-green. Many shops charged photolumes during the day and saved crednotes by using them as supplementary lighting at night. But it was rare to see anyone using nothing *but* photolumes. It added to the creepy sensation tickling Fenlee's spine.

The owner was an older man with a round face and wrinkles so deep it was difficult to tell where his orifices began and ended.

"Nice shop you got here, sir." Fenlee winced as she tried to make small talk. "Say, where is everyone?"

"Are you both daft?" Spittle flicked from the old man's mouth as he berated Fenlee and Elliot. "There was a terrorist attack just two days ago, and the whole district is under tight surveillance. No lockdown, but the curfew starts soon, so of course no one's out. Can't you see all the shops around here are closed?"

"Then why are you still open?" Elliot asked.

"Because I don't care. And if you're not here to buy something, get yourselves gone!"

Fenlee grabbed two chili-flavored protein sticks and put a few crednotes on the counter. "We *are* buying something. And while we're here, tell us how to get where we're going and we'll get on out of your hair." She pulled up her undercity map and overlaid it with a layer of the district, noting the location of an access route. Switching off the undercity layer so as not to arouse suspicion, she asked if he could point out exactly where they were and how best to get to their destination.

A moment of grumbling later, the man identified their current location. He refused to give them the best route to their destination, however. "You'll have to figure that one out for yourself," he said. "You'll never make it before curfew anyway."

Sister and brother hurried out the door and down the street. Trying to keep a low profile, they cut through a worn alley slick with the air's moisture and rich with rancid rot.

"What do you think he meant by 'terrorist attack?'" Elliot was slightly out of breath, struggling to keep up with his sister's pace. She had developed an obvious limp from her makeshift leg, but her eagerness more than made up for it.

"Who knows? Probably Snowdrop or some other pile of

jerks," Fenlee said. "Kinda weird we didn't notice, though, since we were here two days ago…" She trailed off and stopped mid-stride. No, there was no way this could be related to the undercity drone…right?

"What is it?"

"Nothing. Let's just hurry and get back home." Fenlee bit her lip as she walked faster, her leg and hip now aching with each step.

They passed several Sentry drones along the way—far more than usual. The drones went about their business, ignoring them, but their presence set Fenlee on edge. Maybe coming here wasn't worth it. She had dragged her brother into danger two days ago, and here she was again, taking him into…into what? She thought about Cipher and quickly put it out of her mind. If she could dispatch her bot and get him properly trained, she wouldn't need to come here anymore, and that was the whole point.

Maybe it was only her nerves, but Fenlee couldn't remember ever walking through fog this thick. The pressure of the air around her felt like swimming through a near-solid cloud. Whirring above them, just out of sight, was another drone. She couldn't tell what type it was, but after their recent encounter, its presence only added to her anxiety. Sweat and atmospheric moisture beaded on her face. She quickened her pace further and the drone matched it, tailing them for several blocks. They made an abrupt turn through a gate that was rusted in place and entered what used to be a small park. It may have once seen days of manicured flower beds and slotted benches, but it was now an overgrown tangle of dark, cruel-looking plants, piles of refuse, and biological stench. After ensuring Elliot was still with her, she glanced back to find the machine puttering on past with no further regard for them at all.

She stopped to catch her breath and give her leg a quick rest. The drone was probably on some predefined patrol route that happened to coincide with where they were going. What was wrong with her? She had to stop being so damn paranoid.

"I thought for sure that thing was following us," Elliot said. He had his hair in his mouth again.

"Nah, dumb old pile of bolts and blades was just making its rounds," she said. "I figured it'd be best to cut through this way and save us a little time." She pulled up her map with the overlay and studied it for a few seconds. "In fact, the very insertion point we're looking for should be on the other side of this jungle of junk we're in." She pushed herself away from the old stone column she was leaning against and headed off. "Come on, let's do this quick and get back home."

It turned out the map was, in fact, accurate and she had read it correctly. It wasn't long before they exited the other side of the park where two colossal buildings joined together to form a V shape. Barely discernible in the gloom was a heavy-duty ventilation grate firmly bolted to the top of a raised metal box. Fenlee approached and placed her hand across the bars, estimating each bar to be about eight inches away from the next. It was sufficient to keep people out, but there was plenty of space for her little bot to squeeze through.

This area of the district was disused and completely deserted. Fenlee selected it as a location to drop off Cipher for that very reason, figuring it less likely they'd be seen. The only problem was, with so much fog and so few working lights in the area, it was hard to get a sense of much beyond their immediate surroundings.

Fenlee reached in her bag and pulled out Cipher. His legs were curled beneath him for transport, and when she activated him, the eight appendages whipped out and began searching for purchase in the air around her hand. "Whoa, little guy!" she said with a grin. "Relax, we'll get you down there in a second."

The scavenger bot stopped squirming at her words and waited. She had confirmed Cipher's programming earlier in the day during a break at school. Everything was ready to go for his initial run. Fenlee rotated the bot to get him between the bars and set him inside the opening on a small ledge. The magnetic grips on his feet engaged and disengaged for each step as he disappeared down the vertical side of the vent.

"I guess that's that," Fenlee said, putting her pack back on. "Here's hoping this works and there's something to show for it in a couple of days when we come back to pick him up."

Fenlee started walking out of the V-shaped area toward a backstreet that would eventually connect to a main thoroughfare. The night was fully upon them, and now that her task was complete, she was getting nervous about the whole curfew thing. She heard a ruckus behind her and turned to find Elliot searching for something and mumbling to himself.

"Where did…" Elliot trailed off as he looked on the other side of the ventilation box.

"What? What happened?" Fenlee asked.

Elliot gripped the bars on the ventilation grate and looked up at his sister. "Kavi's gone."

CHAPTER 8
ENSNARED

THE MOISTURE IN the cool night air began to settle, leaving a film on their skin. Background sounds were distant and veiled—even the whirring of the drones making their rounds had diminished. Fenlee knew they were alone and safe, but a creepy feeling of isolation and vulnerability made her itch to get back home.

"Did he go down that vent after Cipher?" she asked.

"No," Elliot said. "Or at least, I don't think so…"

"Okay, when did you last see him?" There was no reason a cat couldn't come and go on a whim, but Kavi's sudden departure was creeping her out.

"A while back? He's so light, I didn't even notice he wasn't in my backpack anymore."

Fenlee wasn't certain that she had a "danger sense," exactly,

but on many occasions her own apprehension and awareness had saved her. At that moment, every fiber of her being was telling her to get out. Immediately.

"Elliot, we need to leave," Fenlee said. "Kavi found his way to our place before, so I'm sure if he has any interest in finding you again, he will. But it's way past time for us to get out of here." She pulled gently on her brother's backpack. "Come on. It'll be okay."

As they turned to walk back to the street, Elliot sucked in a sharp breath and stopped. Three silhouettes appeared, blocking their path. It was hard to be sure, but Fenlee thought they were wearing the uniforms of the Cascadian Authority Security Forces. They'd blown the curfew. Hopefully the SecForce officers hadn't been around long enough to see her drop Cipher into the vent.

Fenlee glanced behind her to verify what she already knew: they were cornered. There was no way out, and even the ventilation shaft wouldn't work—the grate was securely bolted with no way to remove it in the next couple of seconds.

The armored figure on the right addressed the shorter middle figure. "What do we do with the other one?" he asked, his voice muffled behind a mask.

"We take them both. I don't know who the other is, but there can be no witnesses," she replied.

Nothing about "no witnesses" sounded good to Fenlee. "Elliot," she whispered, "get behind me." She had no idea what to do, but this group had another thing coming if they thought they were going to harm her brother, SecForce or not.

"You two will come quietly," the woman in the middle said. "Resist and suffer incapacitation."

Fenlee was shaking as she grabbed a flimsy, broken piece of flex-conduit from the ground. "I'm going to charge 'em.

When I do, you run to the right, and don't stop running until you're home."

Elliot tightened his grip on his backpack straps. "What? No, you can't just—"

Fenlee crouched and barreled toward the woman, swinging the piece of conduit like a whip. The woman sidestepped just as Fenlee tripped over a piece of broken pavement. As she fell forward, the man on the left hit her between the shoulder blades with the butt of his weapon. The injury would have been severe if she hadn't already been on her way down. She hit the ground, her ears filled with static, light exploding in her eyes.

"Lee!" Her brother's call sounded distant and pained.

She quickly regained her senses, but was too dazed to react as the man bound her wrists behind her back. She strained to see her brother rooted to the same spot, petrified. *You idiot. Why didn't you run? You stupid, stupid idiot.*

The woman grabbed a wad of Fenlee's hair and yanked her head up from the rough pavement. "That was foolish, but inconsequential," she said, and let Fenlee's head slam back down. More explosions, and everything went blurry.

This was no curfew citation. Fenlee had heard of kidnappers disguised as SecForce taking children and teens alone at night and selling them to high-tier types with too much money. The lucky ones were live-in slaves while others served as toys for the sadistic until the fun ran out. That was the most likely explanation. Icy fear gripped her as she struggled against the bonds. These three may have had the uniforms, but nothing about this was standard procedure.

"Elliot, go! Just run, *please!*" Fenlee breathed the words through clenched teeth. She could only make out her brother's outline as he backed himself further into the narrow V-shaped corner.

Fenlee tried to swim through the mud in her brain and come up with anything at all she could do. She was bound, lying face-down on the ground. Even if she could reach her pockets or pouches, nothing she was carrying would be useful.

This was the second time she'd put Elliot in danger. She was so selfish. *I'm so sorry.*

"Please run. Please, Elliot." She mouthed the words, but nothing came out. Her brother had backed himself against a wall and wasn't moving.

She felt a subtle warmth on her chest—small, but comforting and radiant. Etherclaw?

The three had left her and were slowly closing in on Elliot like a pack of wolves—hungry, but cautious. Were they afraid of him, or was the world just slowing? If this etherclaw thing was real, if it truly required an emotional trigger, it would work now or never. Fenlee closed her eyes and gritted her teeth. She visualized the SecForce trio and…and what? What could she do? Rip them apart like the Guardian drone? She couldn't kill. No way. Maybe…*DROP!*

The man on the right lost his footing but quickly regained control, barely breaking stride. Fenlee didn't know what was real—he could have easily tripped the same way she had.

The two men had their weapons trained on Elliot, and the woman's hand was on her sidearm. "All right, kid," she said. "You're going to lie down on your stomach and stretch your arms out like wings. Now."

Everything was sluggish. Fenlee wondered if her perception hadn't slowed whether she would have missed the sleek figure moving at an impossible speed toward the SecForce trio. The silhouette was rim-lit, the light cutting a sharp outline of what Fenlee decided a human killing machine might look like.

The figure's leg came up with blinding velocity and caught the man on the right in a crushing hook kick to the head. He slammed into the SecForce woman, knocking her flat as he continued to fly past, directly into the wall with enough force to shatter both his helmet and skull. A dark stain remained as his body dropped.

The officer had only partially raised her sidearm before it was kicked out of her hand, clear over Fenlee's head and out of sight. She cried out and backed away.

The other SecForce officer was slow to respond. By the time he rotated to face the dangerous new opponent, his weapon had already been ripped from his hands and a fist was flying into the center of his body armor. His chest compressed with a wet, splintering crunch and only a faint gasp left his lips as he fell into a lifeless heap. Fenlee thought she might puke.

She looked around for the remaining officer, but the woman had fled. The killing machine marched toward her brother, and before Fenlee could even process what was happening, grabbed his arm and helped him stand.

"Get on up, boy. It was beyond stupid for the two of you to come back out here after what you pulled the other day."

The voice sounded familiar, and that confident gait...

"Kyara?" Fenlee found her voice and slowly picked herself up off the ground, grimacing as her body lit up with pain from the movement.

"Who else?" Kyara said. She took a pouch from her belt and sucked down the contents.

"What are you doing here?" Fenlee asked.

"Rescuing you again, obviously. Any other questions will have to wait. Right now, we get you two out of here. One of them escaped, and you can bet reinforcements will have this whole area locked down in no time." She looked over to the metal box with the grate where Fenlee had dropped Cipher and called to the boy kicking his bare feet against the bars. "Come on, Nico. Let's go."

"Good show tonight," Nico said.

"I'm not out here for your entertainment," Kyara replied. "Now get down from there, we don't have much time." She inspected the side of Fenlee's head where she hit the pavement. "Looks like you'll be fine, but you'll need to patch yourself up later." Fenlee noted Kyara's hands were both in perfect shape. At the very least, her knuckles should have been wrecked from the impact of that punch—any normal person would have a broken hand or wrist. The woman didn't even seem out of breath.

Elliot ran to his sister and threw his arms around her. He buried his face in her neck, his warm tears bringing a feeling of humanity to an otherwise inhuman night.

She wrapped her arms tightly around him and blinked back tears of her own. "Elliot, I'm so sorry. I swear I won't put either of us in a situation like that again." She squeezed his small frame closer, pressing her injured cheek against the top of his head, biting her lip through the pain.

"I can't…breathe."

"Oh. Uh, like I said, sorry." Fenlee released her brother, and they exchanged grins.

"Stop wasting what little time we have," Kyara said. "Follow me, stay close, and we'll avoid any more trouble." Without looking back, she vanished into the shroud of fog.

CHAPTER 9
INJUNCTION ZONE

THEY'D BEEN WALKING for almost an hour. Kyara had refused to respond to any questions, insisting everyone remain quiet. The menacing whir of several drones, always just out of sight, kept Fenlee on edge, but Kyara's path always led them safely past. Lights were sparse, and they never encountered another person.

They had long since left the portion of the Waterfront District that was still in use. Here, they were surrounded by abandoned towers and desolate streets. The diffused pulse of platform lights high above and the occasional drone were the only signs of active civilization. It was likely that these areas hadn't been powered in generations.

Plants grew in abundance here, fighting their way through each crack in the cement. Elliot was mesmerized by every patch

of grass or weeds they walked through. Dark amorphous shapes loomed in front of them, swaying in and out of existence in the fog. It was only when they got close enough that Fenlee realized she was looking at a small grove of trees growing out of a sinkhole in the middle of the street.

The trek over broken urban terrain in the shadowy murk wasn't easy, and both brother and sister kept stumbling. Meanwhile, Nico had no trouble prancing about the rough and ruined routes shoeless, while Kyara moved in sure-footed silence. Fenlee's hip ached and she was starting to get irritated. There was no reason to distrust her, and Kyara *had* saved them twice now, but Fenlee needed to know where they were going. She opened her mouth to demand answers, but Kyara spoke first.

"We should be clear of the patrol area now," Kyara said. "It is fine to speak, but you will keep your voices low."

"I…right. Good," Fenlee said. "So, uh, where *are* we headed then?"

"The South Interchange. It will still be very busy at this hour, so you can easily blend in and take a maglev back home."

"Are you crazy? There's a permanent injunction zone between here and there. Elliot and I don't have permits, and I'm guessing you probably don't either."

Kyara grabbed her arm. "Girl, if you do not keep your voice down, they *will* find us!" Her sharp whisper cut through the night and hit Fenlee with enough force to knock her back half a step.

"Sorry," Fenlee said. "But still, you can't just walk through a damn injunction zone."

"True. That is why we will not walk through it."

Then you better have a way to sprout wings and fly over it 'cause I'll be voided before I drag Elliot back underground right now. But there were too many things swirling around in her head to dwell on it at the moment, so she let the thought simmer instead.

"Are you going to tell us who those people were back there?" Fenlee asked.

"SecForce operatives. They're after you." Kyara glanced at Elliot and Fenlee and a flicker of sympathy touched her face. "Well, both of you now."

"What about you?" Fenlee asked.

"They've always been after me."

"What? No, I meant, are you after us? How did you know we were there?"

"Nico told me. I didn't believe him at first because I didn't think either of you could possibly be so stupid. Did you not know the increased security patrols exist entirely because of your little undercity fiasco? They're calling it a terrorist attack, and they are quite determined to find themselves some 'terrorists.'"

"I kind of gathered that, but I still can't say I understand it," Fenlee said. It was unbelievable that a minor incident in a disused part of the undercity could have caused such a response. People went down there often enough and nothing ever happened, apart from the occasional arrest. Sure, she and Elliot had destroyed a drone, but it was only *one* drone, and it was a total accident. "Wait, go back. You're saying Nico found us? How did he know we were there?"

"Nico has some very special talents and is quite adept at using them," Kyara replied.

"Neat for Nico. But that doesn't tell me *how* he knew."

"Later. Now it's my turn for questions. You have etherclaw.

You destroyed a drone with it just two days ago, so I know you can make it work. Why didn't you use it tonight to save yourself and your brother?"

"I tried! It didn't do anything! You said it was tied to emotions, and, well, I was pretty damn emotional just now. But it did flat nothing!"

Kyara stopped and turned to Nico, who was balancing on a crumbling ledge about sixteen feet off the ground. "Come down here!" she called in a loud whisper. He shrugged, leapt to a lower ledge, and jumped, hitting the ground in a silent tuck-and-roll maneuver. "Nico," Kyara said, pointing to Fenlee's chest. "Are you completely certain that is etherclaw?"

"Yup."

"Good. I'm glad you're confident because you will be going back home to stay with her. She needs training."

Nico's body turned into a ragdoll and shambled along beside them like a droopy marionette. "Have to?" he asked.

"Yes, you have to."

Fenlee threw her arms up. "Whoa there. Maybe try checking with us first?" What training did she need? Nico certainly couldn't help her with anything, unless…"Wait a minute, can Nico use etherclaw?"

"Lee," Elliot whispered. "I think it's safe to say Kyara can too."

The realization hit Fenlee like a maglev she should have seen coming from miles away. "Oh, voiding hell. Of course they both can." She put her hands through her utility belt and stared up through the slow-swirling fog. "Everything is completely crazy and makes perfect sense at the same time." She shook her head. It was unbelievable that any of this was real. Her greatest worries should have been focusing on school and looking after her brother while her father was away. Instead, she was in possession of a weird magic alien talisman thingy that granted the owner superpowers, and some shady group of assholes wanted to kidnap or kill her over it.

"What were you two doing down in the undercity the other day?" Fenlee asked.

"We had business in the area," Kyara replied. "As you're well aware, the undercity makes it easier to move undetected. Nico sensed something, so we went to check it out. We found the two of you next to a destroyed Guardian-class drone." She sighed. "I admit, it was not a scene I was expecting."

A deep flood control channel cut through to the group's right, running parallel to the road. There was no median, shoulder, or guardrail, just a steep embankment, patches of which had broken off into piles of rubble at the base of the channel. It smelled like the undercity.

Fenlee kicked at the ground. As though she were supposed to have the skills to take on three armed and experienced SecForce officers. Still, after tonight, she suspected she might need those skills. She knew she had to learn. "But it looked like you were just fighting. I mean, really powerful fighting, but still just kicking and punching and stuff. How do you make it work?"

"I don't hit them as hard as it may appear. Not directly, at least." Kyara clenched her right hand into a tight ball and brought it up in a defensive position next to her cheek. "I compress the air around my fist, my feet, my knees, or any other contact point, and release just prior to impact. Now, watch and listen carefully, because I will only do this once."

Kyara threw her right shoulder forward with her arm and

hand following in a perfect cross punch. The air shifted. It was as though she was moving her hand through a viscous liquid, but instead of getting out of the way, the air gathered at the front of her fist. The moment Kyara was fully extended, a small distortion exploded forth with a soft snap, like when Fenlee's neighbor whipped sheets out her window to rid them of dirt. It all happened in a handful of milliseconds—almost imperceptible, but it was there.

"Close your mouth, girl."

"Sorry," Fenlee said. "I just can't believe this is really real." She pulled her opal from her shirt and held it tight. "What would it take for me to do that?"

"I've spent years working on the technique. It requires calculation and anticipation, both of which require discipline," Kyara said, cocking an eyebrow at Fenlee. "Everyone with an etherclaw bond finds different ways unique to them to make use of it. The things I can do with mine, you may never be able to do with yours, and vice versa. Nico, for example, uses his etherclaw to form a sort of connection with those around him. He can detect other etherclaw users—which is how he knew you were in trouble again tonight—and he can establish empathetic bonds. Don't ask me how. I don't know, and I've never gotten it out of him. Nico is just…Nico." She tapped the silver tattoo running down her shoulder. "Like your opal, mine is a part of me, though, more literally, I suppose. I can't say for certain where Nico draws his etherclaw from, however."

"So, Nico will help me learn?" Fenlee asked.

"He will try," Kyara said, giving Fenlee a heavy side-eye. "But I don't have a great deal of hope, given what he has to work with."

Why was this woman so condescending all the time? Fenlee hated being talked down to, hated being dictated to, and hated being kept in the dark about what was going on. Kyara excelled at achieving all of those things.

"Hey, uh, Kyara," Elliot said, "how did SecForce even know we were here tonight?"

Fenlee rolled her eyes. Elliot was great at sniffing out tension and redirecting. He always tried to defuse things, but she often wished he'd just stay out of it.

"Fair question," Kyara said. "I took the sensor package from the drone your sister destroyed, and I disposed of it. We have no reason right now to think that they have any record of your appearances." She snorted and shook her head. "It seems, however, that particular drone was also equipped with a biosignature sensor and it got a good scan of you two. Those biosig packages aren't common these days, so I wasn't looking for one. Using that data, they matched and tracked you tonight. It was my mistake for being careless."

"I wish you'd warned us about all this before," Fenlee said.

"Knowledge is a blessing and a curse, girl. Sometimes the less you know, the better. I don't know why you have that stone, but you'll have to find your own path. I wanted to stay out of it—I wanted *you* to be able to stay out of it—but now it appears you're at risk. That's why Nico is going to stay with you for a while. He can help you be more prepared at least."

"This is bullshit!" Fenlee couldn't contain her frustration anymore. "We're 'in it' all right, but I don't even know what 'it' is!"

"You're not listening to anything I've been trying to tell you." Kyara's voice was flat.

Fenlee shoved her index finger into Kyara's sternum. "Because you're not *telling* me anything!"

Kyara grabbed Fenlee's chin and pushed. "Back off, girl."

The gash on Fenlee's injured cheek reopened and warmth spread down her chin and neck. Furious tears threatened to cloud her vision, but she forced them back—she refused to embarrass herself in front of this woman. Elliot put his arms around her waist and held her close. His presence and a few deep breaths were enough for her to regain control.

"My brother could have been hurt," she said, keeping her voice low and steady. "If we had known, we wouldn't have come back." Her eyes now dry and hard, she added, "And my name is Fenlee."

"Good," Kyara said. "You'll need that fortitude. But your confidence is misplaced—you have no idea what you've gotten yourself into. A little girl like you has no chance against them, should they come for you again." She walked ahead with Nico skipping along behind.

The streets became cleaner, and several buildings looked as though they'd seen recent use. Distant lights began to appear in the direction they were heading.

Elliot had not let go of his sister's hand. But whether it was out of concern for her, or for his own benefit, she couldn't tell. After several minutes of silence, he whispered, "Are you okay?"

Kyara waved her hand in a slicing motion behind her. "Quiet now, we're getting close," she said.

A wide canal ran alongside them, half-full of slow-moving water. Piles of old scrap formed small islands built of time-forgotten goods. Dark fluid swirled halfway up the windows of an old sunken transport vehicle. Fenlee estimated that would put the depth at about six feet, or a few inches over her head.

With a half-twist, Kyara dropped to a dry ledge about a dozen feet down into the canal. "Come," she said. "We will continue this way." Nico hopped down and landed beside her as though he weighed no more than a feather.

Sister and brother looked at each other. Fenlee still couldn't bring herself to trust Kyara. Back the way they came, dark, foreboding mists hid the patrolling drones, but the path forward led directly into an injunction zone. Her holoquip was no longer calibrated, so she had no way to pinpoint their exact location and, because of the deep fog, she couldn't even look to the upper-tier towers to try and orient herself.

Fenlee bit the inside of her cheek, considering their options. The best case scenario up ahead would be getting turned away for lack of permits, the worst case would be getting apprehended. The latter was more likely at the moment.

She called down to Kyara. "We can't make that jump, and you know it."

Through the gloom, Fenlee was sure she could see the woman smirking. "If you're not up to it, I'll catch you. Hurry and jump."

"I can't jump, Lee," Elliot whispered. "I can barely see where anything is."

There were no other viable options. If they stayed put, they would be stranded, essentially trapped on all sides and unable to fend for themselves. Kyara was cruel, but she'd rescued them twice now. They would have to do this her way for the moment.

Fenlee squeezed Elliot's hand. "Would you feel safer jumping to me?"

"I guess so," he said. "I'd rather not do any jumping at all though."

They would do it Kyara's way, but Fenlee was not about to jump into her arms. "Wait here," she said to Elliot. Squatting down, she took hold of the ledge and carefully lowered her body over the side. It was extra awkward, knowing Kyara was down there watching her. Each move felt clumsier than the last. She maneuvered herself to hang from the ledge, arms fully extended. It was now only about a five-foot drop. She held on a moment longer, anticipating the pain this would cause her left leg.

It's only a few damn feet, Fenlee, you're right there.

She dropped. A shock of pain ran up to her hip, forcing her to stagger backward. Kyara caught her wrist just before she fell off the ledge deeper into the canal. Neither acknowledged the other.

"I'm good, Elliot. All good," Fenlee said. "Go ahead and jump, I've got you."

"Just give me a hand instead, how about that?" Elliot climbed down and hung on the ledge as his sister had done. Fenlee wrapped her arms around his legs and helped lower him.

"Alright, we're down," Fenlee said. "Mind telling us why we're here?"

"Fine," Kyara said, her voice a faint whisper. "But hurry—the fog may disperse soon, and we need it." She pointed to the lights up ahead. "Our best chance through the injunction zone is by way of this canal. The Cascadian Authority will have it locked down as usual, but they don't have the resources to patrol everything. They put on a pretty big show, but they're *weak*." She spat the word as though ejecting a cockroach from her mouth.

"Aren't there at least drones surveilling the canals?" Fenlee asked.

"Ordinarily, yes. But they've repurposed so many to patrol the Waterfront looking for their so-called terrorists that they're in critically short supply elsewhere."

They reached an intersection where the channel flowed into a broader waterway. Many still provided flood mitigation, but these had been repurposed as canals for moving greywater to reclamation plants. Children were always warned away from the greywater trenches, partly because they could drown, partly because they could pick up a skin condition.

It smelled sickly sweet with hints of raw sewage. Elliot was already holding the fabric of his hoodie over his nose and mouth, and she tied her blood-crusted bandana around her face to breathe a little easier.

The group made it close enough to see the boundary of the injunction zone. A fence blocked any further passage down the ledge and went straight across the canal, suspended about two feet above the water.

"We swim through this way," Kyara said.

"No way I'm getting in that! And," Fenlee said, eyeing the fence, "I think I have another idea." The wire links were a cheap, soft composite metal with poor shear strength. Fenlee reached into a pouch, produced her multimini tool, and unfolded a pair of cutters.

Kyara put her hand on Fenlee's arm, making her flinch. "Don't. The noise will draw their attention, and cutting through each ring will take time."

"I know what I'm doing," Fenlee snapped. "This will be dead silent."

Kyara's eyes narrowed, but she withdrew her hand. "Fine. But only if we have a distraction. Nico?"

"Yep." The kid came out of nowhere and scampered up the fence to street level. A small furry head peeked over the side watching them.

"Kavi!" Elliot said.

Kyara clapped her hand over his mouth. "Keep quiet."

Nico bent over to rub noses with the cat, and the two of them ran off toward the injunction zone entryway.

A couple of voices called out then quickly escalated to shouting back and forth. Fenlee heard Nico yelling through the chaos. "Cat! My cat! Come back, cat!"

"Now, girl, cut quickly!" Kyara said.

Fenlee set to work. It turned out Kyara was right: each snap was loud enough to have drawn attention, but Nico's little operation was enough to conceal the noise. She worked as hard and as fast as she could.

The shouting was dying down, but the sound of voices above them was getting closer. Fenlee cut the final ring, and Kyara grabbed the fence before it fell to the ground, moving it out of the way. The three slipped through the gap and into the injunction zone.

The area wasn't very large, just sufficient to stop people from coming through. The injunction zones ostensibly existed to ensure economic balance between the regions in New Cascadia. Goods and services flowed through and could be tracked, with the Cascadian Authority helping to provide oversight, managing supply with demand, and, at times, rationing.

But everyone knew how permits were awarded and the segregation that resulted. There were certain areas in the Cascadian

Civic Zone where injunction checkpoints, such as this, acted more like gates to a prison. The maglev system was the only way to get around freely, but you still needed a pass and were never allowed more than you could easily carry with you. The process for awarding passes and determining what could be "easily carried" was highly subjective.

They reached the opposite perimeter, where Fenlee cut their way out a second time. There wasn't much officer presence here, but she still felt a sense of urgency bearing down on her as she worked.

Once through, the South Interchange opened up before them. It was a sprawling area of commerce constructed during the initial phase of the Cascadian Revitalization Project when Fenlee's father was still young. It had become vibrant in recent decades as trade by sea had started to pick back up, and since most of the older ports in the Waterfront District were unusable.

It was late, but the activity in the Interchange was energetic. Transport bots hauled massive loads of cargo down bustling boulevards, with throngs of people filling the gaps between. A boy, probably about Elliot's age, blew past them on a heavily modded bicycle. Fenlee was impressed that he could move so fast in the crowd. She envied the speed and handling and tried to get a look at the drive configuration before he was out of sight.

By the time they were in view of the maglev station, Nico had caught up to them, appearing out of nowhere with Kavi balanced on his head. Elliot smiled as the cat jumped onto the top of his backpack and snuggled into his hood, purring loudly.

"How did you find him?" Elliot asked. "Or how did he find you?"

Nico shrugged. "Kavi goes where Kavi wants."

"Your ride will be here soon," Kyara said. "Be vigilant. Listen to Nico. Learn from him."

Fenlee pulled out her opal and rotated it between her fingers. "What if I just get rid of it?" She hated the idea. It was like a living piece of her mother. But if parting with the stone would make them safer, she would do it in a heartbeat.

"I would strongly advise against that," Kyara said. Her words were firm, leaving no room for dispute. "You are already marked by powers you cannot imagine. It may be quite some time before they pick up your biosignature again, but they will, and you will be forced to defend yourself. Knowing how to use it properly will be your best, and perhaps only, defense. More than that, once etherclaw has bonded with you, being separated from it for too long is…let us just say it does not end well for the user."

Nico nodded his head in vigorous agreement.

The maglev arrived, and they boarded with a handful of other passengers riding at the late hour.

As the departure notification sounded, Fenlee stared at Kyara, still standing on the platform outside. This callous, hardened woman, improbable partner to this strange little boy, was unlike anyone she's ever met. So Kyara and Nico could both use etherclaw and, presumably, she could too. But that still didn't explain their motivation.

"Why do you keep helping us?" Fenlee called out.

Kyara's face darkened as the maglev door began to close. "Because no one else will."

A storm raged high above the city in the personal office of Dr. Arkamis, on the upper levels of his chateau. Shards from a smashed teacup littered the floor near an antique chesterfield suite of soft buttoned leather. A vase of bloodroot and foxglove sat on a low conversation table next to a tea service, warm chandelier light glinting off its silver filigree. The odor of old incense mingled with the bitter tang of the noxious flowers while polished boots pounded the floor.

Lt. Cano stood stoically while Dr. Morrow reclined into a lavish sofa, watching the cream-cloaked fury thunder around the sitting area.

An hour ago, Cano made contact with the news of the failed abduction. Arkamis had not been taking it well. "How could trained professionals lose to two *children*?!" he screamed.

"It wasn't just a couple of kids," Cano said. "I told you, there was a woman who came out of nowhere and killed *both* of my officers before I even had a chance to respond." She clutched her bandaged hand. "I nearly didn't make it out myself."

Arkamis gripped the back of the sofa where Morrow was sitting. On any other occasion, Morrow's unwashed body leaving greasy residue on his furniture would have driven him mad. At the moment, it was the furthest thing from his thoughts.

So damn close! The child was still alive, but had slipped from his grasp—no, from *Cano's* grasp. To make matters worse, there was outside interference. Did these two children have allies? How much did they know? *Only the calm mind shall prevail. But, damn it, this is what changes the trajectory of humanity.* He needed more information about this woman. He needed a drink.

"Describe this mysterious interloper and precisely what

she did," Arkamis said. He made his way to the wet bar and poured a thin luminous liquid that matched the deep crimson of the foxglove.

Cano took Arkamis step by step through the encounter. The woman who killed the SecForce operatives in the alley sounded very much like a subject from the early days of the Osiris Project he had helped conduct years ago. But most of the tests were failures, and the participants had been terminated.

Arkamis' grip tightened on the goblet as she spoke. It couldn't be. He was sure all the test subjects were accounted for. "Are you certain she wasn't simply bio-reinforced or augmented in some way?" he asked.

"I...I'm not sure." Cano said, cradling her hand. She had taken the time to bandage it but hadn't applied any pain relief. If it was broken, it had not yet been set. Arkamis was glad to see she at least had her priorities in order. "It was dark, and everything moved so quickly. I suppose she could have had some sort of enhancements..." She looked at Morrow's augmentations and shuddered. "...but if so, I didn't see them. Anyway, she seemed to be acting alone."

"You idiot, she had to have been with the child!" Arkamis said. "You had one shot at this—now they'll go underground." The cup felt heavy in his hand, and he wanted to throw it into her composed shell of a face, smashing through the facade to lay bare her fear. "It is beyond my comprehension that you, a trained SecForce lieutenant, were so ill-equipped to deal with this simple matter. Am I seriously to believe you have no night vision or imaging equipment? You didn't so much as bring a drone to assist you?" He shifted toward his counterpart. "Morrow, what sort of amateur have you brought me?"

Morrow laughed, his dull, rotted teeth reflecting nothing in his menacing grin.

Cano stiffened. "We are severely under-resourced, and even basic equipment is nearly impossible to come by. I didn't wish to take a drone with us because I would have had to justify it to my superiors, and its sensors would have picked up everything that happened, risking exposure of the operation."

Arkamis downed another glass. "Your people are dead, and I have no child. Would you call this anything other than a complete failure, Lieutenant Cano?"

The officer shuffled her feet, crunching a piece of broken porcelain. "I don't know, sir. Yes, I mean. It's just, I've never had an unsuccessful mission, so—"

"Then that will be your first and last unsuccessful mission, am I clear?" Arkamis said. He moved close enough to Cano to smell the sweat of the night on her. "Lieutenant, I am a very forgiving person. I am afraid, however, this is not a very forgiving situation." His fingers played with the hilt of his saber. "But don't worry, I'm fully confident you will successfully retrieve the child. Dr. Morrow shall be accompanying you this time."

Morrow's eyes darkened as his lips curled into a smile.

CHAPTER 10
SPARK OF SUCCESS

Fenlee ached in incredible new ways. Each stiff movement felt as though her cartilage had been removed and her muscles pureed into goo. There were occasions where she didn't feel quite comfortable in her own body, but this morning she was a stranger even to herself. The exhaustion had been so complete the previous night that she'd collapsed into bed before taking off her leg or cleaning herself up. The gash on her cheek was oozing, starting to form a crusted line from her cheekbone to her lower jaw. She hoped there was still some suture bond in the cabinet—a clinic visit would eat up a substantial amount of her remaining crednotes which she needed to make last until her father was back.

A few sunbeams did their best to push through the clouds,

but it was a losing battle, each slowly snuffed as late morning showers rolled in. The sounds of people getting along with their daily routines filtered up from the streets below. Neighbors, acquaintances, and thousands she would never meet—all going about their business, oblivious to what she'd just experienced.

Fenlee would have preferred to lie down all day, but she needed to check on the boys. Elliot had gone straight to sleep when they arrived home, and since her father wouldn't be back any time soon, she'd sent Nico to her father's room.

Nico was in the position she'd left him: upside-down on the bed, arms straight out, and drooling like a dog on a sweltering summer day. She hadn't really seen him in the light. Each time they'd met, it had been dark, dismal, and she'd been distracted. He was young—likely less than ten years old—and small, but lanky; lying on the bed, his wingspan exceeded his height. His skin was a darker brown, but she couldn't tell how much of that was a semi-permanent layer of dirt. Crudely dyed green hair that looked like it had gotten caught in a drone rotor suggested he took care of his own grooming. His clothes were a wreck—his shirt was falling apart, and she didn't understand the purpose of the canvas wraps around his arms and legs. The bottoms of his bare feet were a blackened luster, probably as tough as her boots.

What caught her attention more than anything were the scars. Nico's body was covered in pale, poorly healed scars, giving him the appearance of a striped feline, much like Kavi. She had no idea what sort of pain he must have endured, but the thought made her sick. They looked old, from another time—perhaps another life, she hoped.

Elliot was seated at the kitchen table, head down on the

cold metal, fast asleep. Kavi was curled up in his lap, and a pot of room temperature tea with three cups sat nearby. Despite everything, he'd kept to his schedule and prepared breakfast, probably hours ago.

Fenlee took the opportunity while they were still asleep to clean and seal her wound. She scraped the gunk out of the laceration and flushed it several times. It was like pouring fire on raw nerves, but she had taken care of her own injuries frequently and knew what to expect. There wasn't much suture bond left, but it was enough.

"You got hurt."

Nico was standing in the doorway, rubbing his eyes. "Oh, hey, Nico," Fenlee said. "You kind of startled me. You sleep okay?"

"Sorry you got hurt," he said. "We were slow."

"No way, I'm just glad you two were there at all." She ruffled his hair. It was stiff, and she had a strong desire to wash her hands again. "Thanks, kid. We needed you." Fenlee retrieved an old pair of shears from the cabinet. "While you're here, the least I could do is help get you cleaned up a little. What do you think?"

"Mm...okay."

"And maybe a fresh dye job on that hair of yours?"

"Mm...sure."

"Let's start up top first." Fenlee proceeded to comb and chop. The hair was tough to get through, but she was determined and, one by one, matted tangles hit the floor like desiccated insect husks scattering in the breeze. "So, why the green?"

Nico shrugged. "Life is green."

Fenlee wasn't exactly sure what he meant, but for some

reason it reminded her of Elliot. "I see. Wanna try a different color?"

"Nope."

"Want me to re-dye it for you?"

"…okay."

"Great. All I have is the red I use, but I have to run some errands, so I'll add green to the list."

Nico stepped into the shower facility and stood there, unsure what to do. Fortunately, all it took was a slightly awkward explanation and partial demonstration for him to grasp the process, so she left him to it. The kid was so *odd*. He was intelligent, kind, and empathetic, but lacked basic social awareness. There was also something else that she couldn't put her finger on. She knew he could use etherclaw, but couldn't imagine him as a fighter like Kyara. This "training" they were supposed to do was going to be interesting.

Elliot was awake but groggy. While Nico showered, they shared cold tea and discussed the events from the previous night and what to do with their new houseguest. Fenlee didn't mind the kid staying with them, but by no means did she want Kyara to show up unannounced at their door. The woman was hiding something and, until Fenlee knew what, she didn't trust her intentions.

Nico had managed to thoroughly soak the entire bathroom and part of the hallway. He stood in the blower drying off for so long Fenlee sent Elliot in to make sure he was okay.

They went through some of Elliot's old clothes he'd outgrown and settled on a sleeveless hoodie and some tight pants that Nico rolled up to just below the knee. He refused to remove his canvas arm and leg wraps, and shoes of any sort were out of the question.

There was no food in the apartment, so they all left together to remedy the situation. Fenlee wondered how long she might be handling the bill for three instead of two.

Kavi hopped between Elliot's and Nico's shoulders as they walked. Elliot tried to engage the other boy a few times but never got back more than a one- or two-word reply. The light rain formed pools of muck along the gutters, which Nico happily skipped right through with his freshly cleaned feet, much to Fenlee's irritation.

"So, Nico, I guess you're here to help me get this etherclaw thing figured out. How do I start?" she asked. There was no answer. She turned around and there was no Nico. "Nico? Elliot, where'd that kid go?"

Elliot shrugged. "He was right here a second ago—"

Nico sauntered over through the middle of the street, hands stuffed in his pockets, casually dodging bots, drones, and transports. His self-satisfied grin was wrapped around a giant protein stick.

"Nico, where'd you get that prostick?" Fenlee asked.

"Back there. Cart guy."

"With what money?"

"Mm…no money?"

"Nico! You can't do that!"

"So can do that. Just did."

Fenlee palmed her face, wincing as she smacked her own wound. "Okay, let's try, 'shouldn't' do that," she said. "Anyway, you're here to teach me, so maybe we could work on that instead of our thieving skills. Sound good?"

Nico gobbled down the rest of his snack. "M'kay," he said, licking his fingers. "Feel first. Think second."

"I don't know what that means. Care to be more specific?"

Nico put his hand on her chest. "Feel. Angry, sad, happy, scared. Let it happen." He reached up and grabbed her head with both hands. His grip was much stronger than Fenlee would have thought. "*Then* think. *Make* it happen."

"Make *what* happen?" Fenlee asked. "I think you're being too simplistic. I don't get the mechanics of this at all." She pulled out the opal. "How do I use *this*?"

"Nuh-uh," Nico said, pointing to the opal. "Don't focus there. Focus on…" He bit his lip trying to find the words, then leapt up on Fenlee, wrapping his arms around her in a tight hug. "Focus on this."

"Whoa! Okay, okay, I think maybe I get it," Fenlee said. She gave him a little squeeze and set him back on the ground. "So, it's nothing without our feelings. But how do I apply that?"

Nico skipped around and kicked at a piece of garbage. "Mm…gotta be good at things. Gotta understand things. Gotta love things." He spun around at Fenlee. "What things? Figure it out. Use 'em."

It was nearly dark by the time they got back. Fenlee dyed Nico's hair a vivid emerald, made richer by the hints of his natural black hair. She was pleased with her handiwork, but if Nico liked it, he never said as much. He was too enthralled by Elliot's array of plants in the common room and spent most of the evening studying each with a solemn reverence.

The boys both fell into bed early. Fenlee tried, but couldn't make sleep happen. She sat at her workbench, charging and popping a capacitor on her multimini. Over and over again she would attach the coupling from her ambient heat converter, wait almost a minute for the capacitor light to come on, then discharge an instant burst of energy on the metal blade of her tool. The process and repetition helped her think.

She understood etherclaw to be something like the capacitor—a mechanism to aggregate energy and release it with directed purpose. That energy was within her, so she needed to be careful. She would have to ask Nico if there was any risk to herself when using it. Could she deplete her own energy? Would etherclaw just *take* it? What would a human's "energy depletion" mean for the human? She shuddered. You couldn't really recharge a depleted person.

Her mother's old ceramic statue peered down on her from her workbench shelf. She'd never figured out if it was a cat, a fox, or some sort of cat-fox hybrid creature, but it was the only item apart from the opal she had to remember her by.

That, and her mother's looks. Her parents met when her father was working on contract for Norfayne. In his typical style, Max managed to contaminate some rare asteroid samples being offloaded while he was doing maintenance in a hangar. Her mother, Adeline, had recently transferred from the Chinese Provinces to perform astrobiology research for Norfayne in New Cascadia. When she heard some gear-headed oaf had wrecked her samples, she came down to reprimand him in person. It was, for reasons Fenlee never understood, love at first sight.

Her mother was short, with straight black hair and refined features. Her father was pale, redheaded, and, as her mother used to say, "sturdy." Fenlee ended up with her features and his build.

Fenlee knew very little about her mother's life before she met her father, and next to nothing about what she did at Norfayne. She never talked about her past and never discussed her work at home.

She stared at the ceramic creature. *What did you know about all this, Mom? What did you hide from me?*

It was beyond frustrating. She'd been thrown into a situation she wanted no part of and told she had some remarkable tool that only she could use except that she *couldn't* use it. She thought about Nico's words from earlier. That kid was so cryptic. How was she supposed to make sense of any of this without a manual or guide?

He'd said she had to "be good at" or "understand things." She understood mechanical components and electronics just fine, but little else. The light blinked on again, indicating a charge. Her aggravation built to a crescendo. Damn it, if it were really that voiding simple, she could just—

The capacitor jolted, discharging directly into the air.

Her vision went a little weak, and she felt a pang in her stomach. The world outside became silent. Time slowed. The realization of what she'd just done made her jittery. *Voiding hell I made it work. I actually made etherclaw work.*

She stared at her workbench, feeling slightly anemic but invigorated. On her workbench alone were scattered pneumatic assemblies, a micro-gearbox, peltier coolers, RF controllers, and so much more to experiment with. Her fatigue melted away, and she hoped she had enough snacks to last the night.

CHAPTER 11
RINSING WON'T DO, YOU'VE GOT TO SCRUB

"You did it."

Fenlee wiped the sleep out of her eyes and leaned against the wall in the kitchen. The two boys were eating a breakfast of fried rice with puffball mushrooms Elliot had probably pulled from one of his planters. The rich smell of salty oil made her stomach growl, and she loaded up a bowl and sat down.

"How do you know what I did and didn't do?" she asked Nico.

"Last night," he answered, studying a piece of crisp rice balanced on his thumbnail. "You tried. Real hard. You did it." He flicked the small piece of rice in the air and lunged across

the table, catching it on his tongue. Fenlee and Elliot managed to move their bowls out of the way just in time to avoid him.

"What's he talking about?" Elliot asked.

"I got it to work last night," Fenlee said. She pulled the multimini out of her pocket and set it on the table. "Here, watch." Brow knit and hands clenched, she closed her eyes, took a deep breath, and focused. She could feel the opal, hot against her chest. She could see the multimini and see—no, *feel*—all of its internal components. Muscles and brain were tensed. Elliot, Nico, and Kavi sat in silent anticipation. But before she could channel the energy into the multimini, her stomach growled. Loudly.

Elliot burst out laughing. "That's what you've been working on? What an incredible power."

"That's not—ugh! Elliot!"

"Sorry," Elliot said. He was still giggling, but he was the only one. Nico had taken the opportunity to snag Fenlee's rice bowl and had already consumed over half of it.

"Nico! I thought you were here to train me!" Fenlee said. "You're no help."

Kavi hopped up on the table and batted her multimini tool to the floor.

"I am so done with all three of you boys."

With the events of the last two days, Fenlee almost forgot about their dinner with Alex. She quickly bathed, then took a little longer than usual picking out something to wear. This was a mid-tier dinner, so she didn't want to look like some street urchin. And what could she wear for Alex? Not like she needed to wear something *for* Alex. It wasn't like a date, obviously. Just friends, hanging out. Eating dinner and…and what? Why was she so nervous? She rifled through her clothes looking for anything that wasn't cargos and tank tops. She settled on a black and red skirt with ringlets up the sides and a matching jacket with one of her regular tanks underneath. It was way too hot out for the jacket, but it looked good, and she needed the confidence.

Nico was content to stay at the apartment, but leaving him alone was more than a little nerve-wracking. Would they come back home to find their entire home caked in foreign substances? "Using the bathroom correctly" did not appear to be one of Nico's core competencies.

The evening was peaceful and still as they took the public lift up to mid-tier, where Alex and her aunt Lily lived. There was a platform attached to Casper's tower, about 150 stories up. It was smaller and subjacent to the Central Platform, but offered much nicer living than anything below.

As they stepped off the commuter lift, childhood memories poured into Fenlee, leaving a heavy ache in her chest. She grew up in a mid-tier residential zone nearly identical to what lay before her. Tidy lanes separated rows of well-kept apartment buildings interspersed with a fair number of standalone dwellings. Instead of street merchants selling food to people in a hurry, families sipped tea in small cafes. Instead of endless cramped views of steel and structure, they were high enough to see the twelve-mile-wide Void Pillar rising in the eastern mountains, the last sunrays of the day disappearing in its matte black surface.

The Norfayne research scientist salary Fenlee's mother

brought home had afforded her the ability to provide a modest apartment for her family on this level. When she died, there was enough money left for Max to purchase their current low-tier residence, but not much more. It was quaint in comparison, but at least he paid in full and owned it outright.

Fenlee loved the chaos and character of the city's underbelly, but walking up here where the air wasn't as stagnant made her long for her mother and younger, more innocent days. This was where her brother and father belonged, and once she secured a position with Norfayne, she'd see to it they were back on mid-tier.

They arrived at a newer apartment block, likely constructed during the last century as the building materials included metal composite and a distinct lack of cement.

Alex waited for them out front in a wrap of charcoal and fuchsia, somehow both formal and athletic. She was stunning. Fenlee felt like she was in a different world. Maybe she could get away from her own, at least for an evening.

"Hey, you two! Glad you could make it," Alex said.

"Yeah, of course!" Fenlee smiled. "This place is incredible."

"Whoa, Fenlee. What happened to your face?"

And with that, Fenlee was dropped right back into her own world and the events of the past few days. "Oh, yeah, Elliot and I were doing a little exploring, and I fell." She tried to turn slightly to make it less obvious, but there was no hiding a bonded gouge going straight down the side of her head.

"I love the way you two are always out doing stuff and owning your world," Alex said. "And hey, if you're lucky, that might even scar up a little and look pretty cool."

They headed inside, where they met Alex's aunt, Dr. Lily

Blount. She was taller than Alex and softer around the edges, but their smiles were similar and they shared the same calm, passionate eyes. Her hair was in a tight updo, and an endless stream of soft iridescent fabric flowed like liquid around her. Fenlee couldn't find the beginning or end and wondered how the garment was held together.

"Welcome! I'm so glad to see Alexandra bringing some friends around."

"It's very nice to meet you, Ms.—Dr. Blount," Fenlee said with a nod.

"Oh, please. Lily is fine. People insisting on formal titles tend not to have a lot else going on in their lives," Lily said.

"You worked hard for that title, though," Alex said.

"It's just a means to an end, and certainly not *the* end," Lily said. "But back to the real business of the evening. We're going to be having some yassa with Goeli fish and chilis. I hope that works for everyone?"

"Wow. Yes! That definitely works for us!" Fenlee said.

Elliot's eyes lit up. "Do you need any help?" Fenlee couldn't recall if he'd ever had Goeli fish, or fish of any kind for that matter.

"Of course, thank you for offering—Elliot, was it?" Lily asked. "Why don't you start chopping those red chilis? Watch you don't rub your eyes, though, they're a little spicier than normal."

Alex poured cups of hot tea for the two of them. "Come on, Fenlee, I'll show you around."

The home Alex and Lily shared spanned two levels, each larger than the entirety of Fenlee's apartment. Dark trim set off bright, cheery walls, most of which were covered in a variety of artwork. "My aunt collects some, creates some…the really bad pieces are mine," Alex said.

"You've got to be kidding me. There *are* no bad pieces," Fenlee said. It was unbelievable how talented her friend was. Everything she did was perfect. Even her aunt was on a different level. Fenlee had never heard of anyone cooking for pleasure, though sometimes she wondered if Elliot enjoyed it just a little.

The brief tour came to a close, and the two girls ended up on an outside balcony facing east. From their vantage point, Fenlee looked out across the sea of concrete and steel to the massive iron Void Pillar marking the eastern border of the New Cascadia city-state.

"This view is incredible," Fenlee said. "I lived up this high when I was a lot younger, but we never had a place like this. Why bother coming down to the academy? Studying with Casper? You have all this, but you spend all your time down there."

Alex lounged over the balcony railing, swirling her tea. "I guess I never told you. Lily's only here on a work license from Norfayne. First thing she did when we arrived was buy my citizenship, but hers has been harder to come by. I just sleep here. There's a nonexistent address assigned to me somewhere down in lower tier. They won't let my aunt adopt me, since I'm technically a citizen but she's not. It complicates things, but we make it work."

She gave Fenlee a little shoulder nudge. "But hey, at least it means I get to go to school with the two of you, right?" Her tone shifted, her eyes losing their characteristic intensity for a heartbeat. "Really though, I've never felt at ease here. My aunt's great, I don't mean that. I just prefer it down there. The world feels more real, even though you see less of it. And I've never been comfortable living off Norfayne's money."

The evening air stirred, and Fenlee gripped her warm cup tighter in the face of a slight chill. "Yeah. Norfayne's money."

Alex whirled on her. "Oh, yeah! You never told me—how did the drop with your bot go? Did it work? Was it able to collect anything?"

Fenlee grimaced. Apart from nearly getting kidnapped or killed, Cipher was as good as gone. She would never see that little bot again. All the hard work she'd put into creating him over the past year was for nothing. "Right, so, that's an interesting story—"

"Dinner, girls!" Lily called. "Come on in and help me get this plated up."

Pungent aromas of peppery mustard and the smoky sweetness of caramelized onion drew Fenlee to the kitchen like a highly optimized pathfinding algorithm.

"This...this is the best dinner I've ever had!" she said.

"Hah, slow down there, Fenlee," Lily said. "I appreciate your confidence in my abilities, but you haven't even tried it yet. And you should be sure to thank your brother. He's helped a lot and has been a delight to have around in the kitchen."

"Thanks," Elliot said. "I'm happy to come over and help any time. But, um, can I use the restroom real quick?"

"Just down the hall," Alex said. She ladled creamy rice on plates, which her aunt then topped with fish, vegetables, and sauce.

"Your brother was filling me in on quite a few things while you were outside," Lily said.

Fenlee tensed. "Oh? All good, I hope?"

"It's okay, it was all fine stuff," Lily said. "But it sounds like you have a lot going on right now and maybe you could use a hand." Her voice was naturally smooth and reassuring. It made Fenlee feel safe, like a warm blanket and cold night. "I'm sure Alexandra told you, but I'm in biomechatronics research and development at Norfayne. I get to work on a lot of really fascinating stuff, most of which goes to better humanity in some way—at least that's my hope. Anyway, I've been fabricating prototypes of artificial limbs for a current project. If you'd like, I can scan you after dinner and run one off for you this week. It'd be just another disposable experiment as far as my colleagues are concerned, so there won't be any issue. What do you think? If you wear an improperly sized leg like that until your father gets back, it could do lasting damage to your body."

Lily's generosity collided with Fenlee's stressful emotions from the past week. She had been dreading the months ahead stuck using her too-small leg. She couldn't help but start to tear up.

"I'll take that as a yes?" Lily asked.

Fenlee nodded vigorously.

"Good. Maybe it's a bit selfish, but I'd love to see one of my Griffin-series limbs in action too. Which brings us to this etherclaw business."

Okay, Elliot, Fenlee thought. *What did you tell her? You've gotta keep your damn mouth shut.* He was normally so quiet. She wondered what it was about Lily that made him start yammering away all of a sudden.

"Elliot was asking me about it. He said it was of great concern to you," Lily said. "I can't say I have any idea what it is, and I don't recall ever hearing the term. But I may still be of some help. I already have time reserved in the Telluric Library exactly one week from today. You may come as my research assistant if you wish. It would also be the perfect opportunity to pick up your new leg."

Fenlee could not conjure words. *The* Telluric Library? Lily was right. If any information actually existed regarding etherclaw, it would have to be there. "Yeah—yes! Thank you!" She wiped her eyes on her sleeves. "This means so much, I just don't—"

A pained scream ripped down the hallway.

"Elliot!" Fenlee shouted, running toward her brother. They'd been found. The SecForce operatives must have been surveilling the area without them knowing. Fenlee put her hand on her chest. She was barely even a novice with etherclaw, but she would have to give it her all. They had put Lily and Alex in danger just by coming here tonight, and it was up to her to do everything she could to keep the four of them safe.

Elliot stumbled out of the bathroom, doubled over as though he'd just taken a hard groin hit. His pants were mostly up, but his belt was undone. "It's like fire!"

Fenlee stopped halfway down the hall.

Lily leaned on the doorframe, arms crossed. "You didn't wash your hands after cutting those peppers?"

CHAPTER 12
EVERYONE'S A THIEF

THE WEEK PASSED without incident. School brought a semblance of normalcy. Seeing acquaintances and instructors, Fenlee felt as though her world was nearly right again. Casper wouldn't stop asking about Cipher until she bit his head off in irritation. There was no simple way to explain why she couldn't go back and retrieve the scavenger bot. She didn't want to talk about it at school, but found herself constantly bringing up her frustrations with Elliot and Nico at home.

"I bet right now my poor little guy is sitting on that vent at the drop point, waiting for us. Just patiently wondering if we'll ever be back," she'd say. She didn't know whether the self-preservation routines were even sufficient for Cipher to seek out the means to maintain a charge. She preferred not to think about it.

Part-time work at Murdok's ended up being far less exciting than Fenlee hoped. The old shopkeep had her go through large bins of screws, bolts, and fittings, sizing each one according to a reference guide and her own best guess. It was manual, tedious, and boring. At least there was some money involved. The rest, of course, went to pay off the massive debt she had accrued. To have lost Cipher but still have to pay for his components left a bitter taste she had difficulty getting rid of.

Additional etherclaw training followed no particular schedule and occurred at Nico's whim. This wasn't typically a problem, except for the night Fenlee woke up with the kid about half a meter from her face ready to go practice. She had a blunt conversation with him about boundaries shortly thereafter. The improvements were slow, but certain, though Fenlee wished she could speed things up. Nico reiterated throughout the week that one had to "control" it rather than "use" it. Fenlee pondered the distinction, but couldn't make sense of it.

When the Library day finally came, Fenlee's nerves turned her lower digestive system against itself. This could be her chance to figure out what this opal thing really was, but beyond that, she hoped to learn why her mother had it. She was also getting a new leg—a prototype from the top research organization in the world.

"Well? What do you think?" Lily asked.

Fenlee walked about the Blounts' common room, testing out the new leg. It was matte black with a light gray prototype serial number running up the side of the calf—not exactly a high-fashion model, but Fenlee loved the aesthetic. The metal was a custom composite, properly weighted in all the right places. It was the first leg she had ever worn with articulating toes, and she found there was no learning curve controlling them through the nerve interface. There was micro-biofeedback surfacing on the entire leg, allowing her to distinguish between a variety of sensations such as temperature, pressure, pain, and even a tickle. A stabilization assembly around the connection pin was designed to cushion impacts. It was an incredible feat of engineering, and nothing she'd ever imagined she would have the opportunity to wear.

Fenlee didn't know how to thank this woman that she had only met a week ago. She blinked back the dampness in her eyes, refusing to let the floodgates open and get all mushy in front of Alex. "This is just unbelievable," she said. "You have no idea how much this means." Although, she realized, given her line of work, Lily probably knew exactly how much it meant.

Lily wrapped an arm around Fenlee and pulled her close. "I'm so glad you like it," she said. "It's rare that I get to see my work in action, so this isn't selfless, either. I'm thrilled to know you'll get some use out of it." She cocked an eyebrow. "And I'm always open to any feedback you might have."

There were strict protocols in place for anyone visiting the Libraries of the Telluric Ascendancy. Fenlee wore her most formal outfit, but it wasn't sufficient. The library was a religious institution, and specific garments were required. Lily brought out a box with a picture of a scepter with a single wing bisecting a sphere—the emblem of the Telluric Ascendancy. Fenlee knew it was supposed to represent unification and hope, but she always thought it looked like the earth was being ripped apart by a phallic toilet plunger with a bad haircut.

"You can borrow Alex's vesture for today," Lily said.

Fenlee looked at Alex's broad, rounded shoulders and

narrow waist and tried to come up with a way to avoid embarrassment. "I'm not so sure we're the same size," she said.

"Wait until you see it," Alex said. "That floppy mess'll fit anyone."

Anyone, huh? Fenlee's face flushed.

Lily removed a baggy ivory frock and a red collar with long black tails in front and back. Even as a lowly "research assistant," she was expected to look the part of a divine acolyte.

Alex was right: the frock fit fine and allowed easy movement, almost like wearing a loose blanket. The broad collar, on the other hand, was restrictive and stretched from her neck to her shoulders with an oppressive weight.

Lily explained the two articles of clothing were supposed to contrast with one another. "'Freedom through sacrifice' or some such nonsense," she said. "This is just one of the silly games we have to play or the Divine Council will kick us out. Sorry."

Fenlee hadn't been up to the high tier since she was a little girl. Life on the platforms remained so hidden from view it may as well have been another world. There were so few people up that high. No one crowded into anyone else's space, no one seemed particularly hurried, no one wore an expression of stress or struggle.

The Grand Telluric Library of New Cascadia rose before them, all prismatic glass with etched filigree, painting vibrant patterns of every hue on the ground. The lines were colorful, but ended in harsh, conflicting edges like a rainbow over a battlefield. Fenlee's collar felt heavier as she approached.

Heavily armed guards stood at regular intervals around the

perimeter. Drones patrolled in lazy patterns. Fenlee tensed and pulled the frock's deep hood down over her face as she walked behind Lily.

Thick wooden doors with iron inlays glided open on repulsor tracks, allowing them to enter a glass atrium. To either side were more armed guards as well as two hovering Guardian autodrones bristling with weapons and fortified armor. Directly in front, past a security checkpoint, was the entrance to the main library. Fenlee had never seen this level of military-grade protection before, but Lily seemed at ease.

There was a pair of guards and a scanner array between Fenlee and the rest of the library. Lily presented her identification token and her forefinger for bioanalysis.

"Welcome, Dr. Blount," the larger guard said. "And who is this joining you today?"

"This is Fenlee Harper. She's my research assistant, and I expect you to grant her full access."

"Of course. She'll just need to surrender all devices and submit to be scanned."

Fenlee didn't like the sound of that at all. Parting with her tools was worse than going in naked—similar, in many respects. Worse, she didn't want her biomarkers on the official record here. But what choice did she have?

The guards gawked as Fenlee pulled device after device and tool after tool from under her frock, placing them on a tray atop a small bot. It was obvious most patrons of the library did not enter with such an array of apparatus, and Fenlee felt increasingly out of her element. Lily gave her a sideways grin.

After unloading her possessions and receiving a dull, eye-rolling lecture on the rules of the library, Fenlee and Lily were each given three square sheets of paper and a writing instrument. They were admitted with the instructions that they could take whatever notes they wished, constrained to those three sheets.

The library was home to millions of books printed on paper with case binding, each a treasure unto itself. Shelves were arranged in a winding maze, creating partitions for every topic imaginable. There was even a cordoned-off section for the handwritten codices of the Telluric Ascendency. Dense smells of warm vanilla and dusty earth helped smooth out the biting odors of ink and sterilization agents.

The central corridor was oppressively ornate. The symbols and icons of the Ascendency glowered down from their gilded perches. Stiff-backed chairs with fragile spindles and spiraled feet seemed more concerned with their own form over function, unless their function was a *don't-intend-to-sit-here-for-long* ascetic quality. Massive tables lining the broad hall where academics and scribes pored over texts, taking efficient notes as their assistants brought them tea. Fenlee hoped she wouldn't be expected to provide beverage service to anyone.

"There is no electronic representation of the information in this library, Fenlee," Lily said.

Fenlee was so entranced by her surroundings, Lily's soft voice in her ear was startling. "I gathered that. But why?"

"They tightly control the domain of information in this and the handful of other Ascendancy libraries around the world. Some of these books are hundreds of years old and predate the Great Collapse. They offer a rare glimpse into the truths of our world, and those truths are tightly protected." Lily hesitated for a moment then added, "Make certain any notes you take today are your interpretation and not a one-to-one copy of anything. You never know if they'll audit you on your way out. And please don't try to go any further than those little sheets of paper will allow."

"You got it," Fenlee said. "I'm just glad for the chance to even be here."

Lily smiled. "And I'm glad to be able to provide it. Now, go seek the information you need, and meet me back in the main chamber in three hours."

Fenlee had never been in a library before and had only held a few different physical books in her life. As she wandered the halls, she became lost and overwhelmed by the volume of tomes, new and old, that would take thousands of lifetimes for any one person to read.

Her mind drifted to Cipher. If he were here, she could set him to work rapidly scanning and analyzing relevant books to home in on something—*anything*—regarding etherclaw. But he wouldn't have been allowed anywhere near this place anyway.

She wandered back to the main hall and poured herself a cup of tea. It tasted like roasted paper, but at least it was hot. Searching for etherclaw was hopeless; there was no point in trying to find a few drops of water in this unfamiliar sea.

"Do you need some help?"

The library set her nerves on end, and Fenlee jumped for a second time, spilling a bit of tea from her tiny cup. "Excuse me, what?" She spun around to see a boy wearing the same frock and collar she was. He had a pale complexion with short dark hair, piercing blue eyes, and an innocent expression. She couldn't help but be reminded of Elliot. Perhaps that was why the boy's presence immediately put her at ease.

"Hey there," she said. "Yeah, I'm kind of new around here—this is my first time, actually—so I don't really know what I'm doing." She drained her cup and set it down a little too loudly in the saucer.

"I thought you looked out of place," the boy said. "That's why I wondered."

"I came here looking for something, but I've realized I have no idea how to find anything."

The boy nodded. "I've spent a lot of time here helping my father. If you like, maybe I can help you too. Follow me." Without waiting for her, the boy turned and walked through a door off the main hall. Fenlee went after him into a room with rows of terminals. "This is the only area with electronics in the library," the boy said. "Here, you search for what you want and it tells you where to find it."

"Perfect. Got it," Fenlee said. She stood in front of a terminal, but the moment she extended her hands toward it, it flashed "*unauthorized*."

"It's your first time here, so you probably don't have access yet," the boy said. "If you tell me what you're looking for, I'll search for you."

Fenlee didn't want too many people knowing why she was there, but if she didn't take advantage of this boy's offer, she'd be out of options again. There were only two other researchers using terminals and both were hunched over, deeply engaged in their tasks. They probably hadn't even noticed Fenlee enter with the boy.

"Um, try searching for 'etherclaw,'" Fenlee whispered.

The boy stared blankly.

"It's spelled, e-t-h-e-r-c-l-a-w."

"Yeah." The boy scrunched his brow slightly but otherwise didn't move.

"Okay, so, are you going to help me or not?" The boy was starting to make Fenlee feel uncomfortable. Something wasn't right. The weight of her garment bore down on her, and she was suddenly aware of how hot it was where her hair was matted to her neck. She wanted to leave.

"I was just thinking that's a really strange word." He entered the term, but the search returned nothing. He thought for a moment. "The books aren't digitized, so there is no full-text search of the contents, only keywords, and that isn't a keyword." Fenlee thought she saw a flash of regret on his face. "Sorry."

Fenlee sighed. Maybe she was just on edge and the kid was weird. "How about trying it as two words," she suggested. "Like, 'ether' and then 'claw.'"

The boy tried, but again, the search yielded zero results. "Something else you want to try?" he asked.

Fenlee thought, but there really wasn't much of anything. Opals? That would get her thousands of geological references. She didn't have enough info to know what other terms might be relevant. The day was turning out to be a complete waste. What had she truly expected to find here? She wished Alex had come with her—that girl could probably live off a diet of knowledge with all the books she devoured. If there was anything about etherclaw at all here, Alex would know how to find it.

"Thanks anyway," Fenlee said. "I really do appreciate you trying to help." She started for the door. "See you."

"Hey, wait." The boy hesitated. "Let me…" He entered a few terms, just out of sight, then cleared the terminal. "Come on," he said, leaving the room before Fenlee could ask what it was he searched for.

The boy moved quickly, and she did her best to keep up with him down the main corridor and into the labyrinth of stacks. They went down a flight of stairs to another level with far fewer people.

Fenlee was so distracted at how effortless it was to climb stairs with her new leg, she almost lost track of the boy. When she found him again, he was holding a thick black book, but he was still on the move. She caught up to him in a section dedicated to various scientific journals. This floor was not as lavish as the main one above, and this area especially, with rows of metal cases holding millions of papers and journals, felt more like a basement storage area than part of the main library. Everything here looked the same, and Fenlee felt mildly disoriented. The warm vanilla was gone, replaced by a musty smell that created the illusion of being underground rather than hundreds of stories up.

Barely looking at what he was doing, the boy grabbed three journals and spread everything out on a small table. "You should look at these references and see if they have what you need," he said.

"Thanks, I guess," Fenlee said.

"No problem," the boy said. "Glad I can be useful."

She sat down in a considerably less fancy chair than those upstairs as the boy opened each reference to a specific page. Everything in front of her was dated around two hundred years ago, shortly after the Void Pillars were constructed by the Aeons, but just before the Great Collapse.

The journal closest to her contained a paper entitled "Adiabatic Qualities of Foreign Matter Systems" and was written by an author who felt as though the laws of thermodynamics were going soft and everything she knew was a lie. It also didn't appear to be peer-reviewed.

"Hey, why did you give these to me?" Fenlee asked. But when she looked behind her, the boy was nowhere to be seen. She was alone in the stacks.

There was no telling why he grabbed those specific papers and that book, but with nothing else to go on, she kept reading. Whatever the author observed, or thought she had observed, didn't make sense. The paper listed many of the basic formulas Fenlee was familiar with for heat transfer, but then attempted to alter them to explain away various observations. The only problem was the altered formulas directly violated immutable laws of thermodynamics. The woman was crazy—if she had discovered something like that, it would have long since been a central part of every school curriculum.

Fenlee started to toss the journal away in favor of another one when a line of text caught her eye:

...like invisible claws through the ether, reaching out to rip some unknown energy from nearby life...

The phrasing couldn't be a coincidence, especially given the context. She continued on, now glued to the pages. There wasn't much more in that particular paper beyond a few weak attempts to apply mathematical models, a couple of which she copied down on one of the square sheets of paper.

Another journal, dated later, described the process at a higher level, but didn't attempt to model it mathematically:

The ether/claw phenomenon describes the process employed by the Makers of seizing and siphoning the élan vital[3] of biological entities in close proximity[4]. It is not consumption, but rather a redirection of that energy, which is applied directly to a target in order to perform a given task of the Maker's orchestration.

The term "Makers" was vaguely familiar. Fenlee thought she recalled it as the original term given to the Aeons before the world started worshiping them. "Élan vital," on the other hand, was not. She noted both on a piece of her paper to ask Alex about later. The remaining journals didn't make much sense. There were sections on tissue homogenization, transient stem cells, and a wealth of other topics that were completely foreign to her.

Something wasn't right, however. What little information she could make sense of described etherclaw as using bioenergy from *another* entity, not the one controlling the process. Fenlee didn't understand how, when she used it, it seemed to draw on *her* rather than the living stuff nearby as all the articles suggested.

Peeking around the corner, Fenlee eyed a clock that spanned floor to ceiling at the end of an impossibly long aisle of books. She didn't have much time left before she had to meet Lily. As vindicating as it was to find evidence that this was all real, she still felt as though she was missing so much. At this point, she would be walking out of the library with more questions than when she arrived.

Fenlee opened the large black book called *Survey of Origins*. The pages were yellowed with a stale peppery smell. The first half was an anthropological and linguistics study covering a period known as "The Transition," which occurred after the Great Collapse as the world began to stabilize again. But as she flipped through, the book felt less academic and more occult. This was the period that gave rise to the Telluric Ascendancy and the glorification of the Aeons.

Toward the back of the book, several pages had been torn from the binding, leaving jagged bits behind. One scrap remained, about the size of Fenlee's palm, where the tear had been imperfect. There were several lines about the Void Pillars and some other things she wasn't familiar with, but it was difficult to get any meaning without the context of the missing pages.

Fenlee looked at the clock. She was out of time.

Why include this book? There was nothing about etherclaw. Was there something significant about the missing pages?

There was no one else around, so she placed the book in her lap under the table and ripped out the scrap, stuffing it in her boot as discreetly as she could. Taking it was a severe violation, but further study might reveal more about the contents of the missing pages. She was too curious to let it go. But what was that about curiosity killing the cat? Kavi seemed to get along fine though. She had to have it, and besides, it tidied up the book and it was important to leave things in a better state than you found them. Yes, taking the scrap was the right thing to do.

Fenlee tossed the journals and the book into a reshelving bin and raced back upstairs. She arrived, out of breath, to find Lily sitting on the edge of a table waiting for her.

"And how is that new leg treating you? Lily asked.

"Oh, yeah, wow—it's—," Fenlee struggled between breaths.

"It's great. I guess I didn't realize how fast I got here. That's the easiest I've run anywhere since I was a little kid."

"Well, you're probably not supposed to be running in here, but it makes my heart smile to hear it," Lily said. "Did you find what you were after?"

Fenlee held up her papers, one and a half of which were covered in notes. "I found some stuff, yeah. Not exactly what I was expecting. I'd actually like to talk to Alex about a few things if she's around."

"Research is all about digging into the unknown, never being certain what you'll find," Lily said. "Alex has capoeira this afternoon, but I'm sure the two of you can get together soon." She pointed to a clock at the end of the great hall. "Our time's up, and I could get my access revoked if we don't leave when we're supposed to."

Near the entrance stood the same boy who helped her earlier. She tried to get his attention to thank him, but he was deep in a heated conversation with an angry man in Divine Council attire, so she decided to let it go.

Fenlee and Lily turned over their notes for quick review by the guards. She saw her belongings arriving on the little storage bot, waiting for her on the other side of another body scanner.

Oh, voiding hell. No one said we had to get scanned on the way out of this place.

Lily went through the scanner with no issue, and Fenlee followed right behind, trying to keep her breathing natural and her heartbeat calm. She stepped as lightly and casually as she could to minimize the crinkle of paper in her boot. On the other side of the scanner, she started to retrieve her tools and electronics from the tray on top of the bot when a guard captain approached her, staring at her feet.

"One moment," the captain said. "This isn't right."

"Sorry—what, uh, isn't right?" Fenlee choked the words out. Heat climbed up her face and her vision closed in. If she got found out, would they take just her, or Lily as well? And where would that leave Elliot?

"This leg," the captain said, squatting down and tapping Fenlee's new prosthetic with his middle finger. "The model doesn't show up listed in any bio profile. Not sure why it wasn't flagged on the way in." He glared at a set of subordinates behind him.

"Oh, that thing?" Lily walked back over and threw her arm around Fenlee. "You aren't going to find that beauty in any records because it's a prototype. I made it."

"You *made* it?" the guard captain asked.

"Check my profile. It's what I do."

Another guard came forward with a datapad. "She's in biomechatronics at Norfayne, sir."

The captain grunted. "Well, I have to say, it's impressive looking." He stood up and shrugged. "You two take care."

They stepped outside into a dreary afternoon. A light drizzle had dropped the temperature and Fenlee inhaled deeply, savoring the sweet, cool freedom. Despite a few scares and frustrations, she felt good about her discoveries. She couldn't wait to tell her brother.

She arrived back home in the Lower Ashe Ward to find Kavi lounging in the middle of the table, his bristled tongue slurping around his butt. He looked up at her, cocked his head, and went back to his work. She did not understand the appeal of having a cat around.

"Elliot?" Fenlee called, but there was no answer. It didn't take her long to check the entire apartment, but there was no sign of him. She did, however, find a snoozing Nico flopped out in her bed, drooling on her pillow.

"Hey!" Fenlee shouted, yanking him onto the floor. "You have your own bed. What the hell are you doing in here?"

"Smells nice."

"Gross! And no it doesn't, my sheets smell awful!" Fenlee groaned. "Whatever. Just stay out of my room, okay?" He'd hit the floor a lot harder than she meant, so she gently helped him up. "Sorry. I shouldn't have reacted like that. Are you okay?"

Nico gave her a toothy smile and nodded vigorously. Of course he was okay, Fenlee was certain he was made of rubber.

"Have you seen Elliot? I can't find him."

"Left."

"Yeah, thanks. That's pretty apparent. Left to go where?"

Nico looked out the window at the gray wash of buildings. "Dunno."

Elliot crept along the inner curb, sticking so close to the walls that his hoodie kept snagging on a chunk of broken brick here or jagged cement there. He kept his hood pulled low over his face, not only to keep the rain out, but to avoid unwanted looks. There were few people out, even though it was only late afternoon. The occasional Sentry drone circled, but neither human nor machine paid him any attention.

Of all her projects, Fenlee had poured the most time,

energy, and love into Cipher, and Elliot had watched her do it. He knew what it meant to lose the little bot, and Fenlee had lost too much already. She had done so much for him, and he wanted to do this little thing for her. There was no way she could come back into the Waterfront District and hope to make it out again—not after last time. But they would be looking for her, not him. As long as he kept to himself, he should be fine.

But what if she hadn't programmed it correctly? What if that chip thing she got didn't work like she thought? Elliot didn't know the first thing about most of what Fenlee did, but he knew a lot of her projects didn't exactly work as planned. What if Cipher was another flawed experiment, and he was going all this way for nothing?

His stomach tightened with anxiety.

It had already taken longer than he thought to get here. Maybe he had his directions mixed up? He spat out a strand of his hair—Fenlee would lay into him when he got home if there were crimp marks from chewing.

The entire area looked so different during the day. He was lost. There was no way this was the correct route—he would have seen something familiar already. If he backtracked now, maybe he could still find an active maglev station and just forget the whole thing. As he turned to go, he spotted a rusty gate recessed between two buildings.

The park.

He slipped inside and jogged past the same untended flower beds and paths from before until he reached the other side. Before him was the angled alley. Behind him…something felt *off*. He held his breath and listened. But there was nothing beyond the soft, staticky pits and pats of light rain.

He looked in the ventilation grate, but it was too dark to see much. "Hey, uh, Cipher?" Elliot whispered into the shadows. "I don't know if you're in there, but I'm here to take you home." Nothing. Elliot thought for a moment. "I want to take you home to *Fenlee*."

There was a light scratch of metal on metal followed by a series of rapid clicks so quiet they were nearly lost in the rain. Cipher emerged from the depths of the ventilation shaft, but stayed near the back, his dim red eye on Elliot.

"Come on, I'll take you back," Elliot said. "Let's get you snuggled in my pack so you don't get wet."

Cipher took two tentative steps toward Elliot then halted, rotating his optic sensor to focus behind him.

Elliot whipped around, but it was too late. Before him stood the woman from before, this time with three SecForce officers. In front of the group stood a man with thick arms and rounded gut. He had a variety of expensive physical augmentations he'd taken no steps to hide. While some of those on the upper tiers may have been able to afford such things, they usually blended with the rest of the body. This man looked cobbled together, and the incongruity was monstrous. His single red eye was the worst—it raked over Elliot, leaving him feeling vulnerable, as though his whole life and existence had just been exposed.

They had him cornered.

Elliot opened his mouth, but nothing came out. He forgot how to breathe. Had they come for him so they could get to his sister? That had to be it—he was just another low-tier nobody. Out of the corner of his eye, he saw movement inside the vent. Cipher had shut down the light in his optic sensor and positioned himself to get a better look.

"Greetings, Elliot," the augmented man said. "It's been a while. You look as though you don't remember me. That's probably good."

Elliot watched dumbly as the man lifted his arm and shot a thick dart into his neck. The pain was white hot, but only for a moment before everything went black.

CHAPTER 13
MISSING

The last traces of the day were fading, and Elliot still hadn't come back. He would occasionally run out for food or other household supplies, but Fenlee had already checked the local market area and nearby bodegas. His bike was still locked up, so he couldn't have gone far. That kid was great about letting her know where he was going to be; for him to leave without saying anything and for him to be gone so long was not normal.

Fenlee had been pacing for the last half hour, periodically interrogating Nico by repeating the same questions to the boy while he and Kavi both sat on top of the table, watching her.

"Nico, I know we've been through this, and I'm sorry, but do you have any other thoughts or ideas at all?"

"Food?" Nico asked.

His belly had been rumbling on and off. Fenlee supposed she also ought to take care of Kavi. "Yeah, sorry, I guess I'm hungry too. What we should do is start asking around and find out if anyone's seen him. We'll grab something while we're out."

Nico leapt off the table and stood beside the front door. Kavi hopped on his shoulder with perfect balance.

Fenlee asked a few neighbors if they'd seen Elliot around, but no one had. Most of them wouldn't have paid any attention anyway. The old man down the hall didn't even know who she was talking about.

Across the street, the temaki cart man was taking down his sign and closing up for the day. She grabbed Nico's hand and bolted across the street, dodging an irate bicyclist and almost tripping over a slow-moving municipal bot. The temaki man didn't so much as spare her a glance as she nearly slammed into his cart.

"Hey—still got time for one last order?" Fenlee asked.

The man rolled his one good eye and stopped covering up the warm food wells.

"Great. How about two rice rolls? Mushrooms if you got 'em." Fenlee hadn't been involved in feeding Kavi and had no idea what cats ate. "And also maybe a little, um, whatever you have lying around that this little guy would eat?"

It was hard to read the man's expression in the fading light, his face a mass of greasy, folded shadows. But his gnarled hands worked quickly, and he handed Fenlee and Nico each a brown rice and mushroom roll. For Kavi, he scraped the last burned spoonfuls of mashed squash from the bottom of a well and plopped it on the sidewalk beside the cart, drizzling it with fish oil. Fenlee paid him, but he waved off the charge for the cat.

"Thanks. Um, quick question for you," Fenlee said. He had resumed packing up the cart and showed no interest in further engagement, but she needed to try anyway. "We can't find my brother, Elliot, and I was wondering if you'd seen him happen by? I mean, since you're out here all day—"

Without looking up, he pointed down a long avenue to the right. There was only one thing in that direction: the Ashe Ward maglev station.

Fenlee could think of no reason in the world Elliot would need to leave their ward. Anything that he routinely needed was easily accessible by foot or bike—he'd never even traveled alone by maglev. She was incensed. What could he be thinking, going to another ward without her?

There was no point trying to scour the thousands of locations throughout New Cascadia where he could have ended up. She and Nico sat on the front building stoop and ate their wraps in silence while Kavi licked up the bits of rice that fell to the ground.

"Maybe he'll be back around soon. Let's go on up and wait." But the words tasted like a lie. Elliot was brilliant and kind, but socially naive. He lacked certain street charisma and the ability to read his surroundings—skills that were natural to most any kid born down tier. Reporting him to the authorities would be fruitless at best, and likely just make matters worse.

They headed up and Nico went straight to sleep, curled up like a cat under one of Elliot's ferns in the common room. Also like a cat, Fenlee figured he probably slept around sixteen hours a day. She sat at the table, head sunk into her arms, eyes fixed on the door. Kavi jumped up and licked the inside of her ear. It felt gross but somehow soothing, in a weird way.

She was dozing off when Kavi let out a low growl. He was sitting on the edge of the table, attention fixed on an air vent above the cabinets. His tail swished back and forth and his fur stood on end.

"What do you see?" Fenlee whispered to the cat.

The air system was communal—shared among all the building tenants—and on more than one occasion, there'd been a rat or other little creature running around in the ducts. "If it comes out, you're welcome to play mouser." Fenlee picked at a scab on her knuckle and went back to idly contemplating the front door.

A whirring sound in the vent cleared away her exhaustion. *That's no rat.*

She jumped up, flipping over her chair. Kavi snarled, and they both watched as one by one, the bolts securing the vent cover dropped to the counter with four dull metallic thuds. The cover fell, clanging off the counter. Fenlee grabbed her old leg to use as a weapon and held it above her head, ready to pound the intruder to a pulp.

A spindly rod emerged and wrapped itself around the outside of the vent. Then another. A circular sensor glowed red as the little bot carefully maneuvered itself into view.

"Cipher!" Fenlee exclaimed. She dropped the leg and ran to him. "How did you make it back here?" The bot leapt onto the floor and scurried down the hall to her room. By the time she caught up to him, he was already on her workbench with one leg poking at a patch cable.

"Whoa, easy, little guy," Fenlee said. The little bot was dancing around, and kept prodding the cord. "What, you want me to hook you into the terminal?" She hadn't programmed any routines that should have allowed for this behavior. Perhaps the Elixir chip was more powerful than she understood. Was this his way of telling her he needed emergency maintenance?

Clearing the grime out of his I/O port, she patched him in. Nothing happened for several seconds. Then, as Fenlee watched, the diagnostics panels on her terminal were replaced by text output. Cipher was trying to communicate with her.

In the on-screen data dump, she gathered that Cipher had traced his way back home, having observed the route when Fenlee and Elliot dropped him off over a week ago. He had no positioning unit and only basic remapping functions, so Fenlee could not understand how this was possible. Apparently the only reason he remained in the Waterfront District so long was she'd instructed him to await retrieval there. Now something had happened to cause him to override that directive. Words continued to scroll past and then:

They took him.

An iron ball of dread sat thick in Fenlee's stomach. "Who? Who was taken?" But she knew the answer before it was output on the dingy screen. Cipher continued to provide more information about Elliot's captors, but she felt too numb to take it all in.

Damn it, Elliot, why? Of all the pointless, stupid, ridiculous things...

Cipher's storage compartment opened and two small claws dumped out various scavenged objects on the workbench, but Fenlee barely noticed. Her dad was away, she couldn't trust the authorities, and she had no one else she could lean on in a situation like this. She was alone, but as long as it was her they wanted, she was not powerless.

"Elliot's gone."

Fenlee hadn't noticed Nico walk in and had no idea how long he'd been standing there. "Yeah," she said, her voice hoarse.

"It's *them*," Nico said. There was a spark in his inflection that caught Fenlee off guard. Whether it was fear or anger, she couldn't tell.

"Yeah, Nico. It was them."

He put his arm around her waist and squeezed. "Gonna help Elliot."

"It's me they want. Elliot is just a means to an end for them." She ruffled his hair and offered a smile that didn't match the rest of her face. "If they have what they want, they'll let him go. I have to turn myself in."

Nico held his hands up and looked around, flustered. "No! No no. Hafta tell Kyara."

CHAPTER 14
HONORED PRISONER

The room smelled like antiseptic and gear lubricant. Elliot's head felt as though it'd been chewed on by wild dogs. He was scared that if he touched himself he'd come away with blood. No matter anyway because he couldn't feel his hands. Opening his eyes revealed the ceiling of a white metal room, but the brightness made his temples pound. Closing his eyes trapped him in a sea of swirling phosphenes and made him nauseous. Through the buzzing in his ears he could just make out someone talking.

"I'm telling you, Seth, he doesn't remember a thing."

"Cano, what is your take?"

"He seemed paralyzed, sir. It's hard to tell if there was any recognition or not."

"I see. How much longer should he be out, Morrow?"

The man named Morrow laughed. "Oh, he'll be out for a while. Used a dose that'd drop a man three times his weight."

"Then I'll check back later. Keep the room secured and the antieth barriers in place."

The voices faded along with Elliot's senses as he drifted back into unconsciousness.

If he allowed himself to wake up completely, Elliot knew the pain would come back. A warm hand clasped his own while another brushed hair from his forehead and gently dabbed his face with a damp cloth. The light touch soothed him, let him know he wasn't alone. The twisted fusion of pain and comfort reminded him of a life-threatening illness he'd suffered two years before. Fenlee stayed by his side nonstop for three weeks while he got progressively worse until their father was able to secure some black market antibiotics. Maybe he was back home, sick in bed, and all of this was a fever dream. He shut his eyes tight against the truth.

"Elliot." It was a man's voice, rich and refined, but gentle. Maybe even pleasant. "Elliot, there's been a terrible mistake—Dr. Morrow should never have hurt you like that. Please wake up and come back to me."

This was definitely not Fenlee, and he was definitely not home. Whatever reality he was in, he would have to face it. He clenched his jaw against the broken glass in his brain and opened his eyes.

A man sat close, bent over him and silhouetted by the glaring overhead lights. He shifted as Elliot studied him, revealing a pale face framed by jet black hair. Somehow, he knew this man. The recognition boiled his emotions, but he couldn't separate good from bad.

"Oh, Elliot, I'm so glad you're back with us," the man said. "I've been so worried. We've been trying to rescue you for so long now, but we had no idea where you were or how to find you. Words cannot express how happy I am to see you again."

Elliot didn't say anything. He couldn't turn his feelings into thoughts, and certainly not into words. Not yet.

"I see you're having trouble identifying your surroundings." A sadness cast shadows across the man's face. "Perhaps it is to be expected—you've been through so much. It's me, Elliot. Seth Arkamis. Your father."

This didn't make any sense. Elliot had never known a biological father, and while there was something reassuring about this man, Elliot sensed a malevolence under the surface like a sleeping viper always poised to strike.

"No," Elliot said. He felt as though he'd swallowed gravel. "No…I'm Elliot Harper—" Any further words ground to a halt in his throat.

"I see. We have a long way to go, but it's okay now, son. You're home."

Elliot awoke, but this time he was staring at a different ceiling. It was high with dark wooden beams contrasting pearly inlays. This place smelled of sweet honey and mellow tea. He didn't ache anymore. The shards of glass, the buzzing, and the sore throat had all gone away.

There was a *tink clink tink* beside him. He rotated his head, taking care not to aggravate any unknown injuries. Next to the bed was a peculiar girl a year or so older than him sitting cross-legged and looking bored. She wore round black-framed glasses, and her light brown hair wrapped her chin like a heart. Tendrils of steam rose from a small cup as she poured from an expensive-looking teapot. She blew on the surface and downed the entire cup as though it were a shot of liquor. He liked looking at her.

The girl met his eyes and nearly dropped the cup. "Oh! You're awake!"

"Yeah…mostly, anyway."

"Well! Okay then!" She set the cup on the tray next to the bed, picked it up again, appeared to think for a moment, then put it back down. "I'm supposed to give you some tea right when you get up. Right away." She tipped the teapot into the cup, but only a few drops came out. "Oh, fuckleducks. Sorry. Sorry, sorry. That'd be me. No, wait! That'd be *you*! You took so long waking up, I had to drink the tea before it cooled, right? It was the only sensible thing, really."

In spite of everything, Elliot grinned. "It's okay. I think I'm just glad to *be* awake."

'Yeah! You looked roughed up, like really bad. Kinda, I dunno, green? I got you all cleaned up, though."

"Wait. How exactly did you get me 'cleaned up?'"

The girl shot him a toothy smile. "Don't worry, you're scrubbed up and good to go!"

Elliot felt around under the covers and discovered he was wearing nothing but underwear. "Uh, thanks." He pulled the blanket tighter around him. "What's your name? Also, where am I?"

"Right, of course. I'm Loxi, the residential assistant of the esteemed Dr. Arkamis. And you are in his residence and private labs. He lives in this creaky old chateau, and now I guess you do too." She made a dramatic sweeping motion. "And this is your very own room. It's a pleasure to make your acquaintance, Elliot Arkamis."

"Huh? No. Just call me Elliot." He propped himself up on his elbows. The bed alone was as large as his entire closet-turned-bedroom back home. There was real wood furniture and plush crimson and cream carpets on an inky black marble floor. The decor was sparse, but most of it reminded him of the religious paraphernalia in a Telluric Ascendancy temple or community hall run by the Divine Council. The room was warm with the light from a few scattered lamps to counteract the darkness outside.

"How late is it?" Elliot asked.

"It's...not? Oh, right. Windows are dimmed."

She made a simple gesture at a wall panel, which reduced the opacity of a bank of full-length windows running along one side of the room. It was overcast, probably mid-morning, but clear enough to see the tops of platforms and hyperbuildings without having to look up. He was in the high tier. The *extremely* high tier.

Loxi leaned close. "Wow, you know, with your eyes finally open, you really do look a lot like Rook."

"Who?" Elliot's head started to hurt again. "There's way too much going on. Just tell me how I can get out of here."

"Oh. I don't think they want you to leave, so you probably can't. Sorry about that. There are guards and surveillance stuff and even antieth mesh everywhere anyway. You know what? They can probably watch us in here! Isn't that so weird?"

That was a disconcerting thought. He had been assaulted and kidnapped, taken somewhere far above the part of the city he called home, and was now being kept prisoner by a man claiming to be his father in a bedroom that was supposedly his. On top of it all, he had to assume he was being monitored, so any attempts to leave this place were probably doomed to fail.

Loxi stood and brushed crumbs from her lap. Apparently there was supposed to have been food for him as well. "I need to go make you some more tea. In the meantime, maybe try a shower and some fresh clothes? I did my best, but you kinda stink? Your private washroom is through that door. No one's watching you in there. Probably," she said with a wink.

The steam shower and rinse felt amazing. He found a wardrobe that held more clothes than he'd ever owned. Most were formal—he avoided those. Instead, he settled on a black textured shirt with black pants and found his hoodie and boots at the end of the bed. The hoodie might not smell great, but it felt right.

Elliot ran his hand down the slick glass window and surveyed the broad expanse of New Cascadia. The city looked so different from his vantage point, making it hard to pinpoint where he was. The tower the chateau was on appeared largely abandoned. He guessed he was somewhere along the eastern border, but it was impossible to know for sure. Whatever the case, he needed to get back home, back to Fenlee. He just had to figure out how.

Time passed and Elliot waited patiently for the girl to return, but she never came. The bedroom door was on a bio-lock. All Loxi had to do was gesture and the recognition system allowed her access. He mimicked the motion she made with her hand and, to his surprise, the door obeyed, sliding open to a dark hallway beyond. In such systems, access had to be granted individually, which meant someone was allowing him to leave the room. What kind of prisoner was he?

Elliot crept down the hall, hugging the wall and stepping through shadows. He knew he might not make it far, but he wanted to gain a sense of the place before getting caught. Soft music played from somewhere up ahead. The modern orchestration was familiar, but the way it reverberated down the empty passages was eerie and unsettling. He slowed as he heard voices ahead.

A wide archway opened into a sitting room where two figures were in heated discussion. The taller one he knew as Seth Arkamis, the man claiming to be his father. The other was a boy wearing sharp white clothes, nearly form-fitting on his thin figure. He looked like a small version of Arkamis without the cloak. With the boy's back turned, Elliot was unable to make out any other features. He crept to the edge of the arch and listened.

"We have been over this countless times, and I haven't the patience for it," Arkamis said.

The boy shifted his feet and looked at the floor. "I know, but you're wrong! if you would just give me another chance, I could prove—"

"Never presume to tell me I'm wrong." There was no mistaking the staccato clip. The boy straightened his posture and remained silent. "We've spent years on testing, and you *don't* have the ability. And just because he's back around, doesn't mean anything changes for you. Listen, you're an excellent researcher, Rook, and one of the few who can be trusted with what we're doing here. You have a future with Norfayne, but nothing beyond. *Nothing.* Am I clear?"

The boy nodded.

"Good. Scour those ideas from your head. I do not want to revisit this topic again."

The boy spun around and headed straight through the archway. Elliot had no time to try and hide. Their eyes met. Elliot held the boy's gaze, and for a heartbeat it was like looking in a mirror. The boy's face soured before he looked away.

"Look who's awake," the boy said.

Arkamis clasped his hands, his dark scowl disintegrating as a wide grin lit up his face. "Wonderful! It's excellent to see you up and about, Elliot. We should take some time for you and Rook to become reacquainted."

"I've got stuff to do," Rook said. "You know, 'assisting research' and all." He stomped off down the hall before Arkamis could respond.

"I'm sorry you had to witness that, Elliot. Don't worry, beating respect into Rook has had to become something of a tradition around here. But enough of that. Please, take a seat. I'm sure you have questions."

Elliot sank so deep into the sofa cushions he felt ensnared by extravagance. He wanted to know where he was and how to get home, but Arkamis waved off both questions. He wondered what Fenlee would do and figured she'd be throwing punches already. Elliot wasn't sure he could get up from the sofa by himself, let alone benefit from a physical altercation.

"I know you've been through so much, but let us not dwell

on the past," Arkamis said. "With you back, the grand efforts we're making can continue in earnest." He looked over his shoulder and down the hall. "I told that mousey wreck of a girl to bring tea and refreshment some time ago. I don't know where she's off to this time, but you'll have to forgive the inhospitality."

"Are you talking about Loxi?" Elliot asked.

Arkamis rubbed his temple, the scowl returning. "Yes, that would be Loxi. She's both a servant and resident here, and a constant aggravation. If you need anything at all, ask her. Just don't count on the follow-through."

It took all of Elliot's willpower to keep from chewing on the strands of hair tickling the side of his mouth. At least it gave him something to focus on, and he needed that at the moment. For all Arkamis' efforts to be welcoming, Elliot felt something sinister lurking under the thin facade of congeniality; he suspected it wouldn't take much to peel back the layers and reveal a monster within.

Arkamis put his mask back in place in the blink of an eye, and the warmth in his voice returned. "Ah, well. No point in getting sidetracked with trivial matters when we've so much to accomplish," he said. "Let's get down to it, shall we? We have some activities lined up for you. Some procedures you may find a bit unpleasant, but I assure you, they are of great importance." He leaned in and lowered his voice. "Tell me, Elliot, what do you recall of etherclaw?"

CHAPTER 15
SNOWDROP COLLECTIVE

THE SUN WAS beginning to peek over the mountains to the east as Fenlee and Nico made their way on foot over the crumbling roads that served as arteries of commerce in a different age. Remains of structures long ago devoured by plant life created a sea of rolling hills in every direction. Behind them, the urban core of New Cascadia hugged the coastline for over a hundred miles in either direction, with the highest towers lost in the clouds. This was the Eastern Wilderness Zone, the dangerous uninhabited region beyond the megacity itself, but still within the borders of the city-state.

Fenlee had insisted they waste no time finding Kyara after Cipher's report the night before. Nico agreed, and they took the maglev as far east as they could. He then guided her through a

series of short tunnels under the Cascadian Protection Perimeter to bypass the checkpoint. Never in her life had she left the perimeter, and the feeling of walking in lawless, ungoverned territory was at once frightening and invigorating. She knew there were people living outside the urban complex, but they did so at their own peril; there were no services this far out, and no one to help should there be trouble. Still, she saw no other signs of human habitation, and they passed no one on the roads.

Fenlee trudged along as Nico leapt from debris pile to debris pile. Kavi was eager to come with them and had done a fair job of walking most of the way, but he'd slowed over the last couple of miles, so she allowed him to ride in her backpack.

A growing sense of anxiety set Fenlee on edge, tickling the back of her neck until it was impossible to ignore. She tried to brush it off as the stress of Elliot's kidnapping was made worse by being in unfamiliar territory. But it was more than that—she had a strong feeling something was out there watching.

No, she thought, *something's following us. We're being tracked.*

They were crossing an old bridge, stepping through collapsed girders, when Fenlee's backpack growled. Kavi climbed on her head and pushed off, making a flying leap to the top of a steel beam, taking a bit of Fenlee's hair with him.

"Ow! What the hell was that, you dumb furwad?"

Kavi sniffed the still air.

Nico stopped walking. "Uh-oh," he said.

A chill crept up Fenlee's spine, her senses heightened. "What, Nico? What's 'uh-oh?'"

Before he could answer, two massive creatures emerged on the bridge in front of them. They were dog-like, all black apart from a yellow sunburst pattern on their chests to match their yellow eyes. Though she'd never seen one in person, there was no mistaking a solf. Everyone knew of the genetically engineered wolf hybrids once bred as guards and killers for those with the money and influence. The ban on ownership within the urban core was strictly enforced, leaving the highly intelligent creatures to live in packs, roaming the Wilderness Zone.

The pair of solfs bared no teeth as they approached. Two more appeared in Fenlee's periphery—one on each flank. She turned around to find an escape route back the way they came, but another pair emerged to the rear. Six now surrounded them.

They waited until we were in the middle of the bridge...the perfect choke point, Fenlee realized. She and Nico were laughably easy prey.

Nico sat cross-legged, munching on a protein stick while Kavi stood in attack mode with hackles up and claws out. Fenlee refused to end up as dog food or see Nico, or even that damn cat, suffer such a fate. There wasn't much to work with on the bridge beyond broken girders and chunks of cement. If she could use etherclaw to manipulate the girders, however...

Fenlee put her hand to her chest and conjured the feelings she'd need and the focus she'd learned. If she failed here, no one would be coming for Elliot. She didn't want to die, but saving her brother was imperative. A blast of emotions and energy left her body, directed at a girder a few feet in front of the forward pair of solfs.

The sound of steel grinding on cement broke the silence as the girder slid half the distance to the animals. The pair looked down, halted in momentary confusion, and then continued to close in.

Damn. She had to do better than this. But the exertion from shifting the girder even that short distance was extreme; there was no way she could lift and throw it at two of them, let alone the other four.

Nico finished his snack, licked his fingers, and scampered over on all fours to the pair of solfs.

"Nico, no!"

But he was too fast. The boy arched his back and roared at the solfs in his small voice. "*Rawr! Rawr rawr rawr!*"

The solfs lay down with their heads on their paws. The other four trotted over to Nico and dropped into a circle around him.

Fenlee was stunned. "What the voiding hell are you doing?" The massive creatures gave him their undivided attention, as though the kid were relating a captivating story. "This is insane," she mumbled. Kavi, meanwhile, had given up on the solfs and was quietly cleaning himself.

"Prosticks!" Nico called to Fenlee, holding up six fingers.

"Huh?"

"Now."

Of all the situations she'd been in over the past couple of weeks, this had to be the most bizarre. Fenlee rummaged through her backpack and tossed Nico the food. He gave each solf a snack and patted their heads.

"Done," Nico said, and proceeded across the bridge. Fenlee and Kavi followed, edging past the huddle of solfs, who paid them no attention.

When they were no longer in sight of the bridge, Fenlee demanded an explanation. "What happened back there? What exactly did you do?"

Nico shrugged.

"Oh, no. No way. You don't get to just shrug this off. What

were you *doing*, Nico? *Rawr* isn't even the sound dogs make, nor is it an actual word people use, and—"

"Almost there."

"Almost *where?*" Fenlee was done. She'd spent nearly twelve hours walking across rough, dangerous terrain guided by a kid who could talk to murderous wolf-dogs but refused to say where he was taking her. She was tired and sore, and every step they took led them further from her brother. "If we don't get somewhere meaningful soon, I'm turning around."

He pointed east to a series of tall structures and returned to munching on more protein sticks, one in each hand.

"Isn't that the old spaceport? I've seen images, but it hasn't actually been used for anything in generations."

A broadleaf folded into a triangle hit Fenlee in the side of the head. Nico made a face at her, both protein sticks dangling from his mouth like fangs as he skipped along toward their destination.

"Nico, wait!" Fenlee called. She pulled the leaf from her hair and wadded it up. *Argh, that kid!*

It was mid-morning by the time they arrived. Colossal hangars, service buildings, and towers sprawled across the landscape, all monuments to a tragic past. Plants and vines engulfed the old structures like beasts in a monsterous topiary. Anything of value had long since been stripped and repurposed, but the husks of various spacecraft remained.

A few of the old 300-meter Leviathan-class supply shuttles sat on the outskirts of Nico's destination. The shuttle Max had taken with the others from Norfayne Labs was huge, but it couldn't even begin to compare to these.

"I can't believe our ancestors had the technology to even get these things off the ground," Fenlee said. "The fuel alone had to be incredible."

"Mm-hmm," Nico said and led her inside the fuselage of the nearest Leviathan.

The interior was six stories high and felt like being inside the ribcage of some fantastic ancient beast. Rough wooden platforms with shacks on top were built at varying levels, accessible by walkways or rope ladders. Fenlee smelled something cooking and saw a thin swirl of smoke farther down the fuselage. The place appeared otherwise vacant.

Nico jumped in front of her and spread his gangly arms wide. "Here!" he said. Kavi tumbled out of her bag and scratched himself on the side of a wood plank.

"What is this place?" Fenlee asked.

"*This place* is not anywhere you belong."

Fenlee spun and found herself face-to-chest with an ogre of a man, his shoulder-length braids touching the top of her head.

"Uh...hi." Fenlee gulped. "My name is Fenlee Harper and I came with Nico and I need to find Kyara because my brother's missing." The words tumbled out faster than she could control them.

Ugh, Fenlee, spill info on a need-to-know basis. This guy does not *need to know*, she reminded herself.

The man folded his arms. "No idea what you're talking about." His eyes narrowed as he churned through some thought or other. "But since you're with Nico—and *only* since you're with Nico—I'll get Kyara, and she'll figure out if you can be trusted." Behind him, another man of similar build blocked the entrance to the fuselage.

Fenlee sat on the ground and waited. She'd spent the entire night and morning traveling, and her exhaustion exacerbated her impatience. If Kyara didn't know anything or wouldn't help, all of this could have been time spent looking for Elliot. But before she could get herself worked up again, Kyara stormed through, kicking up dust on the dirt and metal floor. She grabbed Fenlee's collar and yanked her to her feet.

"I don't know who I'm more upset with right now: you for coming here, or Nico for bringing you. Explain."

"Nice to see you too, Kyara," Fenlee said, straightening her shirt and straps. "We came because Nico suggested it." She explained how Elliot had been kidnapped and that she was desperate for help or at least information about whoever had taken him.

Kyara listened without interruption. A weariness replaced her anger as Fenlee finished the story. "I tried to keep you out of all of this, Fenlee, I really did. You're young. You have a life ahead of you. But your life's taken a turn beyond your control now."

"Oh, it's all just so terrible." The large man with the braids wiped a tear from his eye. "I'm sorry, I didn't know."

Kyara sighed and gave him the side-eye. "Fenlee, meet Zephyr. Zeph, this is that girl we ran into during last month's rotation."

"I shoulda realized," Zephyr said. "You poor girl. You know, I lost my entire family during the—"

"Zeph, enough." Kyara cut him off. "She's not here for your

tales of misery or glory, and she won't be staying long enough, anyway."

"Now, Kyara," Zephyr said, "she'll be staying long enough for a bite to eat, and I think we owe her at least a basic explanation of what she's wrapped up in."

Kyara and Zephyr locked eyes in silence until the woman finally relented. "Fine. We feed her, then she leaves."

They walked to the rear of the fuselage, where several rabbits were roasting on a spit over a fire. There were at least a dozen or so others in the depths of the old shuttle, doing everything from repairing equipment to hanging clean clothes on lines to dry.

Zephyr seemed to notice Fenlee's curiosity. "It's home for us, at least right now. Most of us are former soldiers that got wrapped up in a bad situation but some, like Nico, have very different backgrounds. And yeah, a few of us can use etherclaw. All these old ships were decommissioned pre-Collapse and left to rot. This place has been picked over and junked for a long time. No one has any interest in coming out here."

"Why *are* you all hiding here?" Fenlee asked.

Kyara shot Zephyr a fierce look, and he seemed to consider his words before answering. "Well, same as you: there are those that want what we got," he said. "To stay safe, we've gone underground."

"This makes a decent hideout, but aren't you afraid you'll get found out?"

"It serves our purposes, at least for now," Zephyr replied. "Commerce and other activity really only runs north and south by way of hypertrain and then west by sea. There ain't really anything out here in the east apart from that old Void Pillar, and the zealots that journey to it are few and far between."

Kyara sliced up a rabbit and shared it with Fenlee, along with a nutrient pack. She dropped a fizzing purification tab into a container of cloudy water that was passed around. Eating cooked animals was a rare experience typically reserved for those with too much money or, like Kyara's group, those who hunted in the Eastern Wilderness Zone. Fenlee's mouth watered, but Nico refused to eat anything that had once been a living, breathing creature.

"Now that Nico has spent some time with you, how is your etherclaw use progressing, Fenlee?" Kyara asked.

"I've figured out how to use it, if that's what you mean," Fenlee said between bites of the crispy meat. "Just not using it very well yet. And it feels slightly different than before. Like, both exhausting and energizing at the same time. Before, with the drone in the undercity, it only felt exhausting."

"Did it now," Kyara said flatly.

"Yeah, and hey, by the way, how exactly does Nico use it?" Fenlee asked. "I can't figure it out, and he won't tell me."

"Ah, Nico," Zephyr said, a fondness in his voice. "Near as we can tell, he's able to control empathetic connections—stuff that no one else can do at all—like communicating feelings, and sensing certain things. No idea where he came from, but we don't ask about each others' backstories around here. But he's a peculiar one, that's for sure."

Kyara stopped eating. "He certainly is," she said, staring at the boy.

Nico sat on a crate, his eyes wide but focused downward, as he shoveled root vegetables and hard biscuits into his mouth.

He looked smaller than usual, barefoot, dirty, and vulnerable as Kyara approached him like prey.

"Something doesn't add up, Nico," Kyara said, circling the boy. "Elliot was taken, presumably as a hostage to get to Fenlee and her etherclaw. However, they have no way to get in contact with her to negotiate. If they did, they would have gone directly to her home—why waste time lying in wait in the Waterfront District?"

Nico took his time gnawing on the outer edge of a misshapen parsnip. Everyone's eyes were on him, even Kavi, who dropped a beetle he'd been playing with.

"I think you need to come clean, Nico," Kyara said. "A couple of weeks ago, when we were in the Waterfront District, you sensed a new etherclaw presence in the undercity. When we went down there, what did you find?"

"Found Elliot. Found Fenlee," he mumbled.

"And which one had the etherclaw, Nico?"

"...both."

"So you found Elliot and realized what he was. Then you discovered that Fenlee happened to have an etherclaw artifact herself, and you seized on that. You covered for him."

Fenlee pushed forward. "Wait a minute, Nico, what are you saying?" The tiny hairs on her arms stood up and she suddenly felt cold, despite the heat of the day. This couldn't be right. Could it? *Not Elliot...*

"He's saying that your brother destroyed the drone," Kyara said. "I had my suspicions."

"But there's no way he could have. I have this." Fenlee pulled out her opal. "And I've been using it too. I might suck at it, but it works. Elliot doesn't have anything like it."

"Elliot doesn't *need* anything like it," Kyara said. "Isn't that right, Nico?"

The boy sat in silence, kicking his feet against the crate. He spit a bit of parsnip stem out of his mouth and nodded. "Uh-huh," he said.

"No, this doesn't make sense." Fenlee shook her head. "You don't know Elliot like I do. What you're saying isn't possible." There was no way her brother could not only wield etherclaw as well, but was also proficient enough to obliterate a large Guardian drone.

"He's not your real brother, is he?" Kyara asked.

"Of course he is!" Fenlee yelled. "You don't know him and what he's been through."

"The lack of biological connection is evident to anyone looking at you, girl. Your 'brother' was almost certainly kidnapped by those working for Dr. Seth Arkamis. He's a research scientist with Norfayne, and an advisor to the Divine Council. He comes from a long line of fools attempting to exploit etherclaw for their own gain. The big difference with Dr. Arkamis is that he tends to succeed where others have failed. Elliot is the product of one of his experiments, nothing more." Her eyes narrowed. "He's not human."

"Aw, come on, Kyara," Zephyr said. "He's perfectly human, don't be like that."

"Is he really, Zeph?" Kyara asked. "When we use etherclaw, the energy comes from our own lifeforce—it is a personal choice and a personal sacrifice. But he's like those damn Aeons. He sucks the energy and life out of others, giving nothing of himself. You know how it works. You've seen it before."

Zephyr put his head in his hands. "Yeah," he said. "It doesn't mean you have to talk about him like that."

"You didn't destroy that drone, Fenlee," Kyara said. "Elliot did. And he drained *your* energy to do it, nearly killing you in the process."

Fenlee forced herself to breathe slow and deep to maintain control and organize her thoughts. *Okay, so who cares if it's all true?* Elliot was her brother, her family. She was getting him back. This changed nothing.

"This changes things," Zephyr said. His braids swished from side to side, beads tapping against each other as he shook his head. "What are we supposed to do now, Kyara?"

"Not a thing. Running rescue jobs is not what Snowdrop is for." Kyara winced as the words left her mouth.

"But we rescue refugees all the time, and—"

"Snowdrop?" Fenlee cut off Zephyr and gestured around her. "Is that what this is? Is that what you all are? You're the voiding *Snowdrop Collective?*" Fenlee screamed and got in Kyara's face. "You're the ones who bombed Norfayne! You're terrorists!"

"We never did that—"

"You killed my mom!"

"Fenlee, enough!" Kyara shouted. "We had nothing to do with that attack—stop being so hot-headed."

"Oh, *you're* one to call me hot-headed!" Fenlee threw a punch at Kyara with her full weight behind it. The impact knocked Fenlee back while Kyara remained firmly planted, absorbing the hit like a brick wall.

"That make you feel better?" Kyara cracked her knuckles. "We can keep going if you need to."

"Stop, Kyara," Zephyr said. "The poor girl has been through enough."

Fenlee kicked the jug of drinking water into the fire. Nico flinched. He sat with his knees pulled tight against his chin, tears running down his face.

Kyara narrowed her eyes. "I think it's time for you to leave."

"Leave this den of murderers? Gladly."

"We don't kill indiscriminately, girl. We're not murderers. We target their etherclaw research and disrupt their experimentation. That's it."

"Yeah, I saw you 'not murdering' those SecForce officers in the alley. You seemed pretty pleased with yourself."

"Oh, girl, you have so much to learn," Kyara said. "We are the antidote to their poison, and we will continue fighting."

"Whatever. I'm outta here." Fenlee grabbed her pack and made for the entrance to the fuselage.

Nico stood up and wiped his eyes. His gaze lingered on Kyara and Zephyr, but after only a moment's hesitation, he balled his fists and stomped off behind Fenlee with Kavi at his feet.

"I'm sorry, Fenlee, I truly am," Kyara called after her. "I hope you have some good memories with Elliot, but that creature is not your brother."

CHAPTER 16
FREE FALL

Fenlee crashed into a thick, dreamless slumber. Her mind wanted to sort through and make sense of the events of the past twenty-four hours, but her body insisted on shutting down.

She awoke to the smell of something burning. It was morning and clear outside, but a slight haze filled the apartment. She leapt from her bed, fastened her leg in place, and ran down the hall to the kitchen. There was a pan with the charred remains of rice, a teapot, and a green-haired boy looking very pleased with himself.

Nico offered Fenlee a cup of acrid fluid. "Tea. Like Elliot."

"Thanks, Nico." The tea was the worst she'd ever had and it burned her throat like liquor, which was exactly what she needed.

He put a plate of seaweed and mushrooms in front of her. "Crunchy."

"Where did you get this stuff? We don't have any of this lying around."

"Shopping!"

"But I didn't give you any money, and you don't have any, so...oh, Nico, you can't just steal. When you want to take something, you have to give them crednotes first." She couldn't bring herself to truly care, and didn't have the energy to mindlessly lecture him. "You know what, thanks for breakfast. It means a lot."

Nico nodded and started eating. The plate in front of him hadn't been touched, and she wondered how long he'd waited for her. The mushrooms were raw and the dried seaweed was unseasoned, but she was impressed to see everything on actual dishes.

"Hey, Nico, if you knew, why didn't you say anything about Elliot before?"

The boy stopped chewing and picked at his plate. "She'd kill him."

"What do you mean?"

"Kyara'd kill him," he whispered.

"But why?" Fenlee asked. "Why does she hate him so much?"

Nico shook his head and remained silent.

If most Snowdrop members were etherclaw users, then why wouldn't they want to rescue him and bring him on as a recruit? What made him so different that Kyara would want to murder him?

But what if Kyara was right about Elliot? Fenlee didn't know his past, but neither did he. Elliot never spoke of his life before they'd met because he couldn't remember. She often wondered if it was because of some psychological trauma or if he was suppressing something unspeakable. It made Fenlee queasy to think about. Whatever the case, she had to get to him as soon as possible.

"I have to run out today and take care of some things. I'll be okay, but I need you to stay here. Watch over Kavi, okay?"

"And I'm telling you no, Fenlee." Murdok resumed sorting a box of tiny resistors into various piles by type.

"And I'm telling you I *need* it. Please!" Fenlee said.

"I don't make fake ID tokens anymore, and even if I did, you don't have any business with one." She dropped her loupes over her eyes, examined a colorful resistor, grimaced, and tossed it in the trash bin. "And anyway, why would I trust you with such a thing when you won't even trust me enough to say why you need it? Hmm?"

"Fine," Fenlee said. "There's this high-tier club I wanna get into."

Murdok's whole body shook so hard with laughter she knocked a pile of resistors onto the floor. "Oh, Fenlee, my Fenlee. You? In one of *those* clubs? I'd pay to see it. Oh, Fenlee, I'd run you off a hundred IDs and come with you just for the amusement."

Fenlee rolled her eyes. "Wow, thanks, Dok. So it's not exactly my thing, I get it."

Murdok removed her loupes to wipe away tears. "But thank you for the mental image. I needed that. Now, if you don't mind, what exactly is your *thing*? Why do I sense such desperation from you? You have deep bags under your eyes, and I can smell you from the other side of the counter. You're not taking care of yourself. What's going on?"

Fenlee relented and told her all about Elliot, finding out the news from Cipher, and even a few details about where he might be. She refrained from mentioning the Snowdrop Collective or any details about etherclaw.

All humor left Murdok's face. When she spoke, her voice was heavy with age and worry. "Not Elliot. Oh, my Fenlee. I'm so terribly sorry. You should have just told me. Of course I'll get you an ID—anything you need."

Murdok activated a switch and a machine emerged from a hidden recess in the counter. She tapped a few commands into the holoquip on her forearm, and the integrated circuit fabricator came to life.

"This thing may be old and clunky, but it'll cut you a token right quick," Murdok said. "While we're waiting, I think there's something else you should be aware of. Have you considered how your little scavenger bot was not only capable of tracking you down across the city and relaying this information, but that it was motivated to do so? I wasn't entirely certain before, but now I am. That's no ordinary Elixir chip, Fenlee. It's modeled after the old Dynamo series."

"You're kidding me," Fenlee said. "It was just stashed with some squished blueberries in the undercity." She had wondered if Nico was the one who hid it, but getting meaningful info from that kid was nearly impossible.

"I don't need to tell you that strong AI like that has been vigorously outlawed since the Great Collapse—it's too powerful—and you may never see the light of day again if the right people ever found out you have it in your possession. I know a thing or two about contraband, and you hold onto that chip at your own risk."

Under any other circumstances, Fenlee would have been ecstatic. But for now, she tucked that bit of knowledge away to revisit when she cared. "I'll keep that in mind. Thanks."

In no time, Murdok fabricated a fake ID token for Fenlee to insert into her holoquip. When she popped it in, her device validated it as authentic. "And this'll allow me access to anywhere on the upper platforms, right?"

"Pretty much anything high-tier, yes. But you still need to watch yourself."

"I really appreciate it, Murdok."

"You're going to need to be armed. Heavily armed. You may need backup. Wait here, I have just the equipment—"

"No! I don't need any weapons. I'm not out to kill anyone, and I wouldn't know how to use them, anyway."

"Is that right? Then what's your plan? You'll get no help from the Cascadian Authority, you know."

"I know." But what *was* her plan? She didn't even know where this Dr. Arkamis guy had his lab. All she knew was that he worked for Norfayne, but Norfayne was huge. At least it was a start.

Murdok pulled out a massive minigun from behind the counter as big as she was tall. "Well, if you change your mind, my little liberator, I gotcha covered."

"Shit, Dok! What the hell is that thing?"

"I call her Princess."

"But why do you even have that? Who are you expecting to have to deal with?"

"This city is full of secrets, Fenlee—many of them deadly. You want to survive, you've got to have a plan for everything."

The lift came to a stop and Fenlee disembarked, stretching her jaw to clear her ears from the increase in elevation. She had never been to the upper tiers alone. Access required either a certified escort or an authorized ID token. Now that she had a token, she hoped she could move about freely.

The upper platforms were supported by thick towers, some of which were half a mile wide. They were constructed during the pre-Collapse period using materials from the original asteroid mining expeditions, necessary due to Earth's resource exhaustion. Only now, after two centuries of stagnation, were humans attempting to collect extraplanetary materials again. Fenlee looked up into the blue sky, taking in the rare unimpeded view. Her father was out there somewhere, helping to support one of those new mining operations. She wondered what he would do if he found out that Elliot had been kidnapped.

It felt like a different world on the high-tier platforms. Maybe there was less street harassment up here, perhaps she was less likely to be mugged, but all the people she encountered had an air of cold indifference, as though they lacked some fundamental element of humanity. The sprawling plazas, the broad avenues, the open green spaces were all beautiful, but also strange and uncomfortable.

Tracking down Elliot meant going to Norfayne Labs, a place Fenlee hadn't ventured to since her mother died. Memories of that terrible day flooded back, but she forced them to remain buried. That was one more thing she couldn't add to her stack at the moment.

Deep breaths. Focus. She could do this. She saved Elliot here once before, and she could do it again.

So far, none of the proximity token scanners complained as she passed. Each time, she tensed and hoped her rise in blood pressure wasn't detectable. She headed toward a skycar station where she could catch a ride to the primary Norfayne campus. The trip would be short, and she realized she still didn't have a real plan. Maybe she could say she was seeking an internship. It was somewhat true—she had hoped to apply for one in the fall. That excuse might work to get her in the door now, but then what?

She was so deep in thought she didn't see the SecForce officer in front of her until she ran directly into him.

"Oh, s-sorry," Fenlee stuttered. "'Scuse me."

"One moment, ma'am," the officer said. "Where are you headed?"

"Nowhere," she said. "Well, I mean, Norfayne. I'm gonna do an internship, maybe?"

"Uh-huh," the officer said. "I don't know of anyone going in for an internship or much of anything up here looking like *that*." He sneered as his eyes raked over her outfit. "And your name?"

In her haste to find Elliot, Fenlee forgot that her clothing alone would make her stand out among the high-tier citizens. She hadn't even cleaned herself in days.

"I'm Fenlee. Fenlee Harper."

"Well, let's see, shall we?" The officer flicked a small heads-up display over one eye and pulled out a holoquip. He was scanning her, and she felt even more exposed. At least when a drone did it, it was more impersonal. This was invasive.

"Name: Fen Lee Harper. Age: Sixteen. Status: lower tier. Academy assignment: trade engineer. Residence: Lower Ashe Ward." The officer looked up from his display. "Do you dispute this?"

Fenlee shuffled her feet. "No, that's all correct."

"Seems to be," the officer said. "Problem is, your ID token doesn't reconcile with the biosignature registered with the library." He stifled a yawn, probably bored from wasting his time on some bottom-dwelling nobody.

"The library?" Fenlee asked. She could feel the hot moisture beginning to accumulate under her arms and in the palms of her hands. Why would he be bringing up the library?

"You were recently registered at the Telluric Ascendancy Library. You were under escort at the time because you're not authorized to be up here. However, your token indicates you've had access for the past four years. So, Fen, which is it?"

Damn it. This wasn't going to work. "Only my mom calls me Fen, and you can go void yourself," she said. "I told you, my name is *Fenlee*."

"You need to watch your pretty little lowfer mouth, young lady," the officer said. He held out his hand. "The token. Now, or you're coming with me."

Fenlee bit down her rage. She wanted to flatten this man. But Elliot needed her, and she would be of no use to him, herself, or anyone, if she was locked up. She popped the token out of her holoquip, dropped it on the ground, and crushed it with the heel of her boot. She didn't owe this man another word. She spun around and headed back to the lift. He said something else to her, but it was only garbage in her ears.

She rushed into the lift in a blind fury. She was angry at the officer, angry at the world, and angry at herself for being so stupid. *And just how exactly did you think that was going to play out, you idiot?*

The lift was bulky and slow. It was one of the newer, poorly constructed public models they had bolted on the sides of the towers since most of the older internal ones could no longer be repaired. People were packed in tight, but she squeezed in a corner and steamed.

You headstrong dumbass. You just wrecked your one shot at getting to Elliot. Burning tears welled up, and she scrubbed them away before they had a chance to streak through the dirt on her face.

She was so wrapped up in her thoughts that she didn't notice at first how quiet the lift had become. She caught a few bits of muttered conversation.

"…That's what happens when you try to do too much too fast…"

"…A shame, another mining setback…"

"…I kept saying Norfayne was going to blow it…"

"…Huh, I think a neighbor of mine was up there…"

"…Shh! Let the rest of us listen…"

All eyes were on an advertisement screen at the front of the lift where a news broadcast had interrupted the cycle of ads.

> *"The new auxiliary orbital platform was recently staffed for maintenance and supply chain fulfillment operations. We have confirmed that all four thousand crew were killed*

in the explosion. Though this is a great loss for Norfayne Labs, the platform was ultimately non-critical and those killed were considered non-essential personnel. Pieces of the destroyed orbital platform may begin falling to Earth over the next several days."

Fenlee bit her lip.

No...Dad.

First her mother, then her brother, now her father. Everyone she loved and everyone who had ever loved her had been taken. No matter what she did, the world insisted on backing her into a corner.

She let out a scream containing every ounce of frustration, anger, and fear she kept sealed away over the years. Bitter rage and resentment poured out of her body.

Someone else's terrorist attack took my mom. Someone else's greed took my brother. Someone else's incompetence took my dad. All of us were only trying to live.

She felt lightheaded and stumbled into the side of the lift car. There was a falling sensation in the pit of her stomach. Screams and shouts filled the lift, but they were largely drowned out by a violent metallic screeching.

There was a warmth in her chest and her hand drifted automatically to the opal around her neck. The realization came with detached clarity, as though she were observing from afar.

Oh. I broke the lift. I've killed us all.

Fenlee thought it strange to be staring death in the face but feeling no panic. What more was there to lose?

She gazed out the lift window at the face of the tower rushing by. Both the standard and emergency braking units had ripped off, leaving only jagged metal and a single slider arm still affixed to the track on the side of the building. The friction from the arm created a blinding shower of sparks and was the only thing keeping them from free fall; it slowed the descent a bit, but not enough to prevent the deaths of all the passengers on impact.

Fenlee's world washed away. Everything she loved had been torn from her, and she'd been powerless to prevent any of it. She couldn't control anything. A tranquility settled over her as she put her hands to the window. Her fingertips pressed against the cool glass and her perception extended outward to the arm and the white-hot metal where it met the track.

Maybe she did have more to lose. Elliot was still alive, damn it, and so were these people. Maybe she could control this.

Battling through her exhaustion, she grasped her remaining energy reserve and held tight.

She clenched her teeth and visualized the arm assembly. Inside was a ratchet system, but without the braking assemblies in place, the arm had broken free. She had created similar mechanisms at home and was familiar with the setup. If she could force the arm to reconnect, it should slow the plummeting car to a normal descent.

She took a deep breath and willed the etherclaw to direct her energy toward the arm, weaving it around the mechanism and pushing with everything she had. The draining sensation came like a gut punch and threatened to knock her down. Around her, the screams of the passengers became muted background static, and creeping tunnel vision pushed her further from reality, as though she were falling down a hole.

The broken arm refused to connect.

It's not gonna end in a stupid lift car.

Fenlee pushed against the window and screamed in defiance. A grating rumble filled the car, harsh vibrations sending passengers tumbling. The arm was moving too fast to connect, but the increased friction against the gear teeth slowed the car substantially.

Fenlee kept pushing.

Seconds later, the lift hit the bottom with a gut-wrenching crunch. Windows shattered and ceiling panels fell on passengers. But apart from a few broken bones, everyone appeared intact.

She needed to eat, or sleep, or to just stop existing for a while. But first she needed out. The sliding doors had buckled on impact forcing passengers to climb their way free. She squeezed through with the rest of the crowd and stumbled out of the lift. There was no destination; she just put one foot in front of the other, dragging herself forward.

The world became darker and Fenlee felt herself falling again. Someone put their arm around her shoulders, and that was when she threw up.

CHAPTER 17
TEST SUBJECT

ELLIOT CHOKED ON bile as electrical pulses racked his body, seizing his muscles. His eyes refused to focus on anything for more than a few seconds before blurring in a monochromatic wash. He was in the middle of a silvery blue room, the edges of which fell into shadow. A familiar smell—sweet, but death-like—was stifling. Terror and fear lurked just outside his periphery.

And he was angry.

Hours ago, in the middle of the night, he'd awoken to the pressure of a burning needle in his neck. The man with the red eye and two others dressed as clinical technicians injected him with a second syringe that knocked him out before he'd even fully regained consciousness. Next thing he knew, he was strapped down tight with a short tube running out of his leg into

a glass cylinder suspended in a viscous green fluid. One of the technicians gave him another injection that made his thoughts and feelings twist into an unmanageable vortex. Raw emotions overwhelmed him. Fury and sorrow took hold, removing any capacity for rational thought. The emotions weren't attached to anything—they simply *were*. No one spoke to him, and everything was cold.

Each electric pulse aggravated his already heightened emotions, and he tried to unleash the feelings inside, but no release would come. The sensation was like gasping for air. Instead, a small amount of his blood was sucked through the tube after each shock, where it froze in the cylinder.

The emotions continued to flow in brutal waves. With every crest, he pulled against his restraints and shook his head, flinging spit in every direction. In the calm of the troughs, he cried. Occasionally the muffled sounds of scratching and hissing broke the quiet, but he could never identify the source.

No one came for him, and the cycle continued until he passed out.

A cool cloth gently dabbed his forehead, and someone was holding his hand. Once again, Elliot didn't want to open his eyes and find himself in the middle of a waking nightmare. He was cold, clammy, and couldn't stop shaking. The nest of soft warm blankets didn't help at all.

He cracked an eye and saw he was back in the bedroom. Loxi was beside him, her brow furrowed in concern.

"Oh, you're up," Loxi said, and pulled her hand away from his. "Here, drink this." She poured a cup of steaming tea then reconsidered. "No, wait, sorry, you're supposed to drink all of *this* first, I think." She gave him a straw attached to a gray bag, and he sucked down salty-sweet water.

He finished the contents of the bag and let his head sink back into the pillow. "What…h-happened to me?" he asked.

"I'm not totally sure." Loxi looked away and fumbled with the tea service. "I'm not totally sure, but I don't like it. They said, 'don't worry, it'll be just like before.' But I don't remember when you were younger, and I really don't know how that's supposed to make it any better. I know it's all part of the project and it's super important, but it's not okay." She picked up his hand again and held it tight. It was softer and warmer than the blanket, and he wanted to curl up into it instead.

"What project are you talking about?" Elliot asked.

"I mean, you're his son, so I don't get why—"

The bedroom door swished open and Rook walked in. Loxi dropped Elliot's hand and cleaned up the gray bag.

Rook gave Loxi a vial without sparing Elliot a glance. "My dad told me to bring you this. You left it."

"Right," Loxi said. "Yep, I will absolutely need this. Thanks, Rook." She swirled the clear liquid around and studied it for a moment. "And what do I do with this again?"

Rook rolled his eyes. "You rub it into his scalp to help with dandruff."

"That seems odd, but okay."

"Oh, come on," Rook said. "You dump it down his throat. It's for the ethersickness."

"Yes! That's right. He would need something for that."

Elliot forced himself up again. "What's ethersickness?" he asked. "Is that why I feel so awful?"

"They said it's a *type* of ethersickness," Loxi said. "But not the kind that'll kill you, so that's good. It'll pass, but until then, I expect you'll feel fairly messed up in all sorts of terrible ways. Now, drink up."

She didn't give Elliot an opportunity to object before squeezing his jaw open and pouring the thick fluid into his mouth. It was bitter and hot going down. The medicine made his tongue feel as thick as his brain.

"You're Rook, right?" Elliot asked, his voice shaky. "Do you know what was going on? Why do they want to hurt me for no reason?"

"No reason? Dad doesn't do things for no reason." Rook spat the words at Elliot and stormed toward the door. "He 'hurts' you because he loves you."

After a couple of days, Elliot was back to walking around on his own without assistance. He was tired of Loxi helping him to the bathroom and grateful to be able to take care of it himself. There was no sign of Dr. Arkamis, Rook, or anyone else besides Loxi, who brought him his food and helped administer the terrible medicine. She would sit with him and talk when he was up for it, but his fatigue made sustained conversation difficult.

With his head finally clear and with little else to do, Elliot had plenty of time to think. Everyone seemed to know him, or at least know *about* him. He had no recollection of this place, but he couldn't deny the threads of familiarity weaving through his mind. Each time he tried to follow one of those threads, it would disappear or shift, always just out of his grasp.

He couldn't figure out the whole etherclaw thing. Dr. Arkamis had asked him what he knew about it, and Elliot had remained silent so as to protect his sister. But the man had made it clear he thought Elliot was in possession of it. But how? Where? He didn't have any special talisman-like object such as Fenlee's opal, or a tattoo like Kyara's, or whatever it was Nico had.

For years, Elliot had tried to remember life before Fenlee and Max, but he could never recall a thing. His earliest memories were cold and bleak until Fenlee pulled him into warmth. Since then, she was family, and that was all that had mattered. He'd given up caring about where he came from or who he was. But now he needed to know. Something terrifying lurked in the depths of his mind, and he was unsure whether it was truly just out of reach, or if he couldn't bring himself to latch onto it.

The door to his room opened, and Loxi walked in with lunch for two. "Good to see you out of bed! Figured I'd eat with you today. I know it's not protocol or whatever, but stuff protocol. I mean, if it's all right with you?"

"Yeah, of course." Elliot liked when Loxi was around but he had a hard time completely trusting her. Not that there was anything that felt off or wrong about her—he just couldn't understand how such a caring and genuine person could work for this cruel group of people. She was a little clumsy and very ordinary, but he always wished she'd stay longer than she did.

The pair sat at a high-top table by the windows in his room, eating fresh bread with seasoned oil and some type of spiced synthetic meat. She poured them both a cold tea with orange cream.

"Seems your father's been away at the other research facility for the last few days," Loxi said, crumbs tumbling down her chin.

"Please don't call him that," Elliot said. "My *father* is on some orbital platform right now. I don't know who that man is."

"Hm. Well, anyway, he only just got back and…" She hesitated, picking a large piece of pepper off her meat.

"And what?" Elliot asked.

"And…"

"And *what*, Loxi?"

"And, do you have a girlfriend?"

Elliot blushed. "What? No…"

"Hm." She put down her fork and studied his face through squinted eyes.

"I mean, not that I wouldn't want one, I guess," Elliot mumbled. His whole body went hot and he looked down at his lap. Why was she asking?

"Oh. I was just wondering because your fath—sorry, *Dr. Arkamis*—was talking to some woman. A SecForce officer, I think? Anyway, she said something about a girl you were with."

Elliot perked up. "Wait, what girl? Do you mean Fenlee?"

"Who? No idea, they didn't mention a name or anything. The officer said something like"—Loxi paused and changed her voice to an authoritative caricature—"*That girl he was with*— oh, 'he' means you, by the way."

"Thanks, I got that."

"Ahem, *that girl he was with popped up on a scan on one of the upper platforms. Sounds like she was super belligerent and blah blah blah and trying to head to Norfayne Labs.*" Loxi changed her voice to imitate a more refined speaker. "And then Dr. Arkamis was all, *well, don't concern yourself with her. If she pops up again, just make her disappear.*" Loxi made a *poof* motion with her hands. "And so anyway, if she was someone important to you, like maybe a *girlfriend*, I guess I just thought you should know."

"Her name's Fenlee, and she's my sister." Elliot shook his head. "I've gotta get out of here before something happens." He felt queasy, his appetite completely gone. What would these people do if they thought Fenlee was somehow in their way?

"I know you wanna get out of here, and maybe I don't blame you at all," Loxi said. "But I told you, this place is locked down pretty tight and mostly under surveillance." She clapped her hand over her mouth. "Oops, I keep forgetting. They could have probably listened to anything we just said if they wanted to." She shrugged. "And anyway, Rook keeps pacing outside your room."

"What? Why? What's his deal, anyway? I don't even know him, but he hates me."

"Rook? Don't worry about him. He's just jealous," Loxi said.

"Of what, exactly? I get kidnapped—literally dragged off the street—and now I'm a prisoner being tortured." Elliot pushed his chair back and walked to the window. He was tired of being cooped up and kept in the dark.

"He's jealous because he's never been able to use his etherclaw. And you can."

"So, I *can* use it? Then what exactly is it?" Elliot asked. "Because I don't have anything on me that has etherclaw in it."

"Hm. You don't know so much, do you?"

"If you know something, Loxi, please tell me."

"I know you're different. It's inside of you, like part of your DNA or something. It's how you were created."

"What? What do you mean, 'created?'"

"I dunno. *Created, born,* whatever. But you and Rook didn't come out of a uterus like the rest of us, Elliot."

Elliot stared out the rain-streaked glass. Life had changed too quickly. It all felt like a dream, and he desperately wanted to go back to the world he knew.

What am I?

Loxi walked over and stood beside him, putting her hand on the small of his back. "I'm sorry. I know you don't understand what's going on. I don't understand everything either. I also didn't mean to get you all worried about your sister."

"I have to get to Fenlee," Elliot said, almost mouthing the words. "I have to get out of here."

Loxi nodded slowly. "Family's important, yeah."

"Can you help me?" Elliot could feel his own frustration in the back of his throat as he spoke. "Please? Can you get me out of here?"

Loxi opened her mouth to say something, reconsidered, and ran back over to the table. "You didn't even touch your meat. Mind if I have a few bites?"

Elliot just stood there. He couldn't understand this girl at all. She bounced from serious and compassionate to peculiar and aloof without notice. "Yeah, sure. I'm not hungry."

She popped a few pieces in her mouth and pushed the rest around on the plate. "I forgot how good this is. I think you should come over and try some."

"Thanks, but I said I'm not hungry."

"You should definitely have a bite."

"Loxi, will you stop? I'm fine."

"Elliot, stop moping. I'm not going to eat all this, I made this meaty pile of flavor just for you, now *sit down and try a bite because I think maybe you will really like it, okay?*" Something about the tone of her voice and look in her eye suggested it might be wise to do as she said.

Elliot headed back to the table, picked up the fork, and went to stab a piece of the meat. He paused when he saw the plate, but only for a fraction of a second. Loxi had roughly arranged the oil and seasonings to spell the words: *3 days.*

CHAPTER 18
REMEMBERING HOW TO BREATHE

FENLEE SAT AT her workbench, slumped over and groggy-eyed, staring at nothing. She had no idea if she'd slept for minutes or days, but she felt unrested regardless. The only reason she was out of bed at all was because lying there for so long had become painful.

It could have been late afternoon or early morning—the daylight filtering down to the lower tiers looked about the same either way. She didn't know how she'd gotten home or into bed. Her leg was still attached and her entire left side ached. Her clothes were glued to her body with sweat and dirt, and her face itched where her suture bond was peeling off.

Her own room was foreign and surreal; reality had careened off a cliff and taken her with it.

So, what now.

Cipher stood on the workbench facing her, his optic sensor slowly pulsating. Behind him was the jar of rice wine from Casper. She picked it up and took a slow sip. The liquid bit into her throat with a cleansing fire. She took another drink, much more this time. It went down easier. Another sip. Maybe she could just kill her feelings. Just for a little while.

Fenlee set the jar down on the bench next to Cipher and rubbed her eyes. As she reached for it again, the little bot kicked out with one leg, shattering the glass and spilling the alcohol onto the floor.

"What the hell, Cipher?" Fenlee said. "Whose side are you on?"

Her bedroom door slid open with a clunk, revealing Nico. He looked down at the shattered jar and sake on the floor and then back up at Fenlee. "You're up," he said.

"Yeah. Guess I'm up," Fenlee replied. She slumped deeper in her chair and shook her head. "What happened? How did I get here, Nico?"

"Temaki man."

"What?"

"Carried you."

Fenlee tried to imagine the old gnarly-looking, eye-patch-wearing street merchant carrying her into her apartment and putting her to bed. "You know what, never mind. Everything is completely weird anyway. Whether it was the temaki man or a pack of wild solfs, I really don't care right now."

Nico stepped through the glass shards to stand beside

Fenlee, neatly dodging each little bit without looking down. "You're not okay," he said softly.

"Good observation, kid," Fenlee said. "No, I'm not okay." She looked at her hands. The dirt in the creases made them look old and worked, like her father's. She took a deep breath. "My dad died, Nico."

"You have a dad?" he asked.

"*Had*," Fenlee replied. "I just told you he died. There was an explosion where he was working and he died. He's dead." The words came easier than she expected, but still felt unreal leaving her mouth.

"Oh no." Nico jumped in her lap and threw his arms around her. As scrawny as he was, he held her with impressive strength. She didn't need this sympathy from him though, not right now. His hair was in her face and smelled worse than she did. She tried to pull away but then felt his chest heaving in silent sobs against her as he cried into her shoulder. She didn't have the energy to wrap her arm around him, and it fell limp beside her. Instead, her own tears came until she was bawling.

Guilt, frustration, anger, and grief all churned and erupted. She hadn't felt this swell of emotions since her mother had died. But now, she had lost everything. There was no path forward, no one to lean on.

After the tears finally subsided, the two sat in silence.

Fenlee gave him a hug and forced the side of her mouth into a half smile. "Thanks, Nico."

Nico bit his lower lip and looked at her. "Elliot?" he asked.

She wiped her face on her sleeve, leaving a long trail of soggy snot and shook her head. "I couldn't get him."

He nodded, then jumped up and ran out of her room. A

moment later he returned with a sopping wet kitchen cloth and proceeded to try and scrub her face.

"Okay, no. Stop, Nico," Fenlee said, trying to fend off the dripping rag. "I'm fine."

"Nope. Get you clean." He grabbed her wrist and pulled her out of the chair, down the hall, and into the bathroom.

"What are you doing?"

Nico struggled to find the words he was looking for. "Gotta...keep moving." He looked down at his feet and twisted his arms in a fidgety knot. "Don't stop. Bad to stop. Don't stop moving. Ever."

The green-haired boy, his scars more pronounced in the cold bathroom light, looked up at her with big, round eyes. Despite, or perhaps because of, whatever he'd been through, he shone with a radiant strength. She knew next to nothing about him, but right now she was glad to have him around. She needed him around. *Don't stop. Keep moving forward.* It was a good thing this kid was here, else...

"All right, Nico. I'll get cleaned up, and then maybe we can find something to eat."

The boy grinned, gave her one quick nod, then left her alone in the bathroom. Fenlee peeled the rest of the suture bond off. The cut down her cheek had healed well, and the scarring would probably be minimal. Her leg was a little swollen but would be fine; it was nothing she hadn't dealt with before. More than anything, she was just dirty. She turned on the shower, the timer ticking down the minutes until the hot water allowance would give out. She stood there, letting the evidence of her failures wash away.

In the darker moments of her life, Fenlee often tried to

think about what her mother would do. But her mom was a research scientist who'd dedicated herself to astrobiology, and her life experiences were vastly different from Fenlee's. Her mom spent as little time as possible around the lower tiers, and she'd certainly never lived in a crap apartment like this one. What would her mother do? *She'd probably be more lost than me.*

Fenlee exhausted the entire hot water allowance, loosely wrapped a towel around her, and left the bathroom. The kitchen was only a few feet down the hall with a clear view of the table, around which sat Nico, Kavi…and Casper and Alex. *Shit.*

Casper turned red and looked down at his lap.

Alex gave Fenlee a sheepish wave. "Hey," she said. "Thought we'd stop by and see how you were doing. Sorry about the timing. We'll just hang out if you want to get dressed?"

"Uh-huh," Fenlee mumbled and ran down the hall to her room. Why would they show up now? She pulled on the door, but it stuck again and wouldn't close. And why hadn't she fixed that damn thing yet?

She threw on some clothes and went back out to the kitchen. Her hair was dripping, and she hadn't bothered brushing it out.

"Yeah, so, hi," Fenlee said. "Guess you've met Nico." These were strangers to him, and she was more than a little upset that he would open the door and let in a couple people he'd never met.

"Ah, so it's Nico, huh?" Casper smiled at the kid. "Yeah, didn't so much get his name, you know? He's a little man of few words. He a friend of Elliot's?"

"Sure, something like that," Fenlee said.

"We didn't mean to barge in or anything." Alex stood up and took Fenlee's hand. "You haven't been at school, and it didn't occur to me at first...Casper mentioned the explosion and I just didn't make the connection. Your dad, Fenlee. I'm so sorry." Alex tightened her grip, and Fenlee started to tear up again.

"Yeah. It's not been a good week." Fenlee jerked her head up and covered her mouth. "Oh, Cas. I forgot your dad was up there too. I'm so sorry."

"Heh, yeah, it's not really that big a deal, you know? Kinda relieving, to be honest."

"How's your mom holding up?" Fenlee asked.

Casper snorted. "Oh, she's fine. In fact, she's been sober and in a better mood than I remember seeing her. Only problem is, now we're not gonna have the old man's income." He looked uncomfortable and changed the subject. "But whatever. Anyway, me and Alex both realized we hadn't really seen you around and figured it'd be good to check in." He craned his neck to survey the hall and common room, which made up the majority of the small apartment. "Where's Ellie? How's he doing with everything?"

"He's not here." She looked to Nico, but his eyes didn't meet hers. He sat motionless, his hands drawn tight under his chin, a pensive expression on his face. What did she expect, that he'd explain for her? Talking about it with Murdok was one thing, but saying it out loud to her friends carried with it an air of finality.

"So he'll be back around soon?" Casper asked.

The back of Fenlee's jaw was stiff and ached from trembling. She tried to open her mouth to respond but couldn't make it work. Nothing was working like it was supposed to.

"Fenlee, what's going on?" Alex put her arm around Fenlee and eased her into a chair.

"I think I need help." Fenlee blurted the words without thinking. "I think I need your help."

Alex's brow creased. "Sure, of course. We're here for you. Right, Cas?"

"For sure. Tell us what's up."

"I just don't know what I'm supposed to do." The room was still, but Fenlee could barely hear her own voice. "He's gone. They took him, and I don't know how to get him back."

Fenlee told them everything. She told them about meeting Kyara and Nico, and how there was more to their experience in the undercity than she'd initially let on. She told them about etherclaw. She told them about Elliot's kidnapping and her futile efforts to find him.

When at last there was nothing more to say, her exhaustion caught up, and her forehead hit the table with a thud. Shrouded on both sides by her hair, she studied the patterns of scratches on the surface an inch from her eyes. *Maybe I could just stay like this. This little spot of table is my new home. Nothing else has to exist.*

But then Alex's strong arms were around her, and Fenlee decided maybe her new home could expand just a little more. Just enough to let in Alex.

"I had no idea." Alex spoke in a gentle whisper. "You should've told us what was going on. We could've helped. We *can* help."

"There's nothing to do," Fenlee said. "Thanks, though."

"Wrong," Alex said. "Look at me, Fenlee."

Fenlee hated to leave her new home on the table. The surface was cold and comforting. *Nothing good lasts, anyway.* She raised her head and was startled by the fire in Alex's eyes.

Alex touched her shoulder. "I am so sorry you've been through all this. But you have these memories you're going to hold onto as tight as you can and never let go. I didn't have a chance to know my parents, though Lily's been something between a mom and a big sister. Either way, family is what you make it. And you still have family out there, so don't you stop fighting until you get him back. And Casper and I will be right there with you. Isn't that right, Cas?"

"Oh, damn," Casper muttered. He thought for a moment, anxiously shaking his leg under the table. "We've known each other a real long time, you know? If there's a way to get family back..." He shook his head as though wrestling with some uncomfortable thought, then perked up and locked eyes with Fenlee. "Yeah. I'm in."

Nico nodded. "Gonna get Elliot."

Fenlee looked around the kitchen at her friends. This small group, each so different, yet each willing to work together to support her. But she didn't want to give in to hope. She couldn't survive another letdown.

"This is all great, but how?" Fenlee felt defeat already trying to take hold again. "I told you, he's somewhere deep in Norfayne Labs, and that place may as well be a fortress. Even if I try again and somehow get in, the whole complex is too massive, and their security is even better than the Cascadian Authority."

Alex squeezed Fenlee's shoulder. "*You* are not going to try again. *We* are going to try again, and we're going to succeed because we're going to go about this strategically. Now come on, we're going to go see my aunt."

Everyone sat together in a small lounge. Nico managed to sneak Kavi along without anyone noticing, though Lily didn't seem to mind at all. He sat cross-legged with the cat in his lap. Casper, meanwhile, had never been in Alex's home, and he squirmed, unsure how to properly sit in such a fancy chair. All listened as Fenlee again related her story, sparing no details.

"Thank you for sharing this, Fenlee," Lily said. "I know something of what you're going through, and I know how impossible a place the world is right now. I also know how insulting it can be to hear 'things will get better,' so I'll spare you empty platitudes." She dabbed her eyes with a translucent teal cloth which appeared to Fenlee to be one of the least absorbent materials she'd ever seen, but it fulfilled its purpose regardless. "I have some questions, but right now you are all guests in my home, and you all need to eat—especially Fenlee. We'll discuss what can be done in a moment."

Lily excused herself to prepare food and drink, leaving the group in silence.

Casper began tapping his nails on a side table. "I have one little question, Fenlee," he said. "What exactly is this etherclaw stuff? Seems pretty central to everything, but you kinda glossed over it."

"It's honestly pretty hard to explain and I'm still not clear on it myself." She turned to Alex. "That day I went to the library with your aunt? I was trying to research etherclaw and get some sense of what the hell it even is."

"Did you find out anything?" Alex asked.

"Maybe? Thanks to this guy," Fenlee said, pointing her thumb at Nico, "I at least have a basic idea of how to use it." She took out her opal and rotated it in her fingers. "This is it, or it's buried in here, I guess. Anyway, it allows you to manipulate the world around you, but there are a couple of constraints. One, you can only affect things you sort of intimately understand."

Casper leaned his head forward in a curious tilt. "What, um, what d'you mean by 'intimately,' exactly?"

"Not whatever you're thinking, that's for damn sure," Fenlee replied. "And the second thing is that it draws on its user as a powersource." She pointed to her heart. "In other words, me. If I use it for more than trivial things, it's exhausting. Beyond that, I know it's connected to the Aeons. In fact, I think it might be part of an Aeon somehow and may have to do with how they operate."

Alex pursed her lips. "You're telling me you have an actual piece of an Aeon? Okay, forgetting for a sec how implausible this sounds, what do you actually *do* with it?"

Fenlee looked at the goggles dangling around Casper's neck. They primarily functioned as a heads-up-display with a few features similar to a holoquip, but they also contained mechanized optics allowing for microscopic and telescopic views. "You take those goggles with you everywhere, huh?" she asked.

Casper shrugged. "Might need 'em, you know?"

"Put them on and look out the window."

"Eh, okay?"

Casper did as she asked. The mechanical components inside were simple enough to control and required very little thought or effort. Fenlee closed her eyes and pictured the inner workings of the goggles.

"I don't get it. There something out here I'm supposed to look at?" Casper jumped back in his seat. "Ahh! It zoomed in! But that's a manual control—did you do that?"

"Now hold your hand in front of your face," Fenlee instructed.

"Okay, but—hey! I can see my skin cells!" Casper ripped off the goggles. "How the hell? Are you seriously doing this, Fenlee?"

"I told you how it works, and now you've had a little demonstration. No more for now, though." Fenlee sunk into her chair. That small effort was more tiring than she'd anticipated.

"What exactly just happened?" Alex asked, more than a little skeptical. "I'm open to new ideas and all, but this sounds like straight magic."

Before Fenlee could respond, Lily walked in with a tray of food and cups of steaming tea. Fenlee knew she needed to eat, but her stomach was still bound up in a tight knot. She nibbled as best she could, but even small bites made her feel sick.

"Fenlee, I'm not sure what to say." Lily passed out the warm cups and set the tray down. "I want to help you, but I don't know how much I can."

"You work for Norfayne, right?" Fenlee tried to tamp down the desperation creeping into her voice. "Maybe you know someone?"

"I work there with over a million others. In the world of Norfayne, I'm no one special." Lily's already firm grip tightened around her cup. "I think you're right to stay away from the authorities on this. If it's true Norfayne is behind Elliot's kidnapping, you'll find no support for his release. They, along with the Divine Council, run just about everything in New Cascadia." She exhaled a bitter sigh. "They make the rules, and their rules will not favor you."

Alex stood up. Her fists were balled and her chin tucked. "To hell with their rules! I am so sick of seeing everyone being taken advantage of by those monsters in power. Don't they know their history? It never ends well! And now Fenlee's brother's been kidnapped—*by them*—and you're saying there's nothing that can be done because of their *rules*?" She was pacing, her muscles tense. Alex was always so composed and level-headed. Fenlee had never seen her like this. She kind of liked it.

"Alexandra, please! That's enough," Lily said. "You know I feel the same way. But you also know the sort of trouble you'll be in if you speak any of that outside these walls. Now, all I was trying to say is that the rules will not work for us, so we will have to figure out how to work *outside* the rules."

Alex exhaled through her teeth. "Sorry, you're right. I don't know what got into me."

"Oh, I know what got into you," Lily said. "The same thing that gets into me every damn day. The difference is, I've learned to control it a bit better."

Fenlee felt a tiny spark of something. The anger around her was energizing and helped to cut through her own despair. Maybe she wasn't as alone as she thought.

Lily's voice returned to a calm, almost melodic tone, and she placed her hand on Fenlee's knee. "Please understand I don't doubt any of your story, but I'm having trouble making sense of Norfayne's interest in Elliot. Maybe you can help me understand."

"All I know is he's being held by someone named Arkamis…Seth Arkamis, I think? There's something about Elliot that he wants, but I don't know what exactly. It has something to do with etherclaw, but Elliot doesn't have any, so…"

A storm cloud shadowed Lily's face. "I see. As large as Norfayne is, Seth Arkamis is a name that even I know. He's bad stuff, Fenlee. There have been many rumors about him over the years, and if even a tenth of them are true—"

"Where is he?" Fenlee interrupted.

"Well, Arkamis' old laboratory was the epicenter of the Snowdrop bombing, and after that, his research was moved to some remote location. If he's truly behind this, it is likely that Elliot is *not* at Norfayne Labs."

The room was silent except for a soft click as Casper messed with his goggles. Nico looked increasingly uncomfortable and was wrapping himself into a ball around Kavi.

Alex leaned against the wall, her brow furrowed in thought. "What all do you know about Elliot's past?" she asked. "Like, from the time before you met?"

Fenlee felt as though she and Elliot had grown up together, as though they'd always known one another. They'd seen each other at their worst and lifted each other up to their best. The pair had a bond that most siblings would envy. But the truth was, he'd only been around half her life.

"He's not my biological brother, but I'm guessing you knew that." Fenlee took a deep breath. "First time I met Elliot was actually at Norfayne Labs, several years ago. The same day my mom died."

CHAPTER 19
SCATTERED FLOWERS

Eight years ago…

"But *why* did you get orchids? I saw how much you paid for them. I thought Mom told you to watch your spending and stuff." Fenlee and her father walked down an icy boulevard on the upper tier. It was uncharacteristically cold, even for winter. Light flurries painted the day gray. While very few flakes were actually sticking, Fenlee was excited—it had been years since she'd seen frozen precipitation. She stuffed her hands deeper into her warm jacket pockets.

Her father laughed. "Aren't you a little young to be getting on my case about finances?" he asked. "Here, take a whiff of this." He shoved the bouquet in Fenlee's face. The purple flow-

ers were velvety against her nose and gave off a spicy fragrance that reminded Fenlee of some of her mother's special teas.

"I thought orchids weren't supposed to smell."

"Most don't. These are pretty hard to find, but worth it. Your mom had one in her hair the first time I met her. She loves 'em, and they remind me of her."

"I thought the first time you met Mom was at the spaceport when she came out to yell at you for messing up one of her research pod thingies."

"You think too much. But…yeah, I guess that's true. What I meant was when we first went out on a date. Well, maybe not the first date. One date, at some point. Anyway, she likes 'em, and it's her birthday." Max gripped the bouquet tighter. "And also, me and her didn't really get off to the best start this morning."

"So that's why you want to surprise her?"

"Yeah. Patch things up, celebrate her birthday. Kind of a two-for-one, right, sweetheart?" Max gave her a little tap on the shoulder. "And besides, if anyone deserves it, it's your mom."

They boarded the skycar to the main Norfayne campus along with engineers and academics. A security guard stationed inside the car looked the two of them up and down. Fenlee couldn't understand why those whose job it was to protect others always made her so uncomfortable. She buried her hand in her father's palm where it was safe and warm and stared out the window.

New Cascadia, the city-state that was her entire world, passed underneath. At their height, the snow and fog obscured the lowest tiers. Every time she came to the upper-most platforms, a sense of unease followed her around. Down below was freedom. People were genuine and real, not like up above where everyone and everything was...false? No, that wasn't quite it. Fenlee had trouble putting the right words to her thoughts.

They disembarked and headed through security to the main reception area. A young woman with white hair and a sour expression greeted them.

"State your business," the woman said, her eyes glued to the holoscreen in front of her.

"We're here to see Adeline Li Harper, Astrobiology Division, please." Max and Fenlee produced their tokens and submitted to a quick bioscan.

"Proceed to the common atrium to your left. She will be notified of your arrival."

"No, that's okay, don't tell her we're here—we'll wait and surprise her when she gets off." Max showed the receptionist the orchids with a big grin on his face.

She was unimpressed. "As you wish. Just don't wander."

The atrium was only partially heated, which made the cold seep in. The glass ceiling several stories above blended into the steel sky beyond. One end was open, revealing dozens of buildings on this side of the complex, including her mother's. Everything about Norfayne always felt sterile and drab, and even more so today.

Father and daughter sat together on a bench, watching a trickle of employees begin to leave for the day. Max was fidgeting with the orchid stems and looked like he might accidentally bruise them. He wasn't one for small talk, but she knew he'd try.

"That thing you've been working on—some kinda tea slicer or something? How's that coming?" he asked. Sure enough, another question he'd already know the answer to if he paid attention.

"It's a tea *separator*, Dad. All it does is get the stems out of the leaves. And it's almost done. I just need a couple more pieces. It's no big deal—pretty much the same as the rice separator I made last year."

"Why do you need to separate rice?" he asked.

Fenlee shrugged. "I don't, I guess." She looked down at her knees. "But I can."

Everyone said she had the brains for her mom's work, but astrobiology was completely uninteresting. Of course, she'd never tell her mom that, and she had become adept at feigning interest whenever her mother explained some new theory or other. Her dad, on the other hand, got to work with his hands. He made stuff *function*. Well, "fixed broken stuff" was probably a more accurate job description. She wanted to create stuff, so it wasn't far off.

But her mom was the one who listened. Despite having no background in mechatronics, she was always engaged. She would set aside time to ask Fenlee what she was working on and even help her research and figure out how to do simple things. On weekends, she would sometimes take Fenlee to surplus or pawn shops to find an odd piece or part. Her father probably could have helped as well, but he often worked late or had to put in extra hours with his drinking pals.

Max was now talking about some incident at work with a misaligned autoloader stripping the pants off a coworker. He was laughing about it, but Fenlee thought it sounded painful and didn't see the humor. She couldn't focus very well, anyway. The air was electric. Her skin tingled and her chest tightened. Something felt wrong.

"And then—you remember Casper's dad, right?" Max continued talking, mostly to himself. "Yeah, me and him helped pick up that big old autoloader and underneath—"

The world around Fenlee became still and hushed as she looked out the far end of the atrium. She watched in slow horror as the fifteen-story tower where her mother worked buckled and collapsed in on itself.

Before she could open her mouth to scream, a silent shockwave ripped through the atrium, followed a moment later by a deafening blast. Father and daughter were both blown off the bench as the glass ceiling fell around them. Everything was twisted and disorienting. Fenlee rolled her head to the side. Through her blurred vision, she watched a few people struggle to stand while others lay still. Several feet away, a man managed to get to his knees, only to be impaled by a massive glass shard that broke free from above.

She heard her father yell, "Adeline!" but her ears were muted and thick. He sounded close. Or maybe miles away? Her brain wouldn't think the way she wanted and her body wasn't responding like she needed.

What is happening.

She pushed herself up on her forearms and looked around. The damage was severe. Several buildings were reduced to nothing more than mountains of rubble, but it was clear her mother's lab was the epicenter of the explosion. Crushed bodies and shattered drones lay everywhere she looked. Her eyes lingered for a moment on the purple orchids scattered nearby among bits of glass.

Then she saw him. Her father's back was to her, but he appeared unhurt. He stood up, limped a few steps, then started running toward what was left of her mother's lab.

"Adeline!" he called without looking back.

"Dad! Dad, wait! I'm right here!" Fenlee tried to scream the words, but her throat felt clamped, and all that came out was a choked whisper.

She crawled to the bench and pulled herself up.

"Daddy, please!" But he was almost out of sight.

She got her footing and struggled out of the atrium after him. It took all her effort to get her legs to cooperate.

There was no longer a security perimeter, and no one was around to stop her, so she went in the same direction as her father. The lab buildings were farther than she realized, and she had to stop several times to catch her breath. Snow gusts blew hard, hindering her progress.

It was difficult to get her bearings in the ruined landscape. The few other people she passed were too busy tending to themselves to notice her. Finally, she reached a broken building she thought was her mother's lab. Girders and support beams protruded like jagged bones in a sea of debris. Chunks of the building's skeletal remains occasionally broke free, crashing nearby.

There was no sign of her father.

Fenlee sat down on a large steel plate and pulled her jacket tight against the cold. Surely her father would come back after he found her mother. He just needed to tend to her mom first.

In the distance, she heard the sounds of emergency support vehicles and at one point several survey drones flew overhead. But those signs of activity diminished, leaving the silence of the snow. No one came.

A child's eternity passed as she sat alone in the chill. Warm drops landed on her small fists, and she realized she was crying.

Several stories above her, a loose girder groaned as gravity overtook it. The screech of angry metal was deafening as it slid free. She looked up in time to see it careening toward her, but she was paralyzed. She couldn't make her body move anymore.

No. Mom might still need me.

Fenlee forced herself to dive out of the way, but she was too slow. The two ton hunk of steel crashed into her, crushing her left leg. The impact smashed her head into the cold ground and her vision bleached to nothing.

She had no idea how long she lay pinned on her side. The pain felt as though it belonged to someone else. It couldn't be her pain, it couldn't be real. But every time she shifted, the aching numbness turned white-hot, threatening her consciousness. She pulled her free leg to her chest and hugged it.

After some time, a shadow fell over her. She looked up to see a young boy, maybe five or six years old. He was barefoot and naked apart from a light wrap around his waist. The wind whipped his small pale body, but the concern in his eyes was for her.

"Are you okay?" the boy asked.

Fenlee shook her head, not knowing what to say. Her leg was shattered and she was colder than she'd ever been in her life. She bit her lip and realized this was what it was like to die. It hurt, and it was lonely.

He put his hands on hers. They were freezing, but clammy with sweat. "It will be okay," he said.

Whoever he was, he seemed lost. Was one of his parents in the explosion? Despite her pain, she desperately wanted to help him. She pulled off her scarf and offered it. "Here, you're too cold."

"But then you'll get cold."

"It doesn't matter."

"It does matter," he said. "Maybe we can be warm together."

He carefully laid down next to her. Fenlee put her arms around him and he snuggled close so the two were facing each other. A line of dried blood ran from each of his ears, but other than that, he seemed okay. Fenlee was small for eight years old, but he was skinny, packing himself in tight enough to squeeze under her coat. He touched her neck and with a gentle hand pulled out the thin, fragile chain she wore, revealing her mother's opal. He knit his eyebrows and gave her a curious look.

The opal radiated warmth as she placed her fingers on it. "That's my mom's. She gave it to me a couple of months ago. We came here today for her birthday, so I wore it and—" Her lip began to quiver, and she couldn't finish.

Fenlee and the boy held each other and cried.

Lily pulled Fenlee into a gentle embrace and then offered her a handkerchief to dry her eyes. "Thank you for sharing that with us. I know how hard it is to talk openly about loss, but I also know how important it is. You're a very brave woman, Fenlee."

Alex nodded in silent agreement while Lily refreshed Fenlee's now-cold tea.

Fenlee hated being the center of attention. But here she was, surrounded by four remarkably different people, two of whom she'd only met in the last few weeks, recounting her most private and emotional memories. She was surprised to realize that she didn't care. The hot teacup felt good in her hands.

She took a sip, letting the warmth and fragrance stimulate her senses, bringing her back to the present.

"I never figured out where my dad ended up that day, and he's never talked about it." It occurred to her that now she'd never know. She'd never have the chance to ask him. "He came back home a couple days later. He entered this bottomless pit of grief and became pretty useless, not even able to work. We exhausted everything my mom had been able to save. I pretty much had to figure out how to take care of Elliot *and* my dad. But Elliot was supportive right back. He wanted to do everything he could to help, and he did. He was always there for me when I had my moments."

"What more did you learn of Elliot's background?" Lily asked.

"We've never really figured out much about him," Fenlee replied. "We tried to reconnect him with his family, but the Cascadian Authority couldn't find a record of him being registered anywhere. Instead of tossing him into some low-tier orphanage or even worse, one of the southern refugee cities"—Fenlee shuddered at the thought—"I talked my dad into adopting him. It didn't take much persuasion because he didn't seem to care about much of anything at the time. Glad it worked out, since Elliot and I have really needed each other over the years. No idea where I'd be without him."

"Do you have any idea *why* though, Fenlee?" Lily asked. "Why would they want to kidnap him?"

"I think…" Fenlee looked at Nico, who nodded. "I think Elliot might have been part of some big project at Norfayne. And now they want him back."

CHAPTER 20
A WALK IN THE GARDEN

Dr. Arkamis came to Elliot's room to collect him for lunch. They ate in silence as Arkamis attended to a number of matters on his holoquip and answered whispered questions from a steady stream of attendants and technicians. This was fine; Elliot didn't have anything much to say to the man anyway. After lunch, instead of sending Elliot back to his room, Arkamis took him for a walk.

The conservatory was a large indoor complex with stone paths weaving through well-manicured beds and under vine-covered trellises. Plants of all types went on as far as Elliot could see. He scrunched his nose at the ripe odors of growth and decay drifting in the humid air. The smooth omniglass facade making up the ceiling and walls gave the impression of

liquid shifting in the light, and he wondered how such a beautiful place could be under the care of such evil people.

It was empty apart from the two of them, but he had the distinct impression they were being watched.

"You always liked plants, Elliot. I thought a stroll through the indoor gardens might do you well. And I believe you're owed a bit of an explanation. I admit, I thought you'd have regained more memories by now, but given the trauma you've been through, perhaps that was foolish of me." Arkamis clasped his hands behind his back, his saber clinking with each step. "You have my sincerest apologies for jumping directly into the experimentation process without getting you reacclimated. I am truly sorry. But, you must understand, we have been behind on our research, and time is not exactly on our side. It won't last, though—we need you for other things." Elliot stumbled forward as Arkamis clapped him on the back. "It's all very exciting business!"

Walking alongside this man he hated while pretending everything was normal made him feel sick and agitated. Elliot focused on the flora around him to calm himself and reached out to touch the petals of a small purple flower.

Arkamis put a finger on his shoulder. "I wouldn't if I were you," he said.

Elliot bristled, shrugging away from the man's hand. "What? Why not?"

"Monkshood." Arkamis picked up a twig and gently prodded the flower. "It contains a fascinating poison. Death is certain if consumed, but merely brushing up against it can leave you numb and struggling to breathe."

Elliot recoiled from the flower and shoved his hands in his pockets.

"Very good. I'd advise you to maintain a look-but-don't-touch attitude while in the garden. Now, to get started, what sorts of questions do you have for me?"

They walked on in silence. Elliot didn't want to converse with this awful human being.

Arkamis slowed his pace. "It's all right, Elliot. I know it's a lot to absorb, but my time is yours. Just tell me what's on your mind."

He had endless questions, so what was he so terrified of knowing? The truth? The only light in the darkness of this high-society nightmare was Loxi. She moved about the estate under the pretense of free will, but he sensed she was as much a prisoner as he was. He didn't know her situation, but he felt a connection to her that he didn't quite understand. And he couldn't get her off his mind.

"Who is Loxi and why is she here?" The words came out faster than Elliot intended. In fact, he wasn't sure he meant for them to come out at all.

Arkamis raised an eyebrow. "Of all the things you must be curious about, I admit that was not what I expected to hear first. But that's fine. My wife died in childbirth. She left me with Loxi."

"Wait, she's your *daughter*?"

"It turns out she's not." Arkamis' lip curled.

Good. Elliot was relieved. That would've meant he and Loxi were siblings, and he didn't want to have to reconcile that with how he was starting to feel about her.

Arkamis' eyes lost focus as he stared across the conservatory.

"I made a foolish promise to watch over her. She owes me. She's owed me since the day she was born. For now, she performs basic servant's duties, and that's all there is to it."

"You're saying she's an indentured servant?" Indentured servitude was not uncommon on the highest tiers, but it made Elliot's heart sink to think of Loxi in that position.

Arkamis ignored the question and pointed down the walkway to a grove of ornamental trees. "You see that stand of small dogwoods?"

Elliot shrugged.

"They're beautiful…from a distance." Arkamis dropped to a whisper. "But let's look closer."

As they approached, Elliot noticed something was wrong with them. A tangled mess was choking out the trees.

"That is cuscuta," Arkamis said, indicating a webwork of thin greenish-yellow vines threading themselves throughout the dogwoods. "It's a parasitic plant that leeches the life from others."

Elliot was disgusted by the satisfied tone in Arkamis' voice. "But why would you want some evil plant in your garden that just kills everything around it?"

"It's hard to distinguish good from evil when survival is at stake. Wouldn't you agree, Elliot?"

"I agree that you're an asshole."

Arkamis arched an eyebrow and tapped his lower lip with his thumb. "I see. Historically, this vine has been known as devil's hair by some, and angel's hair by others. Do you understand, Elliot? It's all about perspective."

"But those trees will die. That's not perspective."

"Eventually, yes, they will die," Arkamis replied. "Here, we allow the superior plants to thrive as they are able, invading others' territory and competing for resources as they will. You can see the outcomes all around you."

"That's not true." Elliot was getting frustrated at the man's self-righteous hypocrisy. "You keep it from going into the other beds. It only grows where you want it to."

"Very observant. Indeed, constraints are necessary in any system, Elliot. Humanity is not unlike cuscuta. But who puts the constraints on us? Who is curating our environment?"

Elliot didn't understand. Arkamis' statements were at odds with one another, and whatever philosophical point he may have been trying to make had Elliot's brain in knots. Regardless of how the man might try and frame it, this was *not* how things were supposed to be. He was walking through a garden of death.

"Stop chewing on your hair!" Arkamis roared and smacked the back of Elliot's head hard enough to push him forward a few steps.

Elliot's adrenaline coursed through him, and it took every ounce of his self-restraint to keep from lashing out, attacking the man, or just running off through the conservatory. He knew nothing good would come from any of those actions.

"My apologies, we should have had that unsightly mop properly cut by now," Arkamis said, adjusting the glove on his hand. "You look lowborn, and I take full responsibility for it."

The paths ran deeper into the conservatory where older trees created natural archways. It was darker here, and the odor became bitter. Elliot would find no peace in this place. He didn't know what Loxi's message in the food meant, but three days would be tomorrow. He tried to focus on that, blocking out the horrors around him.

Subtle movement within a thicket of brambles caught Elliot's attention. Although he had no idea what it was, there was no mistaking the presence of something in the shadows. The hair on the back of his neck stood on end. Arkamis droned on, but Elliot's attention remained fixed on the thorny bushes. Whatever it was had gone.

We're not alone. And whatever that is, it's following us, he thought. Maybe it was just a little lost rabbit? But he doubted in this menacing environment it could be anything so innocent.

A tree of angel's trumpets drooped low over an iron bench. The air was stagnant here, plant life so dense the omniglass was no longer visible around them. It felt like they were outside, deep in some forbidden wood.

Elliot stopped and faced Arkamis. "Okay, fine. You wanted to know what questions I have? Here's one: what am I?"

The silence was eerie. Even in the depths of the bustling city, amid tons of steel and cement, there was always the occasional bird chirping or insect buzzing. But here, even surrounded by life, there was nothing.

Arkamis' eyes darkened as a grin slowly spread across his face. "Well phrased, Elliot. *What* are you indeed?" Arkamis paced in front of Elliot. He resumed tapping his thumb on his chin as a distant look crossed his face. "You are the product of research that began well before my time. Countless subjects have been created with etherclaw-imbued DNA, and each one has been a failure. Until you." He pivoted on his boot heel and regarded Elliot. "Because of this, when your etherclaw is active, it drains the lifeforce from those *around* you instead of your own." His smile darkened to match his eyes. "In this way, you are like the Aeons themselves."

Elliot's knees began to buckle as the world around him took on an unreal quality. He felt faint and sat down on the bench. This whole time, there had been no physical object they were after—*he* was the etherclaw. He knew it was true. He could feel it. But what did this mean? Everyone kept treating him like royalty, but that had nothing to do with him as a person. He wanted to run. His eyes darted from side to side, but each available path led into darkness. He was trapped.

A dry laugh from Arkamis startled Elliot, scattering his thoughts. "It's some heavy stuff, I know," Arkamis said, squatting down beside him. "But it's your raison d'être, Elliot. And it is magnificent."

Elliot realized he still hadn't fully recovered from the last round of experiments as deep exhaustion caught up with him. "I'm just some science experiment then—just some tool for you to use for whatever messed up stuff you're doing. And what even *are* you doing? Why do you need me, anyway?"

"You're not 'just some tool,' Elliot. A good portion of your DNA comes from me. You were born in a tank in a lab, but I regard you as my son. Your mother, if you wish to bother calling her that, was just a technician who happened to meet all the right criteria at the time." Arkamis shrugged. "I never even met her. More importantly, though you and I may share some DNA, yours behaves quite differently. Early researchers wrote it off as 'magic' and abandoned their efforts. But they were foolish to do so. It turns out there's a gray zone between 'magic' and science, and they gave up too quickly."

"Uh huh. So now you're telling me I'm basically a wizard or something? This is messed up. You're messed up."

"No, *not* magic. Not exactly. When you are using etherclaw, it is in an active state, and your DNA goes through a—well, think of it as a shift, of sorts, for a brief period. It morphs into a biological manifestation that we've been entirely unable to synthesize. *That* is why we need you. You see, while your etherclaw is in use, transient stem cells are created in your bone marrow, similar in structure to those found within Aeons. They are quite short-lived, and must be immediately extracted and placed into stasis. That is the process you've been enduring."

"Great. But why?" Elliot knew they'd been collecting something from him; he just hadn't known what. But more importantly, he needed to know the reason.

Arkamis' brow creased, turning his expression severe. "The age of humanity is coming to a necessary close. We have long since exhausted our resources. We're living on borrowed time, Elliot. The Aeons constructed the Void Pillars to mitigate our ecological catastrophe and granted humanity another chance." His face clouded as he continued. "But we humans have a nasty history of repeatedly trying to destroy ourselves. Even now, we teeter on the brink yet again."

Behind Arkamis, deep in the underbrush, Elliot saw another slight movement, but it was too dark to make out any details. As whatever it was backed away, he was certain he saw a glint of metal. *So much for the rabbit*, he thought.

"Does my history lesson bore you, Elliot?"

Elliot's attention snapped back to Arkamis. "No, it's just there's…yeah. Uh, never mind. Keep saying your stuff." At this point, all he wanted was to get out of the conservatory.

"Let's keep it simple then. Consider the refugees to the south. There are thousands—millions worldwide—and each of their lives hang by a thread. They will do what is necessary to survive. We've spent two hundred years building ourselves back up. We cannot survive another Collapse. There is simply not enough left on this earth to go around. It is time for a new species to emerge, one that will act as curators for our environment. You are the first of that species."

"New *species*? Are you saying I'm not even human?"

"I'm saying, Elliot, that you are genetically different enough that you do not qualify as *Homo sapien*. You, and those we create, will walk as gods among humans. You will keep populations in balance and maintain order in this world. Don't you see how marvelous it is? I know you've not quite awakened to the idea yet, but you have the power to control nations. You are both creation and destruction—all it takes is feeding on the energy of those around you. Humans are your resources, and they will bend to your will."

The thought was disgusting. "Yeah? Sounds to me like you just want to enslave everyone."

"There is no choice." Arkamis spoke softly. "As I said, another Collapse will be the end of us all. You, and those who will stand beside you, are the only ones who can protect what remains of humanity from itself."

His whole life, or at least what he could remember of it, Elliot had had no idea who—or what—he truly was. The Harpers had taken him in, and he became one of them: Elliot Harper. Fenlee was more family than this man, or Rook, or anyone else in the world could ever be.

Despite that, Elliot had endured countless sleepless nights

wondering who he really was and where he came from. He always knew he was different somehow. He always felt as though he was hiding a piece of himself, but that piece was forever just out of his grasp. He would lie awake in bed, staring at the ceiling of his room, his door cracked to let in a small amount of light. It was important that he be able to see into the hallway to make sure Fenlee didn't leave in the middle of the night. There was no reason to believe she would, he was just terrified of being left alone.

But there was no comfort in the truth. There was no disputing it, either. He knew it down to his core. It meant he was different—more so than he'd thought possible. He was a unique creature in a world where he'd never quite fit in.

Arkamis sat down, the metallic clang of his saber on the bench pulling Elliot out of his thoughts. "There's one other thing, Elliot. Since I've answered your questions, I now have one for you. There was a girl you were with. Taller than you, perhaps a couple of years older. Black hair with a red stripe in it." He put his arm behind Elliot and leaned into his face. "Who is she?"

Fenlee. What did he want with her? Elliot struggled to come up with a response. He couldn't let them know anything about his sister. Why would they even be interested in her? Because of her opal necklace? Or because she was connected to him? It didn't matter. He would never let them near her.

Elliot squared his small frame and looked Arkamis hard in the eyes. "She's no one you will ever know about."

Elliot's head hurt. His response to the Arkamis's question about Fenlee was not well received, and he was half-dragged straight back to his room. That suited him fine. So much had been dumped on him, and he needed space to process it all. He also couldn't get that creature-like thing that was spying on them out of his mind. It felt familiar somehow. But before he could gather his thoughts, his door burst open and a very angry Rook strode in.

"Have a nice walk?" Rook asked, dripping with sarcasm.

Elliot was in no mood to talk to the boy. "What do you want?" he mumbled.

"Just came by to say hi. Passed dad. Looks like you managed to piss him off quite nicely. You're his favorite little toy, so it must have been hard to do."

"Can you just leave?" Elliot still couldn't figure out why Rook hated him so much. He'd never done anything to him.

"Did he tell you about the experiments?"

"Yeah."

"He tell you about how your etherclaw works?"

"Yes. Now please go."

"Bet he didn't mention where you're getting energy from for those procedures."

Elliot looked up at the boy. He hadn't considered this. If he was being forced to use etherclaw so his stem cells could be collected, and using it meant drawing on the lifeforce of others, then…

He didn't want to know.

"That's right. You're figuring it out. Ever notice you're not alone in there?"

It was hard to recall much from the procedures, mostly

pain and brief lucid flashes. And sounds…not very loud, just out of sight.

Rook dropped his voice to a flat monotone. "I've seen them take their little bodies away afterward, Elliot. Most are probably strays they rounded up, but others were bred and bought. All of them were so broken. Don't worry, they're drugged first so they don't bark and whimper and distract from the process. I've always wondered how much they feel though."

"Stop!" Elliot was shaking. He balled his fists and advanced on Rook.

"Whatcha gonna do, hit me? Oh, you sure are the violent one."

"Shut up!" A whirlwind of sadness and anger twisted Elliot's insides, threatening to rage over. But there was no release like during the extraction procedures. Instead, all he could do was grit his teeth and cry.

"Aw, come on, Elliot, it's okay." Rook laughed. "Wouldn't be the first time you've lost control. We all know what you're capable of. You know why we're here, right? In this chateau, I mean, instead of doing all this back at Norfayne Labs?"

Elliot just stared. His gut was wound up like a tension spring. It suddenly became too much, and he doubled over.

"See, here we're all protected by the antieth mesh everywhere. You can't level this entire complex like you did eight years ago." Rook smirked. "That's right, *you* did that. All of it. Of course, Dad couldn't have the public knowing, so they forged the forensics and pinned it on the Snowdrop Collective."

It all came back to him in a furious surge of emotion. That day. So much pain. Waves of heat followed by emptiness and cold. And then…Fenlee.

"Don't worry, you're not alone. They've experimented on me too, since we were created the same. Only, unlike you, I never really got it to work." Rook paused and scratched his head. "Huh, so, actually, I guess that means we're not the same. I guess that means you *are* alone."

Elliot crumpled in a heap on the cold floor. He could barely breathe.

"Yeah, bet you're pretty tired after such a long day. G'night, brother."

Rook left, and the room went dark and still. The only sound was Elliot, gasping for air as he drowned in his memories.

So Arkamis had been right. He wasn't human at all.

He was a monster.

CHAPTER 21
INFILTRATION

Fenlee arrived back at her apartment drenched in sweat as the hot and muggy evening settled in over Lower Ashe Ward. Cipher was tucked securely in her backpack, and she was anxious to see what data he'd collected. She ran down the hall to her workbench and plugged him in.

A couple of days earlier, shortly after everyone had left Lily's, Alex knocked on Fenlee's door to tell her Lily had found where Arkamis had moved his research operations. His whereabouts turned out to be an open secret around Norfayne, and all she needed to do was ask the right people. There was an old chateau on the easternmost platform in a largely abandoned area bordered by wilderness. Access to the entire platform was restricted.

Lily asked them to be patient and give her time while she tried to get more information. But Fenlee couldn't wait for that. After a brief discussion, they decided to gather information of their own. Alex and Casper were tasked with doing research on the platform and the chateau itself, while Fenlee was to set Cipher loose on a reconnaissance mission. Nico wanted to do something, but Fenlee assured him the best way he could help would be to keep her company while she waited for her scavenger bot to finish his task.

Now that Cipher had returned, Fenlee was more energized than she'd been in a long time. Before releasing him, she'd retrofitted one of his sensor modules with a small video unit she stripped from another one of her projects. There'd been no time to test, so she hoped for the best.

It was impressive he'd made it back at all—one of his legs was completely broken, his battery was nearly depleted, and his casing was scuffed and dented. She promised Cipher she'd repair him better-than-new as soon as they rescued Elliot.

A stream of data flooded her screen. "All right, okay, slow down, Cipher. People can't read that fast, and I'm people." She wiped her brow and leaned closer. There was data on far more than she anticipated. How Cipher had been able to infiltrate and collect this much without getting caught was beyond her.

He'd even managed to map out partial floor plans. The place was much larger than she thought a private residence would be. Given its size, it was relatively empty, apart from an occasional researcher and a handful of armed guards.

The video capture worked, but the cheap optics module hadn't stayed calibrated, and the quality was less than ideal. Still, she got a fair sense of the place: disused labs and storage rooms made up the lower floors and empty, poorly lit halls connecting rooms with garish furnishings made up the top levels.

There was also some sort of indoor garden. Fenlee started to skip past then stopped as two figures caught her eye. The clarity was less than optimal. One was a tall man in a cream-colored outfit, and she was certain the other was Elliot. They were having a contentious conversation, but she couldn't tell what was said. She wished she'd taken the time to configure an audio module. The video cut several times as Cipher repositioned himself to follow the pair.

The last clip was of the man and boy next to a bench under a flowering tree. Cipher had gotten close enough that there was no mistaking it—this was Elliot. He looked upset but unhurt. The man looked less like a scientist and more like some overdressed freak from the Divine Council. She didn't see how he could be Dr. Arkamis—no self-respecting scientist or engineer would go around looking like one of those fanatics.

"Cipher, I don't know how to tell you this, but I think I love you." She kissed her little bot on his optic sensor and ran out of the room. "Nico! Guess what!" He'd been in the kitchen with Kavi earlier when she arrived home, but now he was nowhere to be seen. "Nico? Where'd you go?"

She found him balled up on the floor in a dark corner of the common room under one of Elliot's larger plants. Kavi was licking the inside of his ear.

"Hey, Nico. You okay?"

The boy was listless, lying there staring out the window into the darkness of the night. He glanced at Fenlee and balled himself tighter.

"Elliot keeps hurting," he whispered.

Fenlee tensed. In Cipher's surveillance video, Elliot looked okay. Maybe a little tired, but not like he was in pain. Whatever was going on was clearly upsetting Nico. While she didn't understand his empathetic connections, she did trust him. She put her hand on Nico's back and tried to soothe him. "How is Elliot hurting, Nico? What's happening to him?"

"Can't tell. S'all...fuzzy."

"What do you mean by 'fuzzy?'"

Nico shrugged. "Dunno. He's sad."

Fenlee had been slowly getting used to the feeling of the knife that life stuck in her gut a few days before, but now it was beginning to twist again. There was no waiting. She needed to get her brother back now.

Right. Breathe. She needed a solid plan. She couldn't afford a repeat of her last dumb attempt.

Alex and Casper would be coming over soon to go over what they'd found. Hopefully between all of them, there'd be enough information to proceed. Until then...

"Hey, Nico," Fenlee said. "There's not a whole lot we can do for Elliot at this exact moment, but maybe we can help him another way." She lifted a leaf from a nearby plant. It was drooping and starting to brown. "No one has taken care of Elliot's plants in a while, and the worst thing ever would be if he came home and they were all dead. How would that make the two of us look?"

Nico looked up at Fenlee in horror. "Bad!"

"Right! So I need your help taking care of them. With, maybe, some water?" Fenlee had never done a thing for a plant in her entire life. She'd seen Elliot take care of them countless times but never paid much attention to what he was actually doing.

Nico hopped up and ran into the kitchen. "Water!"

"Yeah, I think we need to pour the water on them. And then we pull out anything that doesn't look right?"

Nico came back with a large aluminum cup so full it was sloshing over and dumped the whole thing into a small cactus.

"Perfect! Elliot'll be so glad to see that we took care of his stuff." She proceeded to pull anything out of the dirt that looked like it didn't belong.

They finished up with all the plants and admired their work. There was standing water in each planter.

"This'll be good," Fenlee said. "The extra water sitting on top will slowly sink in, so we won't have to worry about them for a while." She scratched her chin. "Wonder why Elliot never thought to do that. Guess that's why I'm the engineer."

There was a knock at the front door. Fenlee hit the panel and it slid open, revealing Alex and a very excited Casper.

"I had a lot of luck!" Casper could barely contain himself.

"That's so good to hear," Fenlee said. "And now I know we're definitely looking in the right place. Check this out." Fenlee transferred the video from Cipher to her holoquip and showed them what he'd found.

"Whoa. You're right, that's totally Ellie," Casper said.

"Have you considered a plan?" Alex asked while setting out cups in the kitchen for tea.

"That's why we're here," Fenlee said. "We see what we all got, we make a plan, and we get Elliot back."

Alex smirked. "It's my responsibility to let you know what my aunt said before we go any further. According to her, our best recourse is to file a formal complaint or an investigation request directly with the Divine Council."

"Oh, hell no!" Fenlee was livid. "Did you see that guy Elliot was with in the video? This isn't just Norfayne—the ones that took him are part of the Divine Council! And you know better than anyone how dangerous those theocratic jerks are. I'll do this myself if I have to. I'm done with life taking people away from me."

"Hold up, hold up." Alex waved her hands with a defensive laugh. "I am right there with you! The last place in New Cascadia we need to go for anything is the Divine Council. I just had to relay what Lily said because I told her I would. She doesn't want us getting in over our heads, and I respect that. But she also comes from a family of freedom fighters, and she knows her niece isn't going to just sit on her hands." Alex's lips twisted into a devious smile. "That said, she doesn't exactly know we're planning to do this."

Fenlee took a few breaths. "Sorry," she said. "I kinda went off a little too quick there."

Alex put her arm around Fenlee's shoulders. "Don't worry about it. That fire is what'll get you through all this. It's good to see that energy after the place you were in the other day at my aunt's."

The tea finished steeping, and Alex brought cups for everyone around the table. "Now, let's see what we've got to work with."

Fenlee showed them everything Cipher had collected. "He mapped a lot of the place out, but there are gaps. And you'll notice, it's mostly empty, which is great for us."

Casper went through all the data, carefully studying each detail. He furrowed his brow. "I don't get it. It looks like all their surveillance systems are hardwired—there's no meshnet or anything."

"What does that mean for us?" Fenlee asked.

Casper leaned back in his seat and picked at his ear. "Well, it's good for us because once we get in, I can probably fry the whole system from a single access point. But that's what makes it so weird—no one builds surveillance or communication infrastructure like this because it's so vulnerable. Real easy to tamper with, you know?"

Fenlee thought for a moment. "Unless maybe they had to. Check this out." She scanned through and pulled up some of Cipher's logs. "There's something in that building blocking or muddying transmissions everywhere except a few small rooms and this indoor garden place. I saw some module errors in his logs but skipped over them before."

Maybe it was making Nico's empathetic connection all "fuzzy," too.

Casper nodded. "Yeah, that'd explain the need for hardwired systems, but it's really strange that they'd block everything. They've gotta be hiding some serious stuff in there."

"We'll have to keep this in mind," Alex said. "Want to show her what you found out, Cas?"

"You bet," Casper replied. "The platform the chateau sits on is completely inaccessible except by air transport. Seems the bridges were never repaired after the Great Collapse, so they just left 'em. It's gonna be impossible for us to get in that way. But..." He activated his holoquip's rudimentary projection feature and a complex schematic displayed in the middle of the table.

"That looks like the inside of the tower you live in," Fenlee said.

"Similar, yep. But this one's directly under that chateau."

Fenlee was skeptical. "This is great, but everything here—this entire eastern sector—is within an injunction zone. You have a proposal to get around that little issue?"

"I do, and it's one you're already familiar with. We go *beneath* the injunction zone." Casper swapped the projection for another showing a network of tunnels. "We get to the tower by way of the undercity. Should be easy with all your experience, you know?"

"Got it," Fenlee said. She was starting to feel like this might actually be possible.

"Yep! With my schematics and your recon intel—"

Alex cut him off. "I think you're forgetting some critical information, Cas. We're not done yet."

Casper winced. "Oh, right. Sorry, I'll just…" He made a zipping motion across his lips and sat down.

"I did some research," Alex said. "Contrary to what all the Cascadian Authority reports say, there's still a fairly strong refugee gang presence in that region of the undercity. It backs up to the Eastern Wilderness Zone, so it makes for easy smuggling. SecForce hasn't been able to clear them out, so they just lie and tell everyone it's not a problem." Alex shrugged. "And, as it turns out, it's actually not that much of a problem. They aren't really hurting anyone or causing any harm outside the area. My concern is that we have to march straight through their territory on the way to the tower, and I don't know how well that will go over."

"Oh." Fenlee's shoulders slumped. "I'm sure we can figure

out…something?" The words felt less than convincing as they left her mouth.

"That's not all," Alex said. "I was also able to pull some information on this chateau. Norfayne's owned it for a very long time, but this Dr. Arkamis guy has been using it as a private residence for the past two decades. Prior to that, it was shut down and quarantined by the Cascadian Authority, but any additional info is restricted. It's not just the chateau—all of the other structures on that particular platform have long been abandoned, but there's no indication as to why. Everything I've read about the place is creepy, Fenlee. I don't know what we're going to find there."

Fenlee's gaze drifted from Alex to Casper to Nico. "Okay. Does this change anyone's mind? If you're not in, I totally get it. This is a lot, and I promise I won't think less of you if you back out."

Casper was the first to answer. "I'm with you. We've gotta get Ellie outta there—it'd suck not havin' the little guy around. And I've always wanted to check out the undercity with you too, you know?"

Alex smiled. "It's like I told you before, Fenlee, family is what you make it. Believe me, I get how important this is. Let's do it."

"What about you, Nico?"

The little green-haired boy put two tight fists on the table and gave a deep nod.

Kavi leapt up in front of Fenlee and flicked his tail in her face with a *meow?*

Fenlee laughed. "You too, furwad?"

Life for anyone in the lower tiers of New Cascadia was often hard and full of daily challenges. People got used to it because there were few other options. But everyone also quickly learned to never gamble with unnecessary risks. Not for one second did Fenlee take for granted what it meant for her friends to commit to this.

"You all really are the best," she said. "I honestly have no idea what I'd be doing right now without you." She activated her holoquip. "Right then. We've got the intel, now all we need is a plan."

Elliot lay awake. Violent nightmares had torn him from his sleep. Now, sprawled on top of his covers, he stared at the shadows dancing across the ceiling, scared to dream again.

Memories of the day he'd met Fenlee occupied his mind. They were ill-formed, and didn't fit together quite right, like looking back in time through the jagged fragments of a broken window. But he had enough of a picture of that day to know it was real. He could remember the pain inflicted by those he trusted. He could still see the faces of indifference as those around him took notes and conversed with each other. And he could remember having had enough.

How many lives did he steal to get the energy for a blast powerful enough to level entire buildings? And how many more died in the aftermath? All he knew was Fenlee's mom was among them. There was no other way to look at it: he had killed her.

Less than twenty-four hours ago, all he wanted in the world was to be reunited with Fenlee. Now he didn't know how he could ever face her again.

Elliot watched as one shadow above him detached from the rest. It stretched from the windows, taking its time to reach the far side of the room. Then it quickly receded. A moment later, there was a light thump. He looked in the direction of the windows and saw a dark shape on the floor below a cleanly cut hole in the glass. The figure slowly stood and drifted toward him without making a sound. He caught a glimpse of a silvery pattern on its shoulder, reflecting the nighttime lights of the city.

"Kyara?" Elliot hopped out of bed. "What are you doing here?"

She closed the distance and balled her fist, ready to throw a punch. "Forgive me, kid."

"Wha—"

The impact dropped Elliot hard. Sparks erupted through his vision. He tasted metal and his nose was clogged. Blood pooled on the ground beside him, purple and black in the dim light. Kyara was standing nearby, throwing punches in the air with a confused look on her face.

"Etherclaw doesn't work in here," he mumbled.

"Smart." Kyara drew a long knife from behind her and came at Elliot.

"Wait! Just—if you ever see Fenlee again, please just tell her I'm sorry. Please."

Kyara hesitated. "You're not afraid at all."

Elliot coughed up bits of blood and considered the woman in front of him. This would be a fair end. An easy end. "Found out what I am. Guess that's why you're here." He tried to stand, but fell back down. "It's fine. I deserve this."

She squatted next to him, his blood flowing around her

boots. "You really didn't know before, did you? You weren't hiding it, you really didn't know."

Elliot was getting lightheaded. "Had no memories. Please just do it. I don't want to hurt anyone ever again."

Kyara bent over him in silence. He wondered what it would feel like to die. Would it be more or less painful than how it was for all those he killed? Did dying feel like anything at all? He hoped not, because that would mean—

"Damn it." She resheathed her blade and stood up, giving his bedpost a solid kick before walking back to the window.

When Kyara was halfway across the room, she turned just as Arkamis and three armed guards burst through the bedroom door, weapons drawn.

"There she is! Take her down!" Arkamis yelled.

Two guards fired paralyzing shots. Both hit Kyara in the chest, and she crumpled.

"Cano, see to him," Arkamis said, pointing to Elliot. A familiar-looking woman rushed over to check his vitals.

"Broken nose, possible concussion, minor blood loss," Cano said. "Teeth are intact, though. He should be fine." Elliot ran his tongue along the insides of his teeth just in case. He hadn't thought about that.

"That's good to hear," Arkamis said. He walked over to Kyara, who was splayed out on the floor, fully conscious but unable to move. He turned her head over with his boot to get a look at her.

"Kyara Ravenwolf. What an unexpected surprise. I would offer you refreshment but, unfortunately, I hate you. Tell me, what in the Ascendancy brings you to my humble chateau? I thought you were dead."

"And I thought your etherclaw research had been shut down. You know damn well why I'm here."

"Shut down? Hah! Why, Kyara, I'm better funded, better backed, and have more authority than ever. Just because *you* didn't work out as intended doesn't mean we haven't had great success elsewhere. Isn't that right, Elliot?"

"You murdered my entire team, Arkamis," Kyara spat.

"Kyara, I'm hurt. The term 'murder' suggests such ill intent. The etherclaw integration project you were a part of had over a ninety-five percent failure rate, and you all rebelled. So yes, of course the subjects had to be put down." He shook his head. "But you, unlike the others, appear to be thriving. I suppose we'll need to investigate why that is, won't we?"

Kyara clenched her jaw and remained silent.

"Oh? No comment from our uninvited guest?" Arkamis kicked her in the gut, but she made no sound. "Nothing to say?" He kicked her again. A single convulsion shook her body, but the paralyzing agent still had hold of her.

"Stop it." Blood bubbled on Elliot's lips as he spoke.

"You have something to contribute, Elliot?" Arkamis turned to him with a raised eyebrow.

"Leave her alone."

"No can do. Sorry." Arkamis turned to the pair of guards flanking the doorway. "You two—secure our intruder in one of the lower resource labs. You may wish to refresh the paralysis first."

The guards shot her a second time and dragged her out by her arms.

"Why are you so horrible?" Elliot whispered.

Arkamis walked toward Elliot, each click of his boots on

the floor reverberating through his skull. He knelt beside Elliot and removed a single glove. Smiling, he brushed Elliot's long hair out of his face.

"We are all horrible in our own ways, my boy. All of us. Learn to embrace it—embrace who and *what* you are. You'll feel much better."

CHAPTER 22
FALLING STARS

According to Casper's schematics, the best route into the eastern sections of the undercity was through a disused area on the outskirts. They waited until nightfall and took the maglev to the stop closest to their destination. Sparse industry was the only sign of activity this far out. Myconutrient processing plants and stacked rice paddies were some of the few facilities that looked active, but even those were largely automated and devoid of human presence.

A couple miles to the north was a massive tower, two hundred stories tall. Their line of sight prevented them from seeing the top of the dark, forbidding column and the platform that capped it, but Fenlee knew the chateau was up there. She could feel it.

They walked a half mile north on crumbling roads and through the carcasses of buildings long abandoned to ruin. To their left, the megacity of New Cascadia shone like a supernova. And to their right, the Eastern Wilderness Zone stretched for hundreds of miles past the mountains to the wastelands beyond. It was like navigating the serrated edge of a sharp boundary between worlds.

"Entrance should be coming up soon," Casper said, looking at his holoquip.

"It better be. We're about to run straight into the injunction zone." Fenlee tried to suppress the anxiety before it could seep through the cracks in her confidence. With the tower looming in front of them, the number of obstacles between sister and brother suddenly felt overwhelming.

The plan was simple: they would enter the undercity, go up the tower, access the bottom level of the chateau using an old service channel, disable the surveillance, get Elliot, and get the hell out the way they came. They brought plenty of food and other various supplies to cover contingencies.

Casper wanted to bring some of his homemade sake, but Alex told him to forget it. She and Fenlee also made him leave behind a strange black novelty sword he'd picked up from some overpriced vendor. Alex assured him he'd only wind up hurting himself if he tried to use it, and it would probably shatter on its first impact, anyway.

Kavi rode on Nico's shoulders as the boy plodded along behind them. He'd been quiet since they left. Fenlee wanted to ask if he was okay, but that felt like such as stupid question. Given what they were about to do, none of them were okay.

They took a break on top of a hill of rubble while Casper

checked his map. He pursed his lips. "Should be...there!" Less than twenty feet away, down the other side of the hill, a gaping hole opened into the old undercity.

"*That's* where we're going?" Alex raised an eyebrow. "I'm not saying I expected a welcoming committee, or even stairs, for that matter, but that looks like a death trap."

"I'm guessing you've never been in the undercity before, huh?" Casper asked.

Alex sighed. "Yeah, well, first time for everything. I'm not saying I mind getting dirty, but that doesn't look safe at all."

Nico touched Alex's arm. "Nothing is safe," he whispered.

Casper glanced at his holoquip. "Rain hasn't been too bad, and we're far enough inland that the tunnels shouldn't be flooded. Is everyone ready?"

"What was that?" Fenlee blurted out.

Alex whirled around. "What was what? What did you see?"

"Up there." Fenlee pointed to the eastern sky. Hints of mountains cut an uneven line across the dark horizon. The Void Pillar stood as an ominous backdrop, somehow blacker than night. A bright streak lit up the sky before fading to nothing. After a moment, there was another streak, then several more.

"Are those real shooting stars?" Casper said, sounding awed. "I've never seen any 'cause the city's so bright, you know? And even if it wasn't, with all the damn buildings and everything in the way—"

"Casper." Alex's voice was low and even. "Those are the fragments of the auxiliary platform."

Casper blinked. "Oh. Shit. So you mean..."

"Yeah, Cas."

Fenlee stood on a small mound of pockmarked cement.

Casper walked up beside her, and the pair stared in silence as thin fiery lines traced across the sky. Alex stepped back, giving them both space as the two watched pieces of their lives crash into the atmosphere.

The tunnels were wet, but not flooded. Nico hopped from puddle to puddle, releasing odors of decay with each splash while the rest of the group tried their best to keep their shoes dry. Shadows from their lamps danced along the walls, and everyone's foreheads glistened in the humidity. Casper quickly found that the lamplight overwhelmed his goggles' night vision setting and grumbled in disappointment at having to shut them off.

There were no drones or other security measures in place, but it was still unfamiliar territory and, with the exception of Nico, everyone was on edge. Gaps in the unlit passages had opened over the years, and one misstep in the dark could prove fatal. If the conditions weren't hazardous enough, the warnings about refugee gangs played in the dark corners of Fenlee's mind.

The tunnels they were navigating were first constructed for transportation, then repurposed for flood mitigation years later. Floods were rare, now that sea levels and weather patterns at their latitude had stabilized, and the tunnels were structurally sound in most places. But as they walked, Fenlee wondered if anyone truly lived in such an inhospitable place, or if the rumors of refugee gangs were just that: rumors.

Apart from Casper pointing out directions, no one had spoken since leaving the surface. Watching the chunks of debris light up as they fell to earth somehow made it all real in a way it wasn't before. Fenlee hadn't actually thought she'd see her father again. She hadn't believed he was still alive. But some part of her had still been clinging to the idea of him—an expectation that, despite everything, he'd come walking back through the apartment door in a few months and things would be fine. But that false hope was shattered and laid to rest in radiant display. She wondered how many millions of people watched in awe, and how few mourned.

Fenlee was so turned inward that she had lost focus on her objective. She was there to get her brother, and the three others by her side were braving unknown dangers to back her up. Not the time to wallow.

Casper looked glum. For all the effort he put in to maintaining his facade, Fenlee knew he had to be hurting too.

"Hey, Cas," Fenlee said, moving next to him.

"I don't get it!" Casper was staring at the map projecting from his holoquip. He twisted and turned it around in every direction. A red marker blinked well outside of the blue lines.

"What don't you get?" Fenlee asked.

"This! Here, look." He enlarged the map and they all gathered around the display. "We're here." He pointed to the red dot. "But as you can see, we're not actually *on* the map. In fact, I don't think any of the tunnels we've been going through for the last half hour are."

Alex traced her finger from the mark to the tunnel lines. "We should be able to double back and get on the right track, don't you think?"

Casper grimaced. "With all the rights and lefts we took and branches we passed, do you really think we can just double back without getting more lost?" A mix of frustration and embarrassment was evident in his voice.

"How exactly did you let us all wander off course for so long before realizing we were lost?" Alex asked.

"I was preoccupied, okay?" Casper deactivated the map and kicked the tunnel wall.

Fenlee and Alex exchanged glances. "It's okay, Cas," Fenlee said. This time she did take his hand. "Unless our bearings are off or your holoquip's compass magically stops working underground, we should be under the tower soon if we keep heading in this direction. And we won't be able to miss it when we get there." She mentally kicked herself for not taking the time to repair Cipher before they left. He would have been able to scout ahead and provide them with short-range positioning and orientation data.

Casper withdrew from her and went back to messing with his holoquip. "Sorry. It's just that these are the exact same maps the Cascadian Authority has. They should be right, you know? But these are all…I dunno, they're just messed up."

It was no surprise that the Cascadian Authority had inaccurate layouts of the city. They were understaffed, underfunded, and had to make very efficient use of their limited resources. Of course mapping unused outlying areas would be the lowest priority. The refugee stories made more sense now. The Cascadian Authority probably put the rumors out there to keep everyone away from the eastern edge when the truth was, they had no idea what was out there themselves. As bad as the situation was, Fenlee refused to let it be any more than a minor setback.

"Cas, you did great finding us the entry point—that was what we needed the most. This next part is easy. Our target's just north of our current position, and there's no way we'll be able to miss it." Fenlee looked at each of her friends, but it was obvious they didn't share her optimism. "Let's all take a quick break and grab a little snack."

"I think Fenlee's right." Alex shivered in the damp air. "But the sooner we get there, the better. I'm not really into dark and creepy, and this place is a whole lot of both."

The narrow passages finally gave way to a large room a few hundred feet across. A dark basin covered in metal grating occupied the middle. Fenlee peered over the edge, but her lamplight couldn't penetrate the depth. The guts of ancient flood control machinery lined the walls. Everything here was even older than the undercity she was used to.

Casper kept sighing, and it was starting to irritate Fenlee.

"Spit it out, Cas," she said. "What's going on?"

He sucked his breath in through his teeth. "What's going on is we've been down here an hour now. I originally estimated no more than twenty minutes to enter the undercity, go below the injunction zone, and get to the tower. A whole damn hour, and where are we? There's not even a room like this on the maps I *do* have!"

"Calm down," Alex said. "I think we're just moving slower than we thought. And as much as I'm done with stumbling around down here in the dark, a little patience will get us there sooner—and safer."

Casper waved a hand through his holoquip projection. "I don't even know if this thing is calibrated anymore. Not that it matters anyway, since we don't exactly have a reference point to calibrate against." His shoulders slumped. "I'm only an info thief, not a cartographer, you know?"

"Alex is right," Fenlee said. "And we're not mad at you, so stop being so rough on yourself." She jumped in front of Casper and flashed a surreptitious smile. "And hey, you've always wanted to explore the undercity, right? Well, guess what? This is typically what that exploration turns into, with or without maps. Fun, right?"

They edged around the perimeter to a passage branching off to the north, careful to avoid the gaps in the grates along the way. The route was direct, with fewer side tunnels, and it was wide enough for all four to walk side by side. The additional space and firmer footing allowed them to move faster, but Fenlee was focused instead on the creeping sense of unease chewing at the back of her brain.

This was the first time Fenlee had been in the undercity with anyone besides Elliot. She may have berated her brother from time to time for being overly cautious, but his sensibilities frequently got the two of them out of jams. When they were exploring, she only had him to worry about. Now it wasn't one, but three to look after, and their experience levels were all very different.

Was it a mistake to take them along? *If anything happens to them, it's all my fault. Lily would kill Alex if she knew she was down here—probably kill me too. Casper's already in over his head, and he's starting to realize it. And Nico…well, he seems kind of at home, actually.*

Nico had been quiet and contemplative most of the trip with Kavi sticking close to his side. Fenlee couldn't help thinking that, his appearance notwithstanding, he had a certain maturity beyond any of them. He was an enigma, but his empathy was boundless. And she trusted him. The boy stepped in a pool of muck a couple inches deep that made a nauseating *slurp* as he pulled out his bare foot. He didn't care at all. Fenlee gagged. She was getting that kid some shoes when they got back, and he damn well better wear them.

The tunnels became drier as they continued on. After a few minutes, they arrived at a T intersection with a larger tunnel branching off to the right.

"Which way?" Alex asked. "Any ideas, Fenlee?"

"I might have some ideas," Casper said softly.

"You might," Alex replied. "And I might, as well, but without navigation support, Fenlee is the resident expert here."

Fenlee shined the lamp down both passages. "Well, if I were searching for loot, I'd take the left tunnel because it's smaller and appears to be infrequently used. It'd be less likely to be picked over. But we're trying to get to the underside of that tower, which is major infrastructure, so I'd be more inclined to take the larger tunnel to the right." She pointed to some conduit running down the walls. It was so old and filthy it blended in and was easy to miss. "And if you look closely, you'll notice these pipes also curve to the right from the tunnel we came from." She shrugged. "I mean, I could be wrong, but it seems like the obvious choice."

"Makes sense to me," Alex said.

Everyone headed to the right except Casper. "Yeah, that makes sense and all, but I think we should check out the left for a minute to make sure it's not like, I dunno, a connecting passage or something?" He turned and walked down the left tunnel.

A green-haired blur leapt in front of him.

"Stop!" Nico shouted and threw his lanky arms wide, blocking Casper's path.

"What is wrong with this kid, Fenlee?" Casper said.

"Nothing's wrong with him," Fenlee said. "He's got great intuition. Maybe ask *him* what's up instead of me?"

But they didn't have to ask—Fenlee and Casper saw it at the same time. Mounted about ten inches above the ground on both sides of the tunnel were two small cubes with tiny holes on the front. They were a dull metal, artificially aged to blend into the walls. In the dark, only the most observant could have spotted them.

"Whoa. Okay. And that would be a laser trip line." Fenlee winced. "Good catch, Nico. That could've been pretty bad." She closed her eyes. A small warmth in her chest grew as she reached out to the device. It was similar to many optical and proximity modules she'd constructed in the past. And it was active. *I wonder if I can gently disable it without throwing the trigger—*

Casper broke her concentration. "Yeah, good eye, kid," he said. "Luckily, we can just step over it."

"No, wait!" Alex yelled. She tried to grab Casper's arm, but it was too late. By the time she reached him, he was mid-step across the invisible line.

"What?" Casper pulled out of her grasp. "I'm being careful. This is no big deal!"

"No, Cas, you're not." She pointed above his head. "They're all over the ceiling."

A series of little cubes formed a line directly above Casper's head. Alex ripped open a pouch of nutrient drink mix and tossed the contents toward him. The fine powder revealed a latticework of thin red beams. And Casper was standing in the middle of them.

"Well, that was helpful, Cas," Fenlee said.

Casper was frozen in place, visibly shaking. "Uh, sorry? So, what do we do?"

Fenlee threw her hands up. "Well, it's a good bet SecForce knows we're here, so why don't you tell me what we should do?"

Nico pulled on Fenlee's hand. "Shh!"

Everyone stopped talking. A calm settled over the passageway. At first, there was nothing but silence. Dust motes drifted in the stillness of the lamplight as they stood together, listening. They collectively held their breath as a low hum came from the larger tunnel behind them.

"Really!" Casper whispered, his voice shaky and frantic. "What do we really do now? I'm serious!"

The sound of the drone came from the larger tunnel they had intended to take, so that wasn't an option. The smaller tunnel they were in was clearly set up to detect intruders, and they also had no idea what was down there. The only option that made any sense was to take their chances and go back the way they came.

"We have to be smart about this," Fenlee said. "I think our best bet is to—"

"Run?" Nico asked.

"Run!" Casper and Alex said at once. The two of them took off down the small tunnel. Nico shrugged and followed behind.

Sure. Great. They had absolutely no idea what the hell was down there. She shook her head and followed the group. *Guess it beats running headfirst into the drone.*

The tunnel was, for the most part, straight, and in better

condition than where they came from. They fled without concern for secrecy or stealth—their lamps clanked and their boots smacked against the damp cement flooring.

It didn't take long for Fenlee to get a side cramp from running, and Casper was a wheezing mess. Alex, meanwhile, seemed almost relaxed, breathing slowly through her nose, calmly focused on the tunnel ahead. Fenlee got the sense that her friend was running slower than she'd like on their account. Seeing Alex's serene strength helped put Fenlee at ease.

They rounded a corner and Nico came to a halt. "Uh-oh," he said.

The rest of the group stopped. "Wh…what, Nico?" Fenlee asked, gasping for breath. "I hate when you say 'uh oh.'"

Kavi's hair stood up. He growled into the darkness.

They shone their lamps down the passage, but they couldn't see much apart from some water dripping from the ceiling and the glint of something metallic further down.

"Come on," Casper said. "There's nothing there, but there *is* a drone behind us!"

As he started forward, powerful white lights blasted the group from the direction they were heading. Fenlee put her hand over her eyes, but she was already blinded. When her eyes adjusted and she regained enough sight, she peeked between her fingers and saw the lights approaching. The only other thing she could make out were the muzzles of several guns pointing directly at them.

CHAPTER 23
MISCALCULATION

Elliot paced in anxious circles around his room. Each time he completed the circuit, he caught a glimpse of himself in the mirror. The face staring back terrified him, and he couldn't spare more than a glance on each pass. Shadowy bags under his eyes and bloody splotches across his ashen skin gave the impression of a defeated demon.

Lt. Cano had left a short while earlier after administering basic first aid. She set his nose with an internal nasal cartridge and gave him a shot that eliminated the swelling. The process was quick but extremely painful. Whatever was in the medicine also acted as a stimulant, and now he couldn't settle down.

He gingerly touched his nose, but found his face was just as numb as his mind. Why didn't Kyara follow through? It was

clear she had figured out who he was since the last time he'd seen her. And she and Arkamis certainly knew each other.

She probably knows more about me than I do, he thought. *I'd wanna kill me too.*

The bedroom door slid open with a soft swish. A five-and-a-half foot silhouette stood in the doorway, a few tangles of hair sticking out like oddly placed feathers. Loxi stepped into the room and waved the door shut behind her.

"Elliot, you all ready to go?" she asked, then stopped a few feet from him. "What the..." Her jaw dropped. "What in the Void happened to you?"

Elliot shrugged weakly.

She placed her hands on either side of his jaw and looked him over like a concerned parent. "Did your dad do this? No—was it Rook? This looks like Rook. If he so much as—"

"No, Loxi, it wasn't either of them." Elliot sighed and closed his eyes. "I'm fine. Please forget it."

Loxi scrunched her brow. "You're not fine. Not in a lot of different ways. But I can take a hint." She wet a cloth in the bathroom and cleaned off the blood caked around his cracked lips. "There. Now you look less, I dunno, vampirish."

Vampirish. Thanks. "Did they send you to clean me up again?" Elliot asked.

"Nope! Grab your hoodie if you want it 'cause we're getting out of here!"

"What, now?" Elliot said.

"I told you—*three days*. And I keep my promises. Well, I suppose that wasn't a promise exactly. In fact, I guess it was pretty vague. Could you read it? I've never done food writing before."

Elliot felt like an idiot. Looking back now, given the context of the conversation, of course Loxi meant she was going to try and get him out.

"Thanks, Loxi, but this is probably not the best time. Kyara just tried to break in, and everyone here has to be on high alert."

Loxi bit the inside of her cheek. "Huh? Who's Kyara? Is that your sister?"

"She's—"

"Wait, are you saying your sister beat you up? That's so weird!"

"No, no, she's not my sister at all. She's…I guess I honestly don't really know who she is. But it doesn't matter. We can't leave right now."

"Of course we can," Loxi said. "Dr. Arkamis is gone and everything's all set."

Elliot rubbed his temple where his head still pounded. "He's not gone. He was just in my room about half an hour ago."

Loxi pursed her lips. "Well now, I don't know about that. When he sets a schedule, he keeps to it. And I'm responsible for keeping up with his personal appointments."

"I'm telling you, Loxi, he's definitely still around."

Loxi opened her mouth to speak and closed it again. She did this several times, appearing to reconsider her words. "Well, uh, regardless, I've kinda set some things in motion, and we don't have much of a choice." She hesitated, fidgeting and looking down at the floor. "And I'll be coming with you."

"What are you talking about? What did you 'set in motion?' This room is under surveillance. You realize they're seeing and hearing everything we're doing, right?"

"Nah, we're good. The security team here is pretty small—

old Malcolm's the only one on surveillance right now. I just dropped off his nightly tea with a little bonus. See? Window of opportunity is wide open, but on its way to closing. Come on!"

She grabbed his hand and pulled, but Elliot didn't budge.

"What's wrong, Elliot?" Loxi asked. "Opportunity window? Closing? Let's go!"

Elliot closed his eyes. "I don't know if I can."

After everything he'd learned, after everything he'd done, facing Fenlee and Max was impossible. They'd given him a place to live and a family to be a part of. He'd witnessed Fenlee's pain over the loss of her mother. She put up a strong front, but he'd seen the way she would hold her mother's opal in moments when she thought no one was looking. He knew of the nights she'd quietly cried herself to sleep and the nightmares that would leave her exhausted the next day. And now he knew it was his fault.

Elliot clenched his teeth. "You don't understand, Loxi. Now that I know what I know, it's not like I can just go back to my family."

"I do understand," Loxi said.

"No, you don't."

Loxi placed her index finger over his mouth. "I understand a lot more than you might think." She withdrew her finger, her lips an inch from his. "Whatever happens, you need to trust me, Elliot." She moved closer, her breath soft on his face.

"I...I trust you."

Loxi brushed strands of hair from his face and gently pressed her lips against his. She was the smell of spiced tea and the flavor of sweet vanilla, though the back of his mouth still tasted of harsh coppery rust. Elliot realized he was trembling but managed to steady himself as a soothing warmth flowed through his body. He wanted to collapse, to fall into her. The rest of the world melted away, and he desperately wished to hold on to that moment—*to Loxi*—for as long as he could. But as he licked his cracked lips and tried to kiss her deeper, she stepped away.

"No easy ways out," Loxi whispered. "Not for any of us."

"Wha…what do you mean?"

She grabbed his hand and pulled him toward the door.

They moved cautiously down dark hallways and past empty sitting rooms. Given Kyara's break-in earlier in the evening, Elliot expected to see guards everywhere, or at least patrol bots. But there was no sign of anyone in the quiet mansion. He hadn't figured out their security operations. The few guards he had seen all had Norfayne logos, with the exception of that woman from earlier—Lt. Cano. She was SecForce, which was odd since private and public security tended not to get along.

Elliot still dreaded the idea of facing Fenlee, but his mind kept drifting to Loxi, and the world felt a little lighter than it had in some time. He still didn't fully understand her role at the chateau, but they were leaving together, so he'd probably have plenty of time to ask her later. Other questions bubbled up in his head, the shame of his past momentarily forgotten.

What if she has nowhere to go when we get out? Maybe she could stay with us? I bet Fenlee and dad would be okay with helping someone who needs it. I mean, they helped me. *But the apartment is so small…where would she sleep? She'd have to share a room, and Fenlee doesn't really know her, so…*

"Elliot?" Loxi said.

"Yeah?"

"You're squeezing my hand a little too tight."

"Oh, sorry," he mumbled.

A long, narrow hallway connected the residential wing, where Elliot had been staying, to the central part of the chateau. Thick windows stretched from floor to ceiling on both sides, separated by panels of dark wood with polished metal inlays. The cold nighttime light of the city shone through from the left, painting the floor in contrasting stripes. Outside to their right was an overgrown courtyard fully enclosed by the chateau walls. And still there was no sign of anyone.

Loxi led the way, her hand tightly wrapped around Elliot's. "Hah, I bet old Malcolm's trackers are lighting up right now. You're not really supposed to leave the residential wing unaccompanied." She stopped for a moment. "But you know what? *I'm* accompanying you, so I guess we're all good!"

Elliot peered down the hall, his heart beating in his ears. Something felt wrong. The empty stillness only served to exacerbate his unease. "I've been wondering…why is it so quiet?" he said. "I'm surprised we haven't at least seen small drones or something."

"Oh, that," Loxi said. "There aren't that many people here at any given time. A few technicians, a handful of guards, and that's about it. And drones and bots don't exactly work quite right. The antieth gets to 'em. That stuff doesn't just block etherclaw—it scrambles a lot of different signals. But, as it happens, we're going through the conservatory, the only place here *without* antieth. Well, except for the lower levels." She shivered. "But we definitely don't want to go down there."

No antieth in the conservatory? Then why had Arkamis felt safe walking alone with him? Elliot could have done something if he knew how to control it.

He frowned. But would he have used it? The thought of leeching life from others made him nauseous, but if it meant taking down Arkamis, maybe it was a worthwhile tradeoff.

"There's a loading bay on the far side of the conservatory," Loxi said. "It's kinda small and used to be for dropping off gardening stuff. Nowadays, all deliveries go through the primary loading bay for security reasons or whatever." She dropped her voice and winked. "Thing is, I still have bio access privileges to the old loading bay."

They came to the end of the hall and rounded a corner. A broad staircase flared at the bottom before spilling into an atrium about a hundred feet across and four stories high with corridors branching off in several directions. Cold light filtered through skylights as dust motes drifted through, briefly illuminated like so many stars winking in and out of existence. The seal of the Telluric Ascendancy occupied the floor, its crimson and ivory tilework mostly shrouded in shadow. It was deathly quiet.

"We're almost there," Loxi said as they headed down the stairs.

The old wood creaked with each step down. Elliot grimaced, trying his best to tiptoe.

At the bottom, Loxi paused in the center of the seal. She bit her bottom lip and held her breath.

Elliot had been this way before with Arkamis, but everything looked different in the dark. It was odd that Loxi would get turned around, but maybe she just hadn't been through this part of the chateau at night either. He pointed down a corridor to the right. "I think maybe the conservatory's down there—"

"Shh!" Loxi said.

"Huh?"

Loxi pulled Elliot close and wrapped her arm around his mouth. She looked around, wild-eyed.

"Oush! Ur urting by dose!"

"I said *shh!*" She slowly pulled him backward toward the stairs.

A flicker of light reflecting off something down one of the dark hallways caught Elliot's attention. The flicker blinked and became two yellow eyes. He'd never seen a solf in real life before, but when the massive creature and its starburst chest emerged, there was no doubt in his mind what he was looking at.

The matte black beast was silent as it made its way forward and stopped in the center of the seal.

"O-okay," Loxi said. "I think maybe it just doesn't want us to go this way. Maybe we can slowly back our way up the stairs." She clenched his arm tight, and he could feel her trembling, trying to keep it together.

Elliot turned and looked behind them. "Uh, Loxi…" He elbowed her and pointed to the top of the stairs. Another solf watched them with stoic eyes. They were trapped.

"I had no idea he'd let the solfs out," Loxi whispered. "I'm so sorry."

They've been tracking us since we left my room, Elliot thought. *We never stood a chance.* He looked at the corridor to the right that led to the conservatory. It was about thirty feet from where they stood, and there was a panel beside a recessed door.

"Loxi," Elliot said. "I think if we can figure out how to get over to that hallway, we can shut the solfs on this side and run to the conservatory. They're not even moving. They're just sort of keeping us here. Let's see what happens if we inch our way over. When we get close, we can make a break for it."

Loxi swallowed hard and shook her head. "I don't think you understand solfs. If you move, you'll get us both killed. We might—*might*—be okay if we just stand here and don't move. Any way we play this, they win. You need to trust me."

Elliot was tired of being defeated. This wasn't only about him anymore—Loxi needed to get out of there as much as he did, and he wasn't going to let a couple of dogs stand in the way. If only he could use etherclaw, he could…could what, kill them? And use Loxi's lifeforce to do it? He pushed the idea aside. It was stupid and impossible anyway.

"Let's shift to the right an inch and see what they do," Elliot said. Before Loxi could respond, Elliot moved his feet.

Nothing happened. The solfs continued to eye them but remained still.

"See?" Elliot said. "Let's try another inch."

Loxi groaned, but complied.

Slowly, they made their way closer to the door over the course of several minutes. They were less than fifteen feet away from their destination when the solf in the middle of the room cocked its head.

Elliot whispered in Loxi's ear. "On three, let's run to the door and hit the panel to close it behind us. If we do it together, we should be through it before they can even react."

"Elliot, wait," Loxi said. "You don't understand—"

"One…"

"They'll kill us!"

"Two..."

"You said you'd trust me!"

"Three."

"Elliot, no!" Loxi tried to hold him back, but he pulled away and bolted toward the door.

With blinding speed, the solf in the middle of the floor ran past Elliot and stood in the threshold, blocking his way. Elliot choked on his own breath as he heard a thud and a scream behind him. He turned around and thought he might throw up.

The solf from the top of the stairs was standing on Loxi. Two hundred pounds of muscle and paws the size of her head pinned her face-down to the ground. Her left arm was locked in its teeth and twisted backward at an unnatural angle. But the creature's eyes were on Elliot.

"Loxi!" He stood paralyzed. He couldn't think. Everything happened so fast, and now he couldn't move. He couldn't breathe.

"Thought we were going somewhere?" Arkamis appeared at the top of the stairs, flanked by two guards. He made a motion, and the pair ran over to Elliot, grabbing him by the arms.

"Let her go!" Elliot screamed, pulling against the guards. "That thing's gonna kill her!"

Arkamis took his time coming down the stairs. He shook his head in mock sadness. "Elliot, you must understand that neither of you are going anywhere." He put his hand over his chest. "After all I've done, it pains me to see you trying to leave."

The solf hadn't moved since jumping on Loxi. Her breathing was ragged. A thin stream of blood ran down her forearm where the solf's teeth were embedded. "You were supposed to be gone," she whimpered.

"Gone?" Arkamis said. "Oh, you mean to the North

Research Facility. If you haven't noticed, little girl, everything around here has been quite insane lately. So I'm afraid I've stayed." He loomed over her, and Elliot waited for him to kick her like he did Kyara. Instead, Arkamis laughed. "Clever, slipping a bit of hemlock into Malcolm's tea. He's in the infirmary now. It remains to be seen if you overdid it."

Loxi closed her eyes and her jaw tensed. Elliot knew she didn't mean to do any permanent damage to the man. She was too kind, her heart was too big.

This is all my fault.

"Leave her alone," Elliot squared his shoulders and balled his fists. "She was only trying to help me. It was my idea for us to get out of here. The solf wouldn't have attacked if it wasn't for me, so just let her go!"

Arkamis spared Elliot a brief glance but otherwise ignored him.

"I must say, Loxi, I'm extremely disappointed. Elliot only wants to leave because he doesn't yet understand the magnificence of what we're doing here. We all just need to give him a little patience and some more time. Sadly, little Loxi, right now I'm out of patience, and you're out of time." He bit out the final few words and made a simple hand gesture at the solf. The creature sunk its teeth deeper, shredding bone and tendon with a sickening wet crunch.

Loxi's eyes went wide and her screams filled the atrium. She struggled to twist out from under the solf, but the animal stood firm. The more she flailed, the more blood she lost. After a moment, the exertion was too great, and she lay shaking, staring at Elliot, breathing words he couldn't make out.

His mind ignited. Every emotion welled up inside of him,

building to a fiery crescendo. But the explosion wouldn't come. The etherclaw was in him, it *was* him, but it was restrained, and he couldn't release it. Tears streamed down his face and he went limp in the guards' grasp. This was his fault, and there was nothing he could do to make it right.

Arkamis walked over and gently placed his hand on Elliot's head. "This is a beautiful moment, Elliot. Remember, there is such power in those emotions! Unfortunately, there's also antieth all around you." He nodded to the guards. "Secure him back in his room. I don't care what you do with the other one so long as I never have to see her again."

CHAPTER 24
REFUGEES BELOW

Fenlee sat cross-legged, brow furrowed. Her hand twirled through Kavi's fur as he nuzzled deeper into her lap. Nico lay on his back with his feet in the air, twisting a rusty wire around his fingers while Alex leaned against the wall and Casper paced.

Nothing had gone as planned.

If anything, they were further from rescuing Elliot. Each minute that ticked by felt like another wasted eternity.

The armed group had stuffed them in a tiny storage room in an abandoned underground shopping complex. There wasn't much in the tight space other than some stacks of boxes piled against the walls. Casper had already determined that most of them were empty apart from a few containing tins of long-expired fish paste and one box that held nothing but rusty spoons.

Nico got excited about the food, but Alex remarked that suicide by ancient fish paste didn't sound like a fun way to go.

A thick layer of dust covered the black-and-white floor tiles, and old promotional posters advertising consumer goods from a bygone era had become one with the faded walls. But there were signs of recent occupation as well. Air flowed from a small vent, and Fenlee identified newer conduit running along the ceiling. It smelled at once earthy and synthetic, but overall much cleaner than the rest of the undercity.

"So they're clearly not SecForce, or anyone with the Cascadian Authority," Fenlee said. "Who are we dealing with here?"

Alex shrugged and shook her head.

"Are you all dense?" Casper said. "It's like I said before—they're part of some refugee gang. This is the part where we don't make it out alive, so maybe suicide by fish paste isn't such a bad idea." He picked up one of the old spoons and let it fall with a clank. "They've locked us up with the tools to do it."

"Will you relax?" Alex said. "They're just being careful. From their perspective, *we* were the ones lurking in the shadows."

Nico jumped to his feet and peered at the door. He held the wire next to the knob, studied it for a moment, and tossed it aside. Then, rummaging around in a nearby box, he pulled out a tin of fish paste. Before anyone could stop him, he pressed the pull tab in and peeled off the thin metal lid.

The smell was a combination of sewer backup and every dead thing Fenlee had ever encountered all concentrated into one tiny package. And there was nowhere to run.

"Nico! Why?!" Fenlee said. She wrapped her bandana around her face, and Casper and Alex pulled their shirts over their noses.

Alex craned her neck to try and get fresh air from the vent. "Lovely. Now we're trapped in here with a biohazard."

"I'm gonna be sick," Casper said between gagging noises in the corner.

Nico and Kavi couldn't have cared less about the odor. The boy wiped the mucusy gray film off the inside of the lid and inserted the curled metal between the door and the frame. He worked it back and forth, making slight adjustments. After a few tries, the door popped open.

Two men stood facing them on the other side. The older of the pair had his hand on the outside knob and a confused expression on his face.

"Oh! Heh, breaking free, huh?" the older man said. "We were just coming to get you out—what in the Void is that *smell?*" Both men covered their noses and stepped back as the group fled the storage room, slamming the door shut behind them.

Casper didn't make it far before he doubled over, dry-heaving, and Fenlee ran headfirst into the younger of the men, bowling them both over. After everyone recovered, they relocated to the front room of an old convenience store where a handful of others waited.

"Sorry for cramming y'all in that back room," the older man said. "I'm Sebastian, and this here is Gabriel." He gestured to the younger man.

"Gabe is fine." The younger man leaned against the counter with his arms crossed. He had a pistol strapped to his leg and a small utility bag slung over his shoulder. Fenlee recognized him as a member of the team that found them in the tunnels. He was a few years older and had Casper's build, but with more muscle and less awkwardness. And there was something about him that reminded Fenlee of Nico—they had a similar complexion, but it was the look in their eyes that appeared in momentary flashes almost too brief to notice. Was it pain, or perhaps longing?

Neither of the men seemed particularly worried about keeping Fenlee and her friends confined. Outside the old store, a sprawling underground plaza connected dozens of shops, many of which had been converted to living spaces or made functional in other ways to support the inhabitants. Women and men carried supplies, a couple of kids laughed while being scolded for still being awake, and people more or less went on about their lives like anywhere else in New Cascadia. It all looked so...*normal*.

A little of the tension left Fenlee's shoulders. Maybe they weren't in trouble after all. Casper had been right about refugees living down here, but they sure as hell didn't seem hostile. Regardless, Fenlee decided it'd be best to keep her guard up until they were away from these people and back to the task of rescuing Elliot.

"Sebastian, Gabe," Alex said with a nod. "Good to meet you both. I wonder if you can help us out. See—"

"Who are you really?" Casper cut her off. He was still wide-eyed and looked ready to crap his pants. "What are you doing down here? And what are you gonna do with us?"

Alex grimaced. "Let me introduce Casper, our champion negotiator." She smacked him in the back of the head and rolled her eyes before turning back to Sebastian. "Honestly, your business down here is *your* business, not ours."

Sebastian smiled. "It's fine. He asks perfectly reasonable

questions. We are, after all, the ones who forced you here at gunpoint."

Gabe stretched out on the counter and yawned. Fenlee checked her chronometer. They hadn't lost much time—it was still relatively early. They could still do this. They just needed to keep things moving.

Sebastian glared at Gabe before proceeding. "We're part of the last group of immigrants they allowed into New Cascadia. We arrived a couple decades ago just before they shut down the city-state's southern perimeter. Problem was, we were admitted by mistake, and they never granted us citizenship. We've been living in this sort of quasi-citizen status at the fringe of the city. We do a little hunting in the Wilderness Zone and a little trade with some of the smaller merchant organizations, but we mostly keep to ourselves, and the authorities leave us well enough alone. That's the brief version."

"Thankfully," Gabe muttered. "You don't wanna hear the long version."

Sebastian cleared his throat. "Anyway, you'll have to forgive the welcome you received," he said. "We're always prepared for the day the authorities decide *not* to leave us alone." He put his hands on his hips and widened his stance. "Tell me, what exactly are you doing down here?"

Fenlee opened her mouth to speak, but Casper cut in too quickly. "We're just, you know, scrounging around for old, you know, stuff? Exploring and..." He looked to Fenlee as if she would continue his rambling.

She took stock of the situation. A group of refugees living under the city surely wouldn't hand them over to the SecForce. In the worst case scenario, nothing would happen and they'd be back where they started. But these people knew the layout down there. If they'd be willing to help. Fenlee knew it was a gamble, but she decided the truth might serve them best.

"That's not why we came here," Fenlee said. "We need to get to the underside of the nearby tower." She took a deep breath, knowing her next words could put all of them at risk. "This'll probably sound real weird, but I need to find my brother." She told them as much as she dared, leaving out anything about etherclaw.

Gabe was still lying on the counter, staring at the ceiling. "That's pretty messed up," he said. "But with Norfayne as the baddies? Totally believable."

"Going to the top of that tower is suicide," Sebastian said.

"I thought that's what the fish paste was for—hey!" Casper choked as Fenlee planted a sharp elbow in his ribs.

"We need your help," Fenlee said. "We're further off-track than when we started—we just need to get to the tower. Please?"

Gabe laughed. "You really don't know where you are?"

"Gabe…" Sebastian said.

"This is the old commercial district *underneath* your tower," Gabe said. "Congrats, y'all made it."

Sebastian sighed. "Gabe is right, but you won't be heading any further up. He's here with me now because he's going to escort you out. He'll lead you along a safe path underneath the nearby injunction zone. And then you'll go home."

The hopeful spark faded, and a familiar, painful blend of desperation and frustration crept into the pit of Fenlee's stomach. "But if you just let us go on up—"

Sebastian held up his hand. "I'm sorry, but you're going to be leaving. Now."

🔗

Gabe was armed, and probably stronger than any of them, maybe even Alex. But if they worked together and took him by surprise, perhaps they had a chance. The hallway he led them down was large enough for them to maneuver around him. She didn't want to hurt him, though. He had more right to be down there than they did, and he was just doing his job.

"Not gonna leave." It was the first time Nico had spoken since their capture. The boy's determination caught Fenlee by surprise.

Gabe slowed down. "What did you say?"

Nico looked him in the eyes. "Goin' up the tower."

"Nico's right, Gabe," Fenlee said. "Lead us wherever you want, but we'll just be back. We're not going anywhere."

Gabe narrowed his eyes and smirked. He looked behind them and lowered his voice. "Yeah, I know," he said. "That's why I'm taking you up there instead. Gotta get a little farther then we'll backtrack along a different route. Probably no more than five minutes and we'll be on the main level."

"Seriously?" Fenlee said. She couldn't get a good read on Gabe. What was motivating him to help?

"Shh!" Gabe said. "Yeah, seriously. Still got plenty of eyes and ears in this area, so just shut up and stick with me."

Fenlee grew up spending plenty of time in the towers closer to the heart of the city; Casper's residential tower was almost like a second home. The towers that held the upper-tier platforms were big, but as the group emerged from an underground staircase, she was unprepared for the sight before her. The tower was empty—a gutted, hollow shell. The first eighty floors were simply missing. The vastness was broken only by internal support columns that were somehow still standing strong. Fenlee estimated that her apartment building would fit easily in the space dozens of times over with plenty of room to spare.

Beams of nighttime light from the city shone through holes high above where windows once existed. Dust particles floated in the breeze, and rebar hung from old supports like strands of unkempt hair. The area inside was large enough to support its own ecosystem: plantlife was abundant, and small creatures poked their curious heads up to see who had disturbed their rest.

"Here we are," Gabe said. "SecForce keeps this place cleaned out. They don't run patrols very often, though, so there shouldn't be anything to worry about."

"It's hard to think that humans could have ever created something like this." Fenlee looked around at the mountains of debris. "Did these floors just, like, collapse?"

"Pretty much," Gabe said. He picked up a giant chunk of cement and hurled it against a nearby pile. The thud of the impact blended with the noise from a nearby industrial processing facility. "We figure this is what happened when they tried to reclaim building materials. Got a little too greedy. So yeah, if it's like the other towers where they ripped out the guts, they kept pushing the workers until it all caved in. There're probably, I dunno, hundreds of old skeletons buried under all this garbage. Thousands, maybe." He stomped a few times on a hunk of concrete. "Heh, kinda neat, right?"

"Not at all." Alex squatted down to examine a twisted hunk of metal that may have once been part of someone's kitchen table. "They were so desperate back then to rebuild and make a home for themselves. They sacrificed so much so we could get where we are today."

"Yeah? Coulda used a little more sacrifice, I guess. Lots of people are still desperate." Gabe kicked the dirt and shugged. "Lots of people still don't have a home." He started toward one of the central support columns that was still intact. "Y'all coming or what?"

The column was at least two hundred feet in circumference, but appeared tiny and even flimsy rising up in the heart of the massive tower. An array of lifts was tucked back into a recessed hallway. Years of decay and gravity had caused their doors to buckle and sag, and they sat dark, lifeless, and completely unusable.

Except for a larger service lift at the end.

The door had been ripped away and the interior cleaned out. It still didn't look as though it was anywhere near working order, but it was Gabe's destination.

Casper trudged along behind, face buried in his holoquip, mumbling to himself. "Nothing matches these schematics. These have to predate the damage here."

Gabe removed a wall panel beside the open lift with several switches and dangling patch cables. After fumbling around inside for a moment, a dim light flickered on inside the lift.

"Whoa!" Fenlee stuck her head inside and looked around. "How is this thing working?"

"We retrofitted it a while back," Gabe said. "Took some work, but it let us get to the upper floors. Too bad they'd been looted forever ago. Managed to get some crappy furniture anyway." He waved everyone aboard the lift. "Hands and arms inside the vehicle! Seriously, there's no door, and they'll get ripped off. Now, it's been a while, so let's see if this thing still works."

Gabe looked through a series of exposed wires, each labeled with a tag and grease pencil. He found the two he was looking for and touched the tips together with a spark. The lift lurched, but didn't make it more than about two inches before stalling. He tried again, but the result was the same.

"Shit." Gabe dropped one wire, capped the other and stood in silence, biting his thumb. After a moment he shook his head. "That's about all I got. I'm not exactly mechanically inclined." He kicked at the capped wire on the ground and sighed. "You've got two options. I can show you out like Sebastian wanted, or I can show you the stairs. They're cleared out and usable, but that's an awful lot of floors to climb."

Casper groaned. "I can't make it up half the flights to my own apartment. There's no way we can do two hundred floors."

"Move." Fenlee shouldered past Gabe and ripped off the panel behind the wires. She shoved her arms inside and quickly found what she was looking for: a stubborn direct drive motor, corroded with age.

Easy.

She reached out with the etherclaw and forced the drive to engage. The ancient machinery tried to resist, but with a cumbersome lurch, the drive kicked in, and they began their ascent.

CHAPTER 25
CHATEAU

THEY ARRIVED AT floor one hundred eighty as the brakes engaged with an ear-splitting shriek. Everyone lost their footing, and Casper tumbled onto the floor outside the lift. Unlike the bottom floors, this one was intact, with no city light filtering in. It was pitch black, and the air smelled like dry cardboard and wet socks. Everyone's lamps clicked on one by one as they peered into the darkness.

Fenlee barely needed any time to recover from using her etherclaw. Was she using it more efficiently? There was still so much about it she needed to understand. Whatever the case, she was glad she didn't need to stop for a break.

Gabe led the way. "Chateau basement's gonna be several

floors up from where we are, but it's tricky to find the way. I'll show you."

It was like being back in the depths of the undercity again—dark and disorienting. Ripped-out walls, broken medical equipment, and other signs of looters from ages past littered the walkways.

She felt a hand on the small of her back. "Nice, uh, *equipment*, you got goin' on," Gabe said.

Fenlee swatted his hand away. "When, exactly, did I say you could touch me?" He made her uncomfortable, but they still needed him to play tour guide. She dug her fingernails into the palm of her hand.

"Haha, easy! I didn't mean nuthin'. I was only checkin' out your leg. Real nice equipment. You like, rich or somethin'?"

Fenlee glanced at Alex. "Ah…rich. No. Kind of the opposite. I just happen to know some really good people."

"Huh. Well, I bet they're glad to know you too. Pretty impressive work back there. Dunno what you did, but no one I know could have fixed the lift that quick."

"Yeah. Thanks. I like doing mechanical stuff, so it's no big deal." The whole thing started to feel odd. She had been so desperate to get to the top of the tower that she put her trust—and the safety of her friends—into this guy she didn't know at all. What were his real motivations? He didn't appear to have anything to gain.

"Don't take this the wrong way, but why are you helping us?" she asked. "You don't even know who we are."

Gabe laughed, but there was anger underneath it. "Cascadia's not so bad. But Norfayne can go void itself. If you're doing anything that hurts them, I'm all for it."

"That sounds…personal," Alex said. "I'm not sticking up for them, but what did they ever do to you?"

"You kidding? They steal and withhold resources from people who need them the most. They're the most powerful group in the region, and they take and take and *take*. So, s'pretty simple. Outsiders can only get citizenship rights in New Cascadia based on goods and resources available, right? They tightly control the supply and demand balance. With Norfayne totally devouring everything, Cascadian Authority's cut admittance by millions over the years. Literally millions. Get it? Me, my friends, my family, and tons of others should be citizens. Instead, we're stuck under the damn city, and everyone else is in those awful towns and camps to the south."

Fenlee thought about her mom and Alex's aunt. "Not everyone who works—"

Gabe cut her off. "Oh, and that's not all! We just found out about their whole 'relocation program.' You know, where they take groups of refugees that meet certain requirements and bring them into New Cascadia? Yeah, weirdest thing—no one knows where they end up. They just sorta disappear. I'm tellin' you, they're slowly murdering us or something. But no one cares, 'cause we're *things*, not people, to them." Gabe slammed his fist against a loose wall panel. It broke free and clattered to the floor. "So Norfayne can go void itself and the same for anyone working for them."

"Some people have to take any job they can get." Fenlee knew Gabe was right, but it was more complicated than that, wasn't it? She still blamed the company for her mother's death. And she struggled with the idea of committing to a future there herself. But what choice did she have if she ever wanted to pull her family out of low-tier living?

"Nah, void 'em all," Gabe said. "If you work for 'em, you're either evil, or you've gone and buried your morals so deep you'll never find 'em again."

Fenlee gritted her teeth and looked at Alex, but she was staring at the ground, as though deep in thought. Gabe had just insulted both Lily and Fenlee's own mother. She wanted to bite back at him and say something more, but what was she defending?

"Sorry, Norfayne's totally my trigger." Gabe laughed. "You wanna get me goin', just bring up those bastards."

Fenlee moved closer to Alex and they walked on in silence. They couldn't be far now. Using the data collected from Cipher, they'd determined the bottom levels of the chateau were incorporated into the tower itself.

They climbed several flights of stairs and broke through old utility rooms at the top of the stuffy, humid tower. The top floors had been used as some sort of medical testing facility. Gurneys, stained and smashed, blocked their path and had to be pushed aside. A series of large rusted hooks hung from the ceiling in one room, their shadows performing a macabre dance in the lamp light. An unpleasant chill ran down Fenlee's spine and she looked away.

At the end of a long hall was a set of reinforced metal doors. Fenlee took a deep breath and stared at the red lettering stamped above the handle.

RESTRICTED
NORFAYNE LABORATORIES
PROJECT OSIRIS

"Pretty sure this is what you're looking for." Gabe stood a few feet back from the group, his voice solemn.

"How do you know for sure?" Fenlee asked. "What if this is just some creepy old test chamber or something? What does Project Osiris mean?"

"Dunno what it means. But trust me, this is what you're after. Found it with a friend of mine when we were kids exploring where we shouldn't have. Wasn't locked then, probably isn't now." Gabe shivered. "Anyway, it's all yours, so, good luck."

"You're not coming?" Alex asked.

"Hell no. Y'all are the ones that are insane. I've got a life down there that's just fine, and I'm gonna get back to it."

"Figures," Fenlee said. "So all that 'Norfayne can go void itself' talk was just that: talk." She gave him a dismissive wave. "Thanks for showing us the way."

"Nah, I hate 'em. But I'm not suicidal." He turned to leave but hesitated, his hand on the gun strapped to his leg. "You know what? Here." He unholstered the weapon and offered it to Fenlee.

"Yeah, that's a hard pass." She smiled at Gabe, brief and tight. "We'll be fine."

Casper stepped forward. "You sure, Fenlee?"

"We're not killing anyone, Cas."

"Suit yourself. Later." Gabe winked and strode back down the hall in the direction they came. It didn't take long for his lamp light to disappear.

"Guess that's that." Fenlee turned to face the doors. "Is everyone ready?" Alex, Casper, and Nico nodded in unison. Gabe was wrong about it being unlocked, but it was only secured with a simple clasp that Fenlee made quick work of with her multimini.

Too easy. Norfayne must have been confident no one would ever use this route.

Fenlee jammed her fingers between the doors and pulled sideways. It was heavier than she expected, but with her friends working together, they started to make progress.

Slowly, the door slid open enough to reveal another hallway. But this one was uncluttered, the walls intact, and the floors barely dusty. A dim light shone at the end. There was also an odor of harsh antiseptic and something…animal-like? Kavi crept through first and let out a low, guttural growl.

They'd arrived at the chateau.

CHAPTER 26
CAGED

THE MAGNITUDE OF what they were about to do dropped like a bomb in the pit of Fenlee's stomach as they crossed the threshold from the top of the ruined tower into the bottom of the chateau. The transition made the reality of the situation clear: they were in Norfayne territory now, and not just any Norfayne territory, but one of their top-secret research facilities. If they were caught, getting shot on sight would be the easy way out.

Still, despite the odds, they'd made it this far. And she was determined to take on anything that stood between her and her brother.

Nico held Kavi like a stuffed animal while the other three checked their holoquips. Fenlee shared Cipher's imagery and map data with everyone as they tried to orient themselves. The

little bot hadn't found much in the bottom levels of the chateau apart from a series of storage rooms and some old labs with bizarre equipment.

Fenlee pointed out a terminal on the floor above them for Casper to hook into and attempt to override the security systems. There were also a couple of rooms with something that resembled cages, but it was hard to tell with Cipher's poor infrared imagery if anything was in them.

"All right. So, Cipher discovered something throughout the main levels of the chateau causing signal interference, but it doesn't start for the next few floors—we're basically in the basement of this place." Fenlee rotated her holoquip for everyone to see. "Meaning, we won't be able to rely on the holoquips' short-range comms once we get into the areas upstairs."

Alex nodded. "We stick together, or we risk losing track of each other."

"Exactly. But we're okay for the floor above us at least, so I think for now we should split up so Cas and Nico can work on the security system. And..." Fenlee bit her lip. She doubted Elliot was being caged in the basement, but that room was one of several locations that had stood out when she reviewed Cipher's data. She needed to know for sure. "And I want to check out these rooms just in case. Alex, you think you could give me a hand?"

"That's why I'm here." Alex smiled and cracked her knuckles. "Let's do this thing."

"Great. And Cas, you got this? You have a passkey or something you can use in their systems?" Casper was highly skilled, but Fenlee knew he was prone to overconfidence. She also had enough experience with similar systems to know how easy it would be to trip an anti-tamper alarm.

"Nah, I'd never be able to use one of their passkeys—pretty much impossible to get a hold of, you know? Even if I could, they're probably using moxicrypt algorithms, which are basically impossible to reverse. We don't have time to try and brute-force the system, and we gotta assume it'd fire off countermeasures if we did. But that's not all—"

He could hardly contain his excitement, which concerned Fenlee. "Cas, this is totally interesting, but also totally not the time. Do you have a way to override or not?"

"Ah, yeah, sorry. Basically, instead of trying to steal access using *their* passkeys, I'm injecting my own. We're lucky 'cause access controls in these older systems are tied to the keys, so we don't have to rely on—"

Fenlee didn't have time for him to explain what she already knew. "Sounds great. I know you can do it. Just *please* be careful."

The floor above was a maze of corridors lit by the soft glow of panels along the baseboards. Most of the storage areas they passed were empty, but the entire level showed signs of proper upkeep—floors were scrubbed, room labels were stenciled with relatively fresh paint, and not a single light was out. The area saw use, but was, at least at this hour, deathly quiet.

Fenlee checked her holoquip to make sure she and Alex were still on the right path. It would be easy to get turned around without Cipher's data to guide them. "Sorry for dragging you with me. I honestly don't think we'll find Elliot here, but I just need to know. We'll double back and meet up with the boys once we check."

"Stop apologizing, Fenlee. I keep telling you—me, Nico, and even Cas, we're all here for you and Elliot because we *want* to be." Alex lowered her voice and pointed down the hall. A sliver of light extended from a gap under an unmarked door. "Check it out. I think that's where we need to go."

"It looks like someone might be in there."

"Maybe. Let's just be careful."

Placing her ear against the door, Fenlee held her breath and listened. There was the dull drone of ventilation fans, but if there was anything else to hear, the fans drowned it out. Alex nodded, and then Fenlee waved her hand over the small panel to activate the door.

Inside was a spacious storage room that had been converted into a makeshift lab. Cold overhead lights left no shadows, and the smell of ammonia grated on Fenlee's nasal passages. But what caught her attention were the rows of dogs and cats locked up in cages lining the walls. Each animal looked at the pair of girls in tired resignation. There were several larger cages in the corner to their right. All were empty except for one. A figure in tight bindings sat on the floor, head lowered. Fenlee recognized her immediately.

"Kyara?"

"Fenlee?" The woman lifted her head, and it was the first time Fenlee had seen a look on her face that wasn't some variant of stoic determination or smug confidence.

"Kyara, why the hell are you here?"

But Kyara's confusion quickly turned to panic as her eyes focused behind Fenlee and Alex to the opposite side of the room. A side door slid open, revealing a boy with black hair in formal Telluric Ascendancy attire. He held an old-style logbook in his hands and appeared to have been taking notes on the animals.

"Odd. What are you doing?" The boy sounded only mildly surprised, as though one of the dogs had somehow managed to get out of its cage.

"Hey, wait! You're the kid from the library." Fenlee was stunned. She didn't know what she expected to find in the room, but this certainly wasn't it. "What in the weird hell is going on in this place?"

"Fenlee! Look out!" Kyara shouted to get their attention, but it was too late.

A heavyset augmented man came at Fenlee and Alex from behind, taking the girls by surprise. Before Fenlee could so much as gasp, he grabbed Alex by the hair and whipped her head into a lab table. Her eyes rolled back as she slumped to the ground.

"No!" Fenlee charged at the man, throwing her fists at him.

He shrugged off her attack and smirked.

Fenlee's moment of terror condensed into a ball of rage. She twisted her hips and shoulder as she threw a powerful right hook. Fenlee was no fighter, but the impact would have been enough to knock most normal people out cold. Instead, it connected with the man's ocular augmentation and shattered her knuckles.

The man wasn't amused anymore. "Enough fun."

He grabbed Fenlee's face and lifted her up. The palm of his hand smelled like vinegar and rot. He smashed the back of her head against the wall so hard she felt it in her teeth and the bridge of her nose. She could barely make out his words as her vision faded to black.

"Rook! Stop standing there. Go tell your father. Hurry!"

The world was a ghostly fog. Fenlee couldn't recall where she was or why, only that she was consumed by a threatening sense of urgency. The moment she'd start to home in on what she needed to do, the task or goal would slip away.

She couldn't feel her right hand.

Panic set in. She touched her left hand to her right elbow and slowly moved it down her arm, fearful of what she might find. Everything was intact until she got to her knuckles, which felt like damp seaweed ribbons draped on bits of granite. Pain lanced up her arm at the touch, and it all came back to her: the lab, Kyara, the library boy, and the augmented man tossing Alex like a rag doll.

Fenlee blinked away the blur and forced her vision to clear. She was still on the floor next to where she hit the wall. Kyara was talking to the augmented man, providing violent details on what she intended to do to him once she got out. And then she saw him. His filthy hand was wrapped around Alex's hair as he dragged her unconscious body to one of the empty cages.

All of the sadness, frustration, and fury Fenlee had been suppressing erupted in an unchecked emotional surge. In a fraction of a second, she saw a flash of metal, a servo assembly, and clusters of microscopic wiring. Components fractured and exploded. Her head hurt even worse, and she felt nauseous. Everything faded to black, but only for a moment. She shook it off, then gagged at the sight in front of her.

Bits of brain matter and wet skull fragments lay near what remained of the man's head. A set of cables coming from the back of his neck writhed on the floor like the last gasp of life from a dying animal.

Fenlee's chest was burning.

Oh, shit. No. No no no. I did that.

She never imagined she could use etherclaw to hurt anybody. Not like Kyara did. This wasn't her. This wasn't something she was capable of. And yet, directly across the floor, no more than twenty feet away, lay the lifeless evidence. It was involuntary. She hadn't meant to do it, but it was beyond her control.

"Fenlee. Fenlee, look at me." Kyara was calm and spoke evenly. "You're shaking, Fenlee. Focus on my eyes and take deep breaths with me."

It was true, she realized. Fenlee was shivering head to toe and couldn't make herself stop. Her eyes darted back and forth between the dead man—the man *she* killed—and Kyara. The harsh lab lights bore down, washing out the scene in front of her. The blood was an angry splash of red on a whitish-blue canvas.

"Fenlee. Eyes on me."

She tore her gaze away from the man and locked onto Kyara.

"Good. Now breathe."

It was hard, but she managed to sync her breathing with Kyara's. She felt the coolness of the floor underneath her and the sting of the chemical air in her nose. A few dogs were whimpering over the churn of the ventilation fans. Slowly, and with great effort, she was able to ground herself. The reality of the situation hadn't changed, but she was in control again.

Alex stirred.

Fenlee stood up a little too quickly, but stumbled through

her dizziness and made her way to her friend. She knelt beside Alex and brushed the hair from her face. Alex needed to be okay—she was the strong one, the tough one.

"Hey. Alex. I'm right here with you."

Alex groaned. "Fenlee?" She half spoke, half mouthed the name. "What...what's going on?"

Fenlee blinked away tears and smiled as her friend opened her eyes. She helped Alex sit up and together they leaned against the nearest cage.

"How are you feeling?" Fenlee asked.

"I'm okay. But that guy..." Alex pointed to the broken man on the floor in front of them. "He's definitely not okay. What the hell happened to him?"

"Augmentation malfunction." Kyara responded before Fenlee could even think about how to answer the question. She'd briefly forgotten the woman was sitting bound and quiet in a nearby cage, watching them. But Fenlee was grateful she didn't have to conjure an answer for Alex. She couldn't have her friend know she'd used etherclaw to take the life of another human.

"Huh, yeah." Alex nodded to Kyara. "Makes sense. My aunt's talked about that. A lot of the Norfayne augs are pretty unstable. Weird that it happened when it did. Lucky for us, I guess." She rubbed her temples. "Anyway, you two know each other. That's more than weird. You going to introduce us, Fenlee?"

"Right. This is Kyara. I think I kinda sorta mentioned her before. She knows Nico. She's...complicated."

Kyara's eyebrows shot up. "I'm complicated? Well, it would

certainly *uncomplicate* things for all of us if you would get me out of here."

The cage had an old-style mechanical lock. It'd be simple to remove with her multimini. Fenlee walked over to the cage, took the lock in her hand, and let it fall back against the metal with a clang. "Well, Kyara, I can only think of one reason you'd be here. My brother better be unharmed."

"Your brother is fine."

"Yeah? Why should I trust you?"

"I'm here to take down Dr. Arkamis." Kyara's eyes wandered to the caged animals, each either terrified or sitting in calm resignation awaiting a fate Fenlee could only imagine. "I think you'll agree that man and his experimentation all need to be put to an end." She hesitated. "And…I can lead you to Elliot."

Fenlee flicked open her multimini and held it near the lock. Something wasn't sitting right. Kyara was powerful—she'd seen that demonstrated multiple times. So how was it that a flimsy animal cage could hold her? "Fine. I'll help you get out. But first, I want to know what's stopping you from tearing through those bindings and smashing your way out of here?"

Kyara's lip twisted and she tensed. "Fair question. You're right, ordinarily it wouldn't be a problem to break out. They've managed to develop an etherclaw barrier, and, as far as I can tell, the majority of the chateau floors above are covered in it. I'd heard of this *antieth* but never experienced it firsthand. It seems these bindings have a small amount of it running through them—enough to block my etherclaw, but apparently…" She looked at the dead man and back to Fenlee. "Apparently the proximity effect doesn't extend very far."

That had to be what was blocking transmissions around here. *Okay, fine. So we do this without etherclaw.*

Fenlee clutched the lock in her right hand as best she could and sliced it off. The lock hit the ground and the cage door swung open. Kyara remained sitting on the floor with a neutral expression. The bindings were so tight they were cutting into her skin.

"I don't know if I can cut through these restraints without hurting you."

"I'm not concerned." Kyara sounded almost serene, but Fenlee recoiled when she touched her to begin work on the bindings—the woman's body was loaded like a tension spring ready to snap. Fenlee knew she was taking a risk with Kyara. She didn't know what would set her off. But Kyara didn't seem like the type to lie. If she wanted to kill Elliot, or Fenlee and Alex for that matter, she would have probably been transparent about it, even while bound up and caged. Wouldn't she?

Fenlee gritted her teeth and got to work on the bindings. She cut through the layers, nicking Kyara's arm enough to draw a thin line of blood. The woman was unfazed.

When the bindings fell loose, Kyara stood up and stretched, flexing and relaxing every muscle in her body. Alex may have been fit and toned, but Kyara was a ripped and well-maintained machine of a woman. Fenlee had seen Kyara in action before, but her skintight clothing didn't leave much to the imagination.

Alex, who was still sitting on the floor, looked up at Kyara in awe. "You sure know some interesting people, Fenlee."

Kyara grabbed a satchel on a nearby table and pulled out a small tube. "Here." She snapped it in the middle and gave

Fenlee and Alex each half. "This is a painkiller and energy booster. It will help you until we get out of here."

The strange tube tasted like dirt and cardboard, but Fenlee choked it down regardless. If it could relieve the pain in her hand and head, it would be worth it. She was also still hungry from using the etherclaw and grateful for anything that might help. Kyara was right. Within seconds of swallowing the first bites, she started to feel better.

Alex brushed herself off and looked around the lab. "What do you think they have all these animals for?"

"They slice things open down here to see the effects of etherclaw. I suppose I was queued up." Kyara finished taking inventory of the items in her bag and seemed satisfied nothing was missing. "Let's go." Kyara and Fenlee made for the door.

"Wait," Alex said. "Two things before we go. First, Fenlee, I'm going to wrap your hand."

Fenlee glanced down at her right hand. She could see bits of bone in a couple of places surrounded by puffy, flayed skin. "Probably a good idea. I decked that creep after he knocked you out. Right in his metal aug. The metal part won."

"Must've been a good hit." Alex tore a strip from the bottom of her shirt and wrapped Fenlee's knuckles. "You'll need to keep this on until we can get that fixed up."

And hello, Alex's perfect abs.

Fenlee promised herself that if she managed to get out of this house of horrors alive, she was going to start working out. She winced as Alex bound up her hand. Her knuckles were so badly wrecked she could only bend the tips of her fingers, giving her hand a claw-like appearance.

"There." Alex looped the strip around Fenlee's thumb and

knotted it in her palm. "I've busted some knuckles sparring before, but never anything nearly as bad as this. You'll be all right, though."

For a moment, it felt good to be taken care of. Kyara's cardboard medicine sticks and Alex's shirt bandage weren't exactly the same as a cup of tea and a warm blanket, but in that moment, it was what Fenlee needed. It fortified her courage, driving her self-doubt back into the shadows.

Alex put her hand on a cage holding a small dog. It was missing clumps of fur and trembled at her approach. "Second, we're going to let all these animals out. No one has the right to cage another creature."

There was an edge to Alex's voice Fenlee had never heard before. Her tone made it clear there would be no discussion: they *would* set the animals free.

"And if you release them, then what?" Kyara's expression was pained. "This is the only life they've ever known. They have no concept of freedom. They will not know what to do outside of captivity."

It wasn't that Fenlee didn't want to help the dogs and cats. She thought about Elliot and knew he'd never leave them caged, either. At the same time, she was starting to get nervous about Casper and Nico. Each had a tendency to get into trouble in their own unique ways. They needed to meet back up as soon as possible.

"There *is* no perfect option for them—I get that," Alex said. "When we exit the chateau, we leave the door open. Maybe they find their way out and they're better off, maybe not. But I'm not leaving them like this."

"Fine." Kyara walked over and started flipping open cage latches. "But we need to move quickly."

"What the hell happened to you? And who the hell is this woman? And what the *voiding hell* is with all these animals?" Casper stepped aside as a rawboned German shepherd barreled down the hall, followed by a gray cat that looked like it would happily murder its owner and gnaw on their eyeballs.

"Kyara!"

"Hello, Nico," Kyara replied.

"Wait, how the hell do *they* know each other?" Casper clutched his forehead, clearly beside himself. "Someone fill me in? I'm kinda out of the loop here, you know?"

"Nico, they have functioning antieth technology and they're using it throughout the upper levels." Kyara dug through her bag and pulled out a small comm unit. "Neither this nor etherclaw will function properly. You understand what that means, correct?"

Nico nodded.

Casper waved his arms. "Uh, hello? The loop. I'm not in it. Please assist?"

Kyara keyed some information into the comm. "Arkamis is here, and I'm not leaving with him alive. Whether it's you, me, or…" Kyara looked around at the others. "Whatever the case, my organization needs to know about what I've found here. Zephyr is on standby, but will not commence extraction unless he has a signal from this comm." She closed the comm and looked to each member of the group. "Understood?"

Everyone nodded, but with varying levels of confidence.

Fenlee felt control slipping from her hands. Not that she was a leader in any typical sense, but they were supposed to be concentrating on Elliot, and she and her friends had put together a plan to get him. Now that Kyara was here, things were changing. She had yet to determine whether those changes were for better or worse.

"And Zephyr can get all of us?" Fenlee asked.

"That shouldn't be a problem," Kyara said.

"Including Elliot? I didn't hear you mention him."

Kyara stopped sorting through her bag and looked Fenlee in the eyes. "You're not leaving without Elliot, and I'm not leaving without Arkamis." She gripped Fenlee's shoulder and squeezed. "If we do this right, we all get to leave together."

Casper let out a full-bodied sigh, his arms drooping in a dramatic fashion. "Still don't get what's going on. But whatever. Anyway, you're probably wondering what I've been up to, and you'll be happy to know that security shouldn't be a problem! Just wait till you hear how I figured it out."

Kyara cut him off. "It may not matter. I overheard them talking earlier. Something happened upstairs, and there's no one performing security monitoring right now."

"Huh?" Fenlee blinked. "What do you mean, something happened?"

Kyara shook her head. "I don't know, but it's one more reason we need to move quickly. We also have to assume Arkamis knows we're here and what little security he has is headed to intercept us. Let's go."

"No idea why I came," Casper mumbled to himself, dragging his feet behind the rest of the group. "I don't even exist."

They reoriented their holoquips with the layout provided

by Cipher and headed to the next floor. The halls and rooms were similar to the one below. There were fewer storage rooms and several more labs, but they were all shut down for the night. The group crept quietly around corners. If there were any guards lurking about, they wanted to surprise them, not the other way around.

But the corridors were empty. Fenlee's stomach growled, startling Casper, who clutched tight to Alex's arm. They were all jumpy. Fenlee choked down a wheat bar. She really didn't need her talkative belly to give away their position.

They tried to take a lift, but it was biolocked. Fenlee reached out with her etherclaw, hoping to force the mechanism, but the control was located several floors above and her perception diminished into a static haze. They elected to take the single set of stairs, reasoning that a lift could easily be shut down anyway, trapping them all inside.

Ahead was an intersection of four halls, with those on the left and right branching off into darkness. The stairway ahead was part of the original building. Instead of the sterile basement lab aesthetic, polished redwood with patterned inlays dated it as a relic from the pre-collapse days.

"We are about to enter the main floors." Kyara spoke quietly, but Fenlee detected a hesitancy or unease behind her words. The woman's mask of confidence was showing hairline fractures, and Fenlee didn't like it. "Be prepared," Kyara continued, "and if we encounter anyone or anything, remember…" She trailed off, narrowing her eyes.

"Remember what?" Fenlee asked.

"Shh!" Kyara put her hand up. Her muscles tensed, but her breathing was steady and controlled.

Kavi's hair stood on end.

Nico sniffed the air and closed his eyes.

Something was coming. Fenlee squinted and focused on the top of the staircase.

Alex gasped.

But Alex wasn't looking at the staircase. Out of each dark hall, as though they were perfectly synchronized mirror images, emerged two heavily muscled animals.

Fenlee was faintly aware of Casper trembling behind her. "What do we do?" he whimpered.

Kyara may as well have been carved in stone. "We? We don't do anything," she said.

They'd come so far, but there was nothing—not even Kyara with all her etherclaw-fueled strength—that could defeat these beasts. Unlike the ones in the Wilderness Zone, this was a pair of professionally trained creatures of death. Panic and despair overtook Fenlee as the solfs approached with a slow, menacing grace.

CHAPTER 27
LIES BY OMISSION

No one moved. The solfs circled the group, trapping them in a huddle. They looked nearly identical—carefully genetically coded to meet specific requirements. The only thing setting them apart from each other was the dried blood matted in the fur around one's jaw. Fenlee thought about the dogs and cats they'd just freed and wondered what poor thing it'd been feeding on.

Casper had a death grip on Alex's arm. "They're not supposed to have solfs! That's—"

"Highly illegal, yes," Kyara finished. "Do you think anyone in this entire facility cares for legalities?" She spread her arms low in a protective manner, ready to react if the creatures made

a move. Her defensive posture wouldn't matter if they chose to strike; solfs were far faster than any of them could hope to be.

Fenlee tried her best to think. Her mind was still muddled from the blow she took to the head, but Kyara's medicine was helping cut through the fog. She still had use of etherclaw on this floor, but she didn't see any way to use it effectively against the solfs. Beyond manipulating mechanized electronics, it had proven mostly useless for her. She couldn't even figure out how to do something as simple as detach and drop one of the heavy ceiling panels on the animals. It was true then—etherclaw was strictly limited to a user's intimate knowledge and passion. It was infuriating. Fenlee stood by, as helpless as the others.

One of the solfs stopped circling and stared at Nico. The boy stared back. Neither blinked. No one else in the group dared to breathe.

Nico placed one bare foot in front of the other and slowly approached the solf. The second animal cocked its head and watched. When boy and beast were no more than a foot apart, Nico stopped and sat cross-legged on the floor. The solf towered above him as its counterpart slowly wandered over. Kavi was balancing on Nico's tiny shoulders, and neither cat or boy seemed at all bothered by the situation.

The solfs were focused entirely on Nico.

Kyara motioned toward the stairs. "Go. Slowly," she whispered to the others.

"We can't leave him like this," Fenlee said. The boy looked so vulnerable next to the monstrous creatures. Nico had proven time and again his adaptability and resourcefulness in challenging situations, and he'd dealt with solfs before. But this was different—these weren't wild animals. The creatures in front of them were designed and trained to be guardians and killers with no free will of their own.

"Fenlee." Kyara gently pulled her toward the stairs. "You know he'll be fine."

Sure, okay. But what if he wasn't? He was here in the first place because of Elliot. No, that wasn't exactly right. Nico was here because of *her*.

"He will meet up with us shortly," Kyara said. "Trust him, and trust yourself."

Alex and Casper were already at the top of the stairs. Fenlee looked back at Nico and saw that the solfs were lying down in front of the boy. She wanted to believe that he'd be okay, but the desire to protect him kicked around in her brain refusing to settle.

It was only a single floor up, but the climb felt like scaling a mountain. Each stair was one more step away from her responsibility to the little kid who was now surrounded by some of the most murderous creatures even known to humankind. But ahead was her brother.

Nico can do this. I can do this. I have to do this.

When Fenlee was a few steps away, a recessed steel door shuddered and dropped from the ceiling on the upper landing. It fell fast, but Kyara was faster. She grabbed the bottom of the inch-thick door and, with a grunt, brought it to a halt about two feet from the floor.

"Fenlee!" Kyara said between labored breaths. "Get under there now!"

Kyara and Fenlee were on the same side of the door as Nico. If Fenlee went to the other side with Alex and Casper, she doubted even the three of them would have the strength to hold the door long enough for Kyara to dive under and join them. And no matter what happened, Nico would be trapped.

Fenlee looked around for anything to brace the door, but there was nothing. All the wall panels were secured in place, and there was no furniture in sight.

"Fenlee! Damn it, girl, I am not joking around. You get under there now!"

Kyara's hands started to slip. There was no more time.

"I'm not leaving Nico," Fenlee said. "Or even you, Kyara."

Years of practice before bedtime made it mere muscle memory; she had the process down to a fluid, single-handed motion. With a click and a tug, her leg was off.

Alex and Casper watched her from under the door, eyes growing wide as they realized what Fenlee was about to do.

Kyara's grip slipped just as Fenlee jammed her leg under the door. The top of the prosthetic crunched under the weight, but the internal rods held. The door remained solidly in place as Fenlee and Kyara crawled underneath.

Alex helped Fenlee up. "Way to think on your feet." She looked down at Fenlee's leg. "Or…lack thereof. Sorry. Anyway, you're amazing, Fenlee."

"Yeah, well, navigating the rest of this nightmare without a leg isn't going to be amazing."

"That's what I'm here for." Alex smiled and wrapped an arm around her.

Great. She'd wrecked Lily's military-grade R&D project, and now she'd have to rely on Alex. She smelled awful. But Alex didn't smell great either right now, so at least there was that.

Who was she kidding? She could bury her face in that smell all day.

Deep breaths. This is nothing, right? Remember the insane situation you're in right now? And you're here by choice. What have I done? My leg. Again.

Kyara finished chewing through two of her medicine sticks and started down the hall. "Move it, you three. They know we're here. They're coming."

"How could this happen?" Arkamis paced, grinding the broken fragments of a recently smashed teacup under his boot. "Is this in coordination with that damn Ravenwolf woman? Does she have a team with her?"

An amateur attempt to bypass security had set off a silent alarm, and Lt. Cano had rushed in to inform him. It was infuriating for so many things to go wrong in one night, but even more maddening was Cano's lack of information. Antieth and old architecture be damned—there was no excuse for her, as his new head of security, not to have eyes and ears covering the chateau.

Cano's eyes flicked between the mess on the floor and Arkamis' flushed face. "The basement levels are secure; we've lowered the barriers. The solf units are also conducting a sweep. We're safe here."

"The *basement?* That's not possible—the top of this tower is completely inaccessible. Are Rook and Morrow still down there finishing their nightlies? Did you trap them too?"

"I'm…not sure, sir. Sorry, sir."

A piece of porcelain snapped like a bone under Arkamis' heel. "I want guards posted outside Elliot's room. And I want Kyara killed. She's a fascinating subject, but not worth the risk. Take a team and see to this."

"If she's still caged, sir, then surely that's good enough."

"Hardly, Cano. Don't underestimate her. If she is, in fact, still locked up, then you're in luck. It will be easier to eliminate her."

Cano hesitated. "Yes. Of course."

Arkamis' fingers danced around the hilt of his saber. "How much do I pay you, Lieutenant?"

Cano started to open her mouth to reply but Arkamis didn't allow her the opportunity.

"It's a rhetorical question. Both of us are well aware how stuffed your pockets are with crednotes. What I find curious is, since bringing you on the team here, there has been no end to our troubles. Of course, that's merely *correlation*. But, Cano"—Arkamis spoke through clenched teeth—"I do not like the way it correlates."

"Right. I'll notify SecForce. I can call this in as a terrorist situation and get all the resources we need."

"No! No, you will *not* notify SecForce. They cannot know what we do here. I'll call for reinforcements to come directly from Norfayne. Until they arrive, we have the guards currently on rotation, my pair of solfs, and…*you*." He stabbed his index finger at her collarbone. "Find out what's going on and put an end to it immediately. If our research is compromised, you cannot begin to fathom the damage it will do to the world."

The door slid open, and an out-of-breath Rook entered. He stared at the broken teacup.

"Yes, Rook?" Arkamis said. "You have something to say? You were in the basement with Morrow. Care to provide us with any insight as to what's going on?"

"Well, I uh…"

"Spit it out! Right now, there is a team of infiltrators on the lower floors, and we have to assume their objective is Elliot. For his protection, you need to tell us what you know."

"I, um, didn't really see anything. I just came to say goodnight."

Arkamis and Cano exchanged confused looks. Rook was extremely intelligent, but his behavior was often perplexing. He lacked social tact and had notoriously bad timing.

"Goodnight?" Arkamis shook his head. "I see. Then get to your room, lock the door, and keep yourself safe." He picked up a teacup fragment. It was large enough to make out the swirling cream and crimson patterns. "Get moving, Cano," he muttered. "If you can't take care of this, we will all be answering for your failure."

Rook and Cano left Arkamis alone. He looked out over the city, the nighttime lights now muted through a settling fog. Norfayne may have been tasked with reconstructing human technology, but he, Dr. Seth Arkamis, was in charge of something decidedly nonhuman. While they were busy reconstructing the past, he would be the one to lead the world into the future. If only the world would back off and give him the opportunity to get there.

He rubbed his forehead.

The night had been altogether exhausting.

"Is the little guy gonna be okay back there by himself?" Casper asked.

"For sure," Fenlee said. "Nico's got this. There's a lot about him that you don't know." But there was a lot about him that she didn't know, either. She tried to sound confident, but Casper's expression made it clear he wasn't buying it.

"Fenlee's right," Kyara said. "Focus on the objective."

The objective had been to sneak in, find Elliot, and sneak back out. Now that they were in, it was obvious how foolish the plan had been in its simplicity. A single rookie guard could have taken them all down. But now they were in it deep. There were no do-overs. Fenlee was supposed to be leading this operation, but she was down a hand and a leg. She felt so weak having to rely on Alex.

"I know you think you were helping, sacrificing your leg back there," Kyara said. "And don't misunderstand—you've impressed me, Fenlee. I never would have expected, given your inexperience, you would be able to successfully infiltrate a place like this. But losing the leg was a bad call. Now you've become a burden to the rest of us, and it was completely avoidable."

Why can't that woman just accept that maybe I helped?

"She's not a burden at all." Alex tightened her arm around Fenlee.

"It's good you feel that way, since she's become your responsibility. Now be ready. Elliot's room should be close…assuming they haven't moved him." Kyara stopped behind a pillar and motioned for the group to stop. "They've posted guards, so it's safe to say he's still there."

Around the corner was a long, broad hall lined with archways and fancy bits of uncomfortable-looking furniture. A little over a hundred feet away, a group of three people spoke in low voices beside a closed door. Two wore dark uniforms, the other a technician's lab coat. From what Fenlee could make out, it sounded as though the technician was upset because she wasn't allowed to retrieve something from the lower labs. One of the guards promised to escort her after the "threat" was neutralized.

Casper bent around the corner and squinted through his goggles. "I count one long gun, a small sidearm—hey!"

Kyara slapped her hand over his mouth and whipped him back around the corner. "Are you an idiot? This isn't a game. Stay. Put." She pulled two matte black knives from her bag and tucked them into her belt.

"What are you planning?" Fenlee asked.

Kyara narrowed her eyes. "Anyone can be sucker-punched."

They watched from behind the column as Kyara edged around archways and flowed behind small benches and side tables like a liquid shadow.

The guards were positioned at an angle, their backs turned. The technician stood opposite them, engaged in a monologue about wage fairness and how it made sense to get rid of her apartment because she slept in the lab most nights. She sounded desperate for human interaction.

Fenlee winced. *Leave. Please go. You're not supposed to be here.* The technician was only minding her own business, caught up in conversation after a late night of work. There was no need for her to be involved.

"Gimme those." Fenlee yanked Casper's goggles to her eyes to get a better look at Kyara. Apart from a slight choking sound as the strap pulled on his neck, Casper didn't protest.

Kyara was about fifteen feet away from the guards, but she was nearly impossible to make out; her bodysuit's stealth feature interfered with infrared and other detection mechanisms. Fenlee watched her pull out one of the knives and hold it, blade in hand. This slinking about in the shadows approach was decidedly different from the etherclaw-wielding force of fury version of Kyara that Fenlee had seen before.

Fenlee didn't want to see any more death. But before she could put the goggles down, Kyara launched her attack. The first knife flew at the technician, burying itself hilt-deep under her chin. Her eyes went wide and her body convulsed as she collapsed.

Before either guard could react, the second knife came flying, but it missed its target, instead embedding itself in the door frame. Kyara was on top of the guards before they could bring their weapons to bear. She ripped the rifle from the first guard's hands and used the butt to crush his throat. He staggered back in an agonized daze.

The second guard was fumbling for his pistol when she grabbed his arm, pulling it back, wrenching it from its socket. He howled. She pulled the knife from the door frame and flipped the grip over in her hand. With a slicing punch to the remaining guard's neck, she destroyed his ability to make any further sound. He clawed at his throat and fell to the ground.

A moment ago, the technician was a living, breathing woman. Someone with a name, someone just trying to make it through another day. There wasn't supposed to be any killing. Death was not part of the plan.

"What the *hell*, Kyara?" Fenlee and the others rushed over. "I get taking out the guys with guns, but that technician was just doing her job!"

"All three of them were 'just doing their jobs.'" Kyara took a pulse to ensure each was, in fact, dead, and proceeded to clean her knives. "How much torment does she bear responsibility for? How much pain and suffering would she continue to inflict because of her *job*, Fenlee? It's likely she has more blood on her hands than the other two combined. And she had to go anyway. She would have been the first to scream."

"Well, still. I don't like it."

"Good," Kyara said. She waved her hand in front of the panel beside the door, but nothing happened. "Locked. We're going to have to override it." She jammed a knife into the panel to pry it off.

Casper activated his holoquip. "I can probably bypass it if you give me a sec."

"I don't think it's locked," Fenlee said. "It's just not responding to us."

Kyara picked up one of the guards and waved his hand in front of the bio detector, but again, the door remained shut.

"Are you serious?" Fenlee rolled her eyes. "Move over and let the *burden* do it." She flipped open her multimini and, one-handed, stabbed it into the door. Then, one-legged, braced herself to tug it sideways. *I'm coming, Elliot.*

She gritted her teeth and yanked. It moved an inch, causing her to stumble back. Alex put her hands over Fenlee's and helped pull. After a few more attempts, the door reluctantly gave.

The room before them was dark, despite the dim light from windows lining the opposite wall. A small figure sat silhouetted on the side of a poster bed. He looked up and stared. Strands of hair fell from his mouth as the cold light caught the edge of his cheek. His pale skin was puffy and glistening.

"Lee?"

Fenlee rushed to her brother, half-dragging Alex with her for support.

They threw themselves into each other's arms. The silence in the room was broken only by Elliot's muffled sobs into Fenlee's shoulder. She'd done it. Despite every obstacle, she'd found her brother.

And he looked completely shattered.

I don't know what they've done to you, Elliot, but I swear I'll keep you safe no matter what.

Elliot backed away and scrubbed the tears from his eyes with the palm of his hand. "Why are you here?"

"What do you mean?" Fenlee gave him a sideways smile. "You're family, Elliot. Where else would I be?"

"How did you even make it here? And what happened to your leg?"

"What *hasn't* happened to my leg? I'm fine, but what happened to your nose?"

Elliot glanced at Kyara. "It's fine. I'm fine too, Lee. Painkillers. I don't feel anything."

"You're not fine. But we'll get you fixed up when we get out of here. We need to hurry."

"I can't."

"You can't what?"

Elliot's gaze drifted to his feet. "I can't go with you."

CHAPTER 28
CONFRONTATION

"I don't understand. Of course you're coming with us." Fenlee wiped blood-tinged snot from Elliot's upper lip. He was the same fragile, vulnerable kid he was the day they first met. They needed each other, so what was this barrier that he was putting up?

"Lee," Elliot mumbled. "I'm not who you think I am."

"No. Maybe they've made you think things that aren't true, but…" Fenlee felt her grip on the situation slipping. She was frazzled as it was, and this was not a battle she'd anticipated having to fight. "I know you, Elliot—the real you. Whatever they've done to you is over now."

Elliot shook his head. "All I do is destroy and hurt people. You have no idea."

Kyara marched over and got in Elliot's face. "Your sister has been through hell to reach you. I know what you're thinking, deep down—oh, believe me, little boy, I know all about the weight you carry. But look around." She gestured to Fenlee, Alex, and Casper. "The world is so much bigger than just you. So, the choice is yours: you can cave to your own doubt and selfishness, or you can conquer your past by standing up and moving forward."

Elliot looked over his shoulder and out the window to the sprawling city beyond. "I just can't lose anyone else." He softly exhaled the words, as though they hurt.

"I'm here now, and I'll be there with you on the other side of all this," Fenlee said. "No matter what."

He lowered his head, but Fenlee caught a glint of desperate hope in his eyes. "You promise?"

"Promise."

"If you two have it all figured out, we need to move." Kyara was at the door, casting glances down the hallway. "We're lucky there are so few people here, but that won't last."

"Where are we supposed to go now?" Casper asked.

"I'll escort you to an exit, and then you're on your own," Kyara said. "I have my own business to finish."

"The conservatory," Elliot said.

"What?" Kyara asked.

"We can exit out of the conservatory. I think. There's a loading bay or something on the far side, but it's bio locked. Etherclaw isn't blocked in there, though."

"Fine. Let's not waste any more time."

The conservatory smelled noxious and floral, like an over-perfumed corpse.

"Don't touch any plants," Elliot said. "Everything here will make you sick, kill you, or make you wish it'd killed you." One of his hands was around Fenlee, helping her walk; the other was a white-knuckled fist. His eyes darted in every direction.

Casper scrunched his shoulders and shivered.

"These people are sadistic," Alex said.

"I keep telling you this." Kyara kept pausing to wait for the rest of the group to catch up. "It takes a great deal of effort and intent to construct a garden one can only describe as evil."

"What about Nico?" Fenlee asked. "I told you, we're not leaving without him."

"And I told you, Nico will be fine. Let me worry about him."

Fenlee shook her head. "Not gonna work. We don't leave anyone behind."

"You're in no shape to do much of anything," Kyara said. "If you care for Nico, your brother, or the rest of your friends, you will leave this place as quickly as you can."

Fenlee was relieved to have rescued Elliot, but with Nico missing, the tension in her stomach remained persistent. She couldn't convince herself that it was okay to leave without him.

Elliot shuffled along beside Fenlee, his chest shaking as though holding back tears. "We don't…leave anyone behind."

"What? Elliot, you're mumbling," Fenlee said.

"I…I don't know. It's nothing. I can't do anything."

She couldn't begin to imagine all he'd been through, but she could see his recovery was going to take some time. "Hey, it's going to be okay. Once we get back home, I'm all yours, and together we're going to talk and work through everything."

Elliot nodded, but Fenlee sensed every step he took caused him some unspoken pain. She gave him a reassuring squeeze and they continued to push forward.

The conservatory roof was transparent, but the canopy of trees became thicker as they continued, blocking all but a few shafts of cold nighttime light. Casper started to turn on his lamp, but Kyara stopped him.

The place was surreal, like a forest from a dark dream on the edge of reality. A chill rippled down Fenlee's spine, and she tightened her grip on Elliot.

"How much further, Ellie?" Casper asked.

"I don't really know. I haven't been to the loading bay, just…"

"Just what?"

Elliot's voice wavered. "I just heard from someone that it was there. I don't really know, I guess."

"You guess. Great. We've done about a dozen things that could get us arrested, we've almost been killed, we have a trail of bodies behind us, and now you're all, 'well, *maybe* this is the way out.'" Casper's voice continued to escalate as he waved his arms nearly hitting Alex in the face. "Nothing is going like we planned, so it's no surprise if we get stuck in this death jungle for the rest of forever."

"Cas! Enough!" Alex elbowed him in the ribs. "What is wrong with you? Yeah, a lot has happened, but we're all in this together. Don't fall apart on us here at the end."

"Keep your voices down." Kyara peered behind them into the gloom. "Move faster. Go."

A light reflected off the foliage as a uniformed guard rounded the path behind them.

"They're over here!" the guard called behind him.

Kyara was in front of him in a heartbeat. She threw a punch, but it went wide as the guard ducked to the side. He pivoted and raised his gun, but Kyara kicked it out of his hand. She faltered but quickly regained control and squared off before him.

"Damn it, Elliot," Kyara said. "You said etherclaw wasn't blocked here!"

"I thought it wasn't! I don't know what's wrong!"

"It's blocked wherever I want it to be blocked." A man in a cream cloak with a saber at his side walked around the bend. Four guards flanked him, their weapons aimed at Fenlee and her friends.

With Kyara momentarily distracted, her opponent rushed her. She reacted just in time and bent low, using his momentum to throw him off the path, head-first into a bush with broad, heart-shaped leaves.

His agonized screams filled the conservatory. It was an insane, inhuman sound. The only time Fenlee recalled hearing anything similar was years ago when she once took a wrong turn in the Lunarinto Market. A gang of local vigilantes had pinned down a thief and were severing his fingers. Memories of the raw, animalistic shrieks still gave her nightmares.

The lead officer watched, horrified, as the guard writhed in pain. "Dr. Arkamis, should we retrieve him?"

"No, of course not!" Arkamis said. "Shoot him."

"What? But he's one of ours."

"Don't be an idiot, Cano!" Arkamis pulled the gun from her hand and fired rounds into the screaming guard.

Cano watched, mouth gaping, until the guard stopped moving.

"He landed in a patch of *dendrocnide moroides*—otherwise known as the suicide plant." Arkamis passed her gun back. "I did him, and us, a favor." He clasped his hands and returned his attention to Fenlee and her fellow trespassers. "Lieutenant Cano tracked you here. She tells me you left two guards and a highly valuable researcher dead outside Elliot's room. And I don't even want to know what mess you've made of my lower levels. Now, will someone tell me why you filthy poor-bred scum are scurrying around my chateau?"

The guards and Lt. Cano positioned themselves around the group, cutting off any escape. Fenlee thought fast.

We're so close. We just need an out. They have lamps, but visibility still sucks. We're surrounded by death plants, they have guns pointed at us, and we're unarmed. And…unlegged. Ugh. Not a lot to work with. So what is Kyara thinking? She has to have something in mind to get us out of this. Right?

But Kyara stood frozen, expressionless except for a vicious edge cutting across her eyes as she stared at Arkamis.

"No one is willing to speak up?" Arkamis paced and tapped the hilt of his saber. "You know, never mind." He flicked his wrist in their direction. "Kill them all, except the boy."

Kyara grabbed Elliot, pulling him to her chest. With the sudden lack of support, Fenlee collapsed. By the time she recovered and looked up, Kyara's knife was pressed to Elliot's throat, and she'd backed the two of them away from the group.

"Stop!" Arkamis commanded his guards. "On second thought, let's hold fire for a moment. It appears Miss Ravenwolf has decided to make a rather bold move instead."

"Kyara! What the hell are you doing?" Fenlee was always wary of Kyara, but this was betrayal. Her brother had been wrenched away from her again, and she was powerless to do anything about what was unfolding in front of her.

Alex started to help Fenlee up, but a guard pointed his rifle in their direction, halting her in her tracks.

Elliot hung limp in Kyara's arms. He mouthed *I'm sorry* to Fenlee over and over, though it seemed more like a plea than an apology.

"Come now, Kyara, you know how all this will play out." Arkamis tapped the hilt of his saber and smiled. "You're powerless around me."

Kyara's eyes widened. "It's your damn sword. It's antieth-infused." She sneered. "You know, for someone so obsessed with etherclaw, you certainly are terrified of it."

"Terrified?" Arkamis laughed. "Hardly. I, among all of you, understand and respect it. This," he said, unsheathing the saber, "is merely insurance."

"You're a depraved coward."

"Am I? You're the one holding a knife to my boy's throat!" Arkamis extended his arm, pointing the tip of the sword at Kyara's head. "Hand him over."

"Why? So you can siphon off his etherclaw and create more of us?"

"Oh, Kyara. I'm not interested in creating any more of *you*. The current iteration of humans is far too flawed." His eyes raked over Fenlee and her friends with contempt. "Just look at yourselves. Why modify humans when we can create our own?"

"You won't ever understand humanity."

"Hand over the boy, and you can join us. You are a marvelous study, Kyara. Unlike…others, you have surpassed expectations in every way. You can help build a new future alongside us." Arkamis smiled, but Fenlee noticed his grip tighten, his hand jammed up against the saber's crossguard. "I assure you that what we're doing here is for the ultimate benefit of all humankind."

"Uh-huh," Alex said. "That stink on you isn't exactly *noblesse oblige*." Her arms were crossed, and she wore a defiant expression. Her confident demeanor was contagious.

Fenlee sat up and pinched her nose. "Yeah," she said. "Will someone wrap this guy's face in a diaper, please?"

"What did you say?" Arkamis whipped around and closed the distance between him and Fenlee, his brow twisted in indignation.

"For the last couple of weeks, I've been covered in blood, muck, sweat, dirt, and plenty of tears, but being drenched in the bullshit coming from your mouth has got to be the worst." Nothing about this man scared her. Arkamis embodied everything Fenlee hated about upper-tier Cascadians. He was just some self-important ass hiding his own weakness behind an archaic weapon.

Arkamis shifted the tip of his saber to point at Fenlee. "Who is this girl?"

"She's my sister!" Elliot yelled.

"Sister? What an odd thing to say, Elliot. You don't have a sister." Arkamis thrust the saber downward, clear through Fenlee's abdomen to scrape on the stone path behind her.

Fenlee gasped. The pain was there, but it was surreal, detached. It was as though she were experiencing someone else's pain by proxy.

This wasn't real. This wasn't real. Right?

But when she touched her stomach, her hand came away

covered in very real blood. Ignoring the guards, Alex ran to her side and used her bare hands to put pressure on the stab wound.

"No!" Elliot screamed from across the path. He tried to wrench away from Kyara, but she held him tight.

"It's okay, Fenlee, I'm right here," Alex said. "Just breathe slowly, and make sure you stay with me." But Fenlee could feel her friend trembling, her stubborn strength of a moment ago completely gone.

"It isn't supposed to go like this." Casper breathed the words, staring down at Fenlee. The color drained from his face, and perspiration beaded on his forehead.

"You know what I think, Kyara? I think that you won't kill him." Arkamis said. A drop of blood fell from his saber as he raised it and approached Kyara. "A bullet might miss, but I won't."

"You really want to make that bet?" Kyara pressed the knife deeper into Elliot's neck, drawing a thin line of blood. But her eyes shot back and forth between Fenlee and Arkamis. Her body tensed as he approached.

Something caught Arkamis' eye and he paused, squinting into the darkness back down the path. A small cat with bright emerald eyes dashed toward them.

"What is that creature doing in here?" Arkamis said.

Everything unraveled at once.

Kavi was only one of many. Behind him came the pack of animals they'd released in the basement lab. They looked hungry, feral, and angry. A large brown dog with patchy fur leapt on the nearest guard, tearing at his throat. The other guards shot wildly into the animals, mostly missing.

The two solfs from earlier brought up the rear. The guards

panicked and focused their fire on the massive beasts. But the solfs were far too agile, and easily dodged the bullets. In seconds, they were on the nearest guards, ripping them to pieces.

"Kill them, you idiots! They're just animals!" Arkamis said, kicking a small terrier off his leg.

With Arkamis' attention on the animals, a green-haired blur flew at him from the opposite direction. Leaping through the air, Nico swiped the saber from Arkamis' hand and dashed off down the path.

With the saber gone, Kyara wasted no time. "Go to your sister!" she said, shoving Elliot out of the way.

Arkamis' fury turned to shock and terror as Kyara closed the distance between the two of them.

Dust kicked up on the path as Kyara's feet slid into a wide stance. She was all offense. Her hips rotated forward as she threw all of her weight into a concussive punch to Arkamis' chest. There was a thunderous crack as an air pocket exploded and ribs were crushed.

Arkamis flew into the woods. There was a crash as he hit a tree, snapping his back. He fell, landing in the nest of suicide plants beside the dead guard. His eyes bulged out of their sockets as blood foamed from his mouth. He lay on his deathbed, unable to move, unable to scream.

Cano fled as the solfs destroyed the remaining guard. The other animals gnawed on the carcasses of the dead, while Kavi licked his paws, clearly pleased with himself.

With the swirl of chaos coming to an end, Fenlee's pain began to take over. It was becoming nearly impossible to focus.

"We're done here." Kyara pulled a comm unit out of her bag

and keyed in a quick sequence. "Rendezvous beacon's active. Let's go."

Kyara started to pick up Fenlee, but Alex wouldn't have it. "No. I'll carry her," Alex said.

"Fine, just keep up. Elliot, go beside her and keep pressure on the wound so your sister doesn't bleed out."

Nico met them at the loading bay in the back of the conservatory. He was already messing with the access panel by the door but having no luck.

"Nice work, Nico," Kyara said. "Though a little sooner would have been appreciated. I don't feel good about buying time with a hostage." She backed up an arm's length from the large reinforced door. "Stand aside."

Kyara let loose a flurry of punches until the door buckled and finally gave.

"I probably could've gotten that, you know," Casper mumbled.

"Sometimes brute force is best."

Dawn was breaking as they left the chateau. The morning shadow of the Void Pillar cloaked the Eastern Wilderness Zone as swirling mists burned off around its perimeter. Fenlee felt as though she was teetering on the edge of the world, looking off the side of the platform into the expanse beyond. Freedom beckoned, but Fenlee was fading and she knew it.

As they stepped out into the light, weary and wounded, a SecForce Shryke emerged before them, rising up the side of the tower. The combat craft hovered, guns pointed their direction.

CHAPTER 29
TO SAVE THOSE WE LOVE

THE SHRYKE WAS an older model and not in the best shape. A ramp dropped from it with a heavy groan, as though the craft was too tired to carry its own weight. Boots thudded down the incline and a well-muscled man descended, backlit by the rising sun.

"Well, good morning! Find some new friends, Kyara?" Zephyr yelled over the rumble of the Shryke's engines. "Quite a crew! Glad I brought this old junker and not the patrol skiff—that'd've been a little too cozy."

Zephyr's face darkened when he saw Fenlee. He rushed over and placed his hand on her forehead. His palm was rough, but warm and gentle. "She's going into shock. What in the world happened?"

"I'll explain once we're away," Kyara said. "Tell me you brought a stabilization kit."

"I've got triage supplies, yeah. Let's get her on board."

The Shryke grumbled about lifting off, but soon Zephyr had it flying away from the city, low over the overgrown ruins of the Eastern Wilderness Zone. The main hold was designed to transport about eight soldiers and their equipment. With room for two more in the cockpit and one in the rear turret, there was plenty of space to accommodate all of them with Fenlee lying flat on the floor.

Kyara injected Fenlee with something that numbed the pain then inserted an expansion cartridge into the wound. The intense pressure in her abdomen made Fenlee feel sick.

"Thanks," Fenlee said, though it was hard to work her jaw. "Pretty much…out of endorphins…over here."

"How is she?" Zephyr called from the cockpit.

"She's hypovolemic," Kyara said. "I can slow the blood loss, but not stop it. You need to get this thing moving faster."

Fenlee tried to concentrate on everyone's faces, but had to blink away the blur every few seconds to bring things back into focus. Elliot and Nico sat opposite Kyara, both holding her good hand. They looked as unrelated as two boys could, but their expressions were carved from the same emotion. They needed her, and they did not want to let go.

The thought of leaving Elliot, or even Nico, was far more excruciating than the injuries she'd suffered. But her willpower could only get her so far. So she continued to blink, refocus, and hold on.

"Uh, some not-so-good news," Zephyr said. "Looks like

we've got a little entourage. Couple of Sentry-class drones back there tailing us, but they're keeping their distance."

Casper leapt up and scrambled to the back of the craft. "I'll take the rear turret!"

"Yeah, good luck with that, kid," Zephyr mumbled.

"Hey! There's no rear turret!" Casper ran back up front.

"Yep," Zephyr said. "This may be a Shryke, but we dug it outta the scrap heap, and it's missing a few factory-installed essentials."

"Then just spin us around and shoot 'em!"

"Hah! Those old guns on top don't work either. And if I whipped around too fast, this whole thing's liable to break into pieces."

"This isn't funny," Casper said. "What the hell are we supposed to do?"

Zephyr laughed. "Oh, not much, I guess. Can't outrun or outlast 'em. Plasma engine was a mess when we salvaged it, so we retrofitted the whole deal to use fuel cells. Simple enough tech, but pretty pricey."

The discussion between Casper and Zephyr in the cockpit became nothing more than background murmur as Fenlee's senses dulled.

Kyara knelt close to Elliot. "We need your help here. Nico and I can't manipulate etherclaw in the same way you can. You're the only one on board who can take out those drones."

"Why should he do anything you say?" Alex interjected. "You tried to kill him!"

"As I told Nico, it was to buy us time," Kyara said. The annoyance in her voice was directed more at herself than at Alex. "I'm not proud of it, but I didn't see any other option.

Regardless, this isn't about me—this is about everyone on board this craft."

"You don't understand." Elliot looked down at Fenlee, his eyes were red from fatigue and too many tears. "I can't. When I use it, it doesn't take my energy, it steals from everyone around me."

Nico put his arm around Elliot. His eyes poured sympathy. "It's okay," he whispered in Elliot's ear. "I know."

"Let me make this clear," Kyara said. "These Sentries will track us until our fuel cells expire and we're forced to land. Once our position is known, a strike team will be on top of us. And it's not like this is SecForce coming to arrest us. This is Norfayne backed by the Divine Council, which means either immediate elimination or far worse if they decide to take us alive. You need to use it, Elliot."

"I don't know how!" Elliot yelled in frustration. "I've never been in control of it!"

"Just *try*," Kyara said. "It won't take much energy, and we'll all be fine."

Elliot squeezed Fenlee's hand, but she lacked the strength to squeeze back. "She won't be," he said, his voice barely audible.

"Hey." Zephyr leaned his head back into the hold. "Any ideas back there? We can't let these drones follow us back to base. And I'm gonna have to set this thing down pretty soon or it'll set itself down."

Fenlee's looked at the faces gathered around her. Elliot, Alex, Nico, and even Casper. These were the people she cared for more than anyone else in the world. They'd risked so much for her. Without them, life was nothing.

Drones were such simple devices. Sure, the higher-end ones

ran on micro-plasma and repulsor tech, but few could afford to use those. No, the majority were like the ones behind them now: prop-and-motor style with modular fittings to swap out sensors, weapons, or other devices. They were so delicate. All it took was for the drive unit to be slightly out of alignment and…

Fenlee closed her eyes. She was so cold. Her hand wouldn't move to the opal, now hanging sideways over her chest. It didn't matter. She could feel the warmth from it spreading through her body. It felt like when her mother used to hold her when she was sick or afraid. Her tension and worry disappeared, and she fell into the heat of its embrace.

The last fragments of her perception zeroed out.

Then everything became nothing.

The night had not gone as Rook planned. He thought the group of intruders was there for Elliot—nothing more than a bunch of his friends trying to rescue him. Of course Elliot would have friends. When he opened the door to his father's study, it occurred to him that there were two outcomes: the group would succeed and remove Elliot, or they would fail and his father would be even more upset with his brother. Either way, Rook would come out better for it.

He never imagined it would lead to his father's death.

Rook wasn't good at emotion. He knew how to get angry, but it was never the kind of anger his father wanted to see. He'd experienced sadness, but always in an abstract sort of way. No one ever spent the effort teaching him how to understand emotions, so he looked upon many of his feelings as cumbersome and strange.

After Norfayne evacuated the chateau, he became lost, unsure what to do next. None of the doctors would answer his questions. It was as though he didn't exist. He glanced at the faces of guards he recognized, all lying unconscious on life support. Even that irritating servant girl was among them, now ashen and unmoving with tubes and blinking apparatus sticking out of her. But he couldn't find his father.

He wandered deeper into the complex, down endless halls until he located the morgue.

Seeing his father's broken body laid out on the medical slab was more than Rook could handle. Norfayne medical staff milled around in the background, indifferent. For them, it was just another day. Their reality was not one Rook shared, and he resented them for it.

Rook felt himself slipping, losing control. All of his thoughts, feelings, and fears balled up inside him. It was too much. He couldn't get it sorted out or just make it all go away like he'd done in the past.

For years, Rook had studied etherclaw, and his academic knowledge was extensive. Though he understood it well and knew it was a part of who he was, it always remained trapped inside of him, just out of reach.

Tonight was his catalyst.

His rage and love collided, exploding in a shockwave. He unleashed the etherclaw built into his very core and poured the world around him into his father. The feeling was liberating. It was as though his inner self, buried deep his entire life, was now free. He breathed deep as energy coursed through him and wondered why Elliot had resisted such an empowering feeling.

The morgue was silent. Rook looked at the desiccated

bodies of doctors and nurses behind him. A lab tech he'd once tried to befriend lay crumpled in a fetal position, a look of shock permanently etched into her face. With their élan vital fully drained, there was hardly anything left of the people they once were.

A rasping breath startled Rook, and he turned back around.

His father's eyelids fought against the crust of dried blood and, one at a time, opened. Arkamis looked lost for a few moments as though his mind was putting itself back together. Rook stared, petrified.

"Rook. You've done it," Arkamis said with a dry and grating whisper. "I always knew—" His words gave way to a coughing fit; his lungs rattled and his body shook. When he recovered, a smile touched his cracked lips.

"I'm so proud of you. We have a bright future together, son."

EPILOGUE

Thin sunbeams danced through treetops as the autumn breeze picked up, bringing a slight chill to the air. Fenlee sat across from Alex in a small park near her friend's mid-tier home. The four months since escaping the chateau had flown by, leaving the two with few spare moments to catch up. It was a rare day where neither of them had much of anything going on, so Alex had invited Fenlee over after the academy let out.

"How's the new leg?" Alex asked. She poured steaming tea into a cup and passed it to Fenlee. "I know it's nothing like the other one."

"No, it's great!" Fenlee blew on the tea and took a tiny sip. "I mean, sure, nothing compares to that other one, but it's definitely the *second* best I've ever had. You and Lily are both incredible. I've missed seeing you." She felt her face flush. "Mm...tea's hot."

After field surgery in Snowdrop's makeshift medical facil-

ity, Fenlee healed quickly and returned home feeling physically better, but still without a leg. She hid the loss from Lily out of guilt. Alex, meanwhile, explained the situation to her aunt, and in a few days' time, presented Fenlee with a newly fabricated leg. It wasn't elaborate, it wasn't fashionable, but it fit perfectly, and she was grateful for it.

"Well, I'm glad you could make some time," Alex said. "I know how busy you are. And the offer still stands—if you need any help, just let me know. Lily asks about you and those two boys all the time."

"I know, I know, but we're all fine. Elliot takes care of the cooking and cleaning and Nico takes care of...well... we have him properly using the toilet now, so, progress?" Fenlee shrugged.

Like before, Nico had no desire to stay with Snowdrop. He'd followed her back and had been living with them since. It was like having another adopted brother. She and Elliot had made it clear that he was welcome to stay with them as long as he wanted. And having him around made the apartment feel less empty with her father gone. Though she let him use her dad's old bedroom, most mornings she found him curled up with Kavi nestled under Elliot's plants.

"Speaking of Elliot, how is he?" Alex asked. "Has he opened up at all?"

"Nico and I apparently over-watered some of his fancy flora while he was gone. That sure didn't go over well. Really, who knew you could give a dumb plant too much water?" Fenlee swirled the tea around, furrowing her brow in thought. She bent her head, and a freshly dyed red curl fell loose. "I'm worried about him. Whatever he's holding in, he's nowhere close to letting it out. I know he's got to be traumatized, I just don't know how to help him. He was so upset when he learned about my dad. And honestly, I'm still trying to figure out how to deal with all that."

There was also the matter of the augmented creep in the chateau basement. She hadn't meant to kill him, but what other option had there been? That was another thing she hadn't dealt with. Kyara was the only one who knew the truth and, for now, Fenlee wanted to keep it that way. She tucked the loose hair behind her ear and forced a smile.

"It's not all as bad as I'm making it sound. I mean, yeah, some days we're all a depressed mess, but mostly…I dunno. It's like I said, we're all fine. We're making it work. And I can't really explain it, but I think Nico grounds us in some weird way."

"You're doing everything you can for Elliot just by being there for him. And don't forget, those boys are there for you too."

Fenlee slumped. "I know. It's just, he'll seem fine, but whenever I ask him anything about what happened, he shuts down."

"You can't bear all this weight on your shoulders." Alex leaned forward and put her hand on Fenlee's knee. "Things have happened that are well beyond your control."

"Yeah. I can't stop long enough to even figure stuff out, let alone control anything. If I could—" Fenlee's stomach growled. Both girls sat up.

"Ah." Alex dug into her bag and handed Fenlee two green and brown sticks. "Now that's something we can control. Here you go. Seaweed sizzle. Extra *extra* salty."

"Thanks." Fenlee bit off a piece and let the toasted briny flavor linger on her tongue. It was amazing how much better the same food was up on mid-tier. "Have you talked to Cas at all? I've tried a few times, but he hasn't really said much."

"Yeah, he's been pretty quiet," Alex said. "I think losing his dad is hitting him harder than he lets on. His mom is gone most of the time these days, so it's just him. He goes to academy, then back home and does who knows what."

Fenlee promised herself she'd find a way to make time for him. It was easy to forget she wasn't the only one struggling with grief. Still, given the circumstances, life was as normal and stable now as she could hope for. The apartment was paid for, so all she had to worry about covering was food and a general service bill paid to the complex. Murdok allowed Fenlee to increase her part-time hours, and she sent Cipher on scavenging missions, reselling whatever he'd bring back. It turned out the little bot was much better at assessing value than she was. Between making ends meet and keeping up with her academy work, she was exhausted and had no time to herself.

She'd also decided there was no way she could ever work for Norfayne. That was supposed to be her ticket out of low-tier living, but she was done with that wicked corporation. Further, she'd realized she was already surrounded by people who cared about her—everyone from Murdok to the enigmatic temaki man—and they were all part of her community. With Elliot and Nico, she had everything she needed right where she was.

"Oh, hey, before I forget, you're going to love this." Fenlee finished crunching on the tightly wound stick of roasted seaweed and pulled a scrap of ruined paper from her pocket. "I found this molded to the inside of my boot the other day."

Alex squinted at the torn paper trying to read what was left of the smeared lettering. "Um, okay? What am I looking at here? Why will I love this?"

"Remember when I went to the library with Lily?" Fenlee told Alex about her etherclaw research and the book with the missing pages. "And, well, at the time it seemed like a great idea to snag this little piece of the page."

Alex's jaw could've hit the ground. "Fenlee Harper! You stole this! They could have disappeared you for that."

"Yes. As you know, I have a reputation for always taking the rational course of action."

Alex laughed. "Yeah, well, your decisions come from your heart, and that's what I love about you. But still…" She shook her head.

"Eh, I made it out. Somehow. Anyway, I swiped it because, at the time, I'd hoped I could show it to you and, I don't know, you'd use some of your magical history knowledge to give me some brilliant insight into etherclaw. Of course, I forgot about it, and now my foot sweat has made it totally unreadable." She shrugged and stuffed it back in her pocket. "Dumb, I know. But the thing of it is, I don't really care anymore. I can use my etherclaw for little day-to-day things, and that's more than enough for me."

"I don't know how much more you *need* to know," Alex said. "You seem to have a pretty good grasp of the whole etherclaw thing. I mean, the way you dropped those two drones that were after us?" Alex shook her head. "Unbelievable."

"Thanks. But I hardly remember any of it."

"It was a miracle they were able to get you patched up. I still can't believe how much blood you lost."

"Gallons. Had to be. I wake up every morning feeling sorry

for Zephyr and the hours he had to have spent scrubbing my bodily fluids off the deck of that Shryke."

"He was a weird one. But I'm sure he was happily whistling away while doing it."

"Hah, yeah. Really though, I wouldn't call it a miracle. Maybe a little luck, but I'm pretty sure I made it out alive 'cause I was surrounded by people who knew what they were doing."

"Whatever the case, you're tough, Fenlee. Toughest I know."

Fenlee looked down at her feet. Here she was, now seventeen years old, covered mind and body with scars she never asked for. "I don't feel it, though." She opened her mouth to continue, but she wasn't sure how to finish her thought out loud.

"What's wrong?"

"I'm sorry I dragged everyone into all this. I was so naïve. Any one of us could have been killed. Easily. I'm such an idiot."

"Fenlee!" Alex pounded the ground with her fist, emphasizing her words. "You're *no such thing*! We got Elliot back, right? And, not only that, but I think we dealt a very real blow to some of the messed up stuff Norfayne's been doing." She pursed her lips and refilled their cups with the last of the tea. "I'd call us heroes. You know, rescuing the innocent and taking down the bad guys? We're pretty amazing, if you ask me."

She knew Alex was right—it *was* amazing. It was horrible, stupid, and overwhelming if she thought about it too long, but it was incredible to consider what they'd accomplished together. And none of it would have been possible without going against the odds, ignoring risks, and facing their fears.

"Then here's to us, the unsung Heroes of New Cascadia!"

Fenlee said. She and Alex laughed and clinked their cups in a toast.

Dry leaves rustled as the breeze picked up again. Another day was coming to a close, and she still had responsibilities to attend to at home. The tea was lukewarm but not yet cool. There were only a few moments Fenlee had ever wished she could capture and hold on to, and this was one.

It wasn't the life she'd ever expected, but it was hers. And she wasn't afraid to live it.

ABOUT THE AUTHOR

MATTY ROBERTS began their career in journalism where they earned an Emmy and had the privilege of working on several other award-winning projects. They hold an MS from Johns Hopkins University and are now an engineer in renewable energy in Denver, Colorado where they live with their wonderful partner, two extraordinary kids, and the best doggie ever.

In addition to writing, engineering, and parenting, Matty is a vegan enby nerd who is in love with this world and will forever be doing all they can to make it a better place. And they may be known to occasionally play in a punk band here or there.

Finally, a deep and gracious **THANK YOU** to all of the readers, reviewers, editors, friends, family, and others who helped along the way. Your efforts, feedback, and love made this book possible.

www.mattyroberts.io.

CPSIA information can be obtained
at www.ICGtesting.com
Printed in the USA
LVHW011736280722
724616LV00002B/277